The crystal on the table shimmered and began to glow with a blue flame. Kerwin sat a long time, while the woman stared into the stone and murmured to herself. Finally, it occurred to him that she was in a trance and might answer his questions, the questions no one else would answer.

"Who am I?" he asked.

"You are the one who was sent," she said low and thickly. "It was a trap that missed its firing. They didn't know, the proud Com'yn. Cleindori. . . ."

The lights in the crystal seemed to coagulate suddenly into a brilliant flash of flame. Dazed, he straightened and passed his hand slowly across his eyes. Confused, he shook his head.

The woman had collapsed across the table, and Kerwin reached out to shake her shoulder. With a nightmarish slow grace, she slid down and toppled sideways to the floor.

She was dead.

THE
BLOODY
SUN

MARION ZIMMER BRADLEY

ace books
A Division of Charter Communications Inc.
1120 Avenue of the Americas
New York, N.Y. 10036

THE BLOODY SUN

THE STRANGER WHO COMES HOME
DOES NOT MAKE HIMSELF AT HOME
BUT MAKES HOME STRANGE

PROLOGUE

THIS IS the way it was.

You were an orphan of space. For all you knew, you might have been born on one of the Big Ships—the Big Ships of Terra, that made the long runs between stars, doing the business of the Terran Empire.

The first home you knew was the Spacemen's Orphanage, where you learned loneliness. Before that, somewhere, there had been strange colors and lights, confused images of people and places that sank into oblivion when you tried to focus on them; nightmares that sometimes made you sit up and shriek out in terror before you got yourself all the way awake and saw the clean quiet dormitory around you.

The other children were the abandoned flotsam of the arrogant and mobile race of Earth, and you were one of them. But outside lay the darkly beautiful world you had seen, that you still saw in your dreams. You knew somehow that you were different. You belonged to that world outside, that sky, that sun; not the clean white world in the Terran Trade City.

But the dreams faded to memories of dreams, and then to memories of memories. You only knew that *once* you had remembered something different than this.

You learned not to ask about your parents, but you guessed. Oh yes, you guessed. And as soon as you were old enough to endure the thrust of a spacedrive kicking away from a planet, they stuck your arm full of needles and they carried you, like a piece of sacked luggage, aboard one of the Big Ships.

And when you woke up, with a fuzzy sick headache and the feeling that someone had sliced a big hunk out of your life, the ship was making planet-fall for Earth, and there was an elderly couple waiting for the grandson they had never seen.

They said you were twelve or so. They said you were Jeffrey Andrew Kerwin, Jr. That was what they'd called you in the spacemen's orphanage, so you didn't argue. They showed you a picture of Jeff Kerwin, Sr., who'd run away as a cargo boy on a starship almost twenty years ago. That helped, some. They were kind to you. They put you in his room, and sent you to his school, and not more than once a week did they remind you, by word or look that you weren't—that you never could be—the son they had lost. The son who had abandoned them for the stars.

And they never answered questions about your mother, either. They couldn't. They didn't know and they didn't care. You were Jeff Kerwin, of Earth. And that was all they wanted of you.

If if had come when you were younger, it might have been enough. You were hungry to belong somewhere.

But the sky of Earth was a cold burning blue; the hills were a cold, unfriendly green, and the pale-blazing, yellow sun hurt your eyes even when you hid them behind dark glasses. You missed the cold, and the winds that swept down from the high, splintered teeth of the mountain skyline; you missed the dusty dim sky and the lowered, blazing crimson eye of the sun. Your grandparents didn't want you to talk about Darkover or think about Darkover, and once when you saved up your pocket-money and bought views taken in the Rim planets, they took the pictures away from you. You belonged here on Earth. Or so they told you.

Only you knew otherwise; and as soon as you were old

6

enough, you left. You knew that you were breaking their hearts again, but you left. You had to. You knew, if they didn't, that Jeff Kerwin, Jr., wasn't the boy they loved.

Probably the first Jeff Kerwin, your father, hadn't been, either. . . .

First there was a civilian's job there on Earth, and you worked hard and you kept your mouth shut when the arrogant *Terranan* made jokes about your height or smiled at the Darkovan accent you'd never quite lost.

And then one day you boarded another of the Big Ships, warranted in the Civil Service of the Terran Empire, sky-lifting at incredible velocities for stars that were names in the roll-call of your dreams. And you watched the hated sun of Earth dwindle to a dim star, and then to nothing.

Not Darkover, yet. But a world with a red sun and a purple sky, and a subordinate's job on a world of stinks and electric storms, and albino women cloistered behind high walls.

And after that, there was a good job in the Spaceport Co-Ordination office of a world where men carried knives and women walked with fettered hands and the chiming of little silver chains. You had liked it there. You'd had plenty of fights and plenty of women. Behind the quiet civil clerk there was a roughneck buried, and on that world he got loose now and then. You'd had good times. You could have stayed there and been happy.

But there was still the compulsion driving you; the restlessness. And by now the apprentice years were over. Until now, you'd gone where they told you. Now they asked you, within reason, where you wanted to go.

And you never hesitated.

"Darkover."

The man in Personnel had stared awhile. "Why in the devil would anyone want to go there? It's a hell of a planet—cold as sin, among other things. The place is barbaric—big sections of it barred off to Earthmen, and you aren't safe a step outside the Trade City. I've never been there myself, but I hear the place is always in an uproar. Added to which, there's practically no trade with the Darkovans, which means

Empire ships only touch down there once in a while. If you go there, you might be stuck for years before they could locate a replacement for you, after you get tired of it. Look," he added persuasively, "Rigel 9 is crying out for good men, and you could get ahead there—maybe work up to Legate. Why waste yourself on a half-frozen lump of dust out at the edge of nowhere?"

You waited a moment, and then you told him.

"I was born on Darkover."

"Oh. One of *those*. I see."

You wanted to smash that smirk off his pink face, but you didn't. You stood there and watched him scrawl his name on your transfer application. And then, after getting unwound from too much red tape, there was another of the Big Ships, and a growing excitement that gnawed at you, so that you haunted the observation dome, searching for a red coal that gradually grew to a blaze filling all your sky. And then, after a time that seemed endless, the ship dropped lazily toward a great crimson planet that wore a necklace of four tiny moons, rubies set in the pendant of a carmine sky.

And you were home again.

CHAPTER ONE

THE *Southern Crown* made planet-fall at high noon on day-side. Jeff Kerwin, swinging efficiently down the narrow steel rungs of the ladder from the airlock, dropped to the ground and took a deep breath. It had seemed that the very air should hold something rich and different and familiar and strange.

But it was just air. It smelled good, but after weeks of the canned air inside the spaceship, any air would smell good. He inhaled it again, searching for some hint of his elusive memory in the fragrance. It was cold and bracing, with a hint of pollen and dust; but mostly it held the impersonal chemical stinks of any spaceport. Hot tar. Concrete dust. The stinging ozone of liquid oxygen vaporizing from bleeder valves.

Might as well be back Earthside! Just another spaceport!

Well, what the hell? He told himself roughly to come off it.

The way you built it up in your mind, getting back to Darkover, you made it such a big deal that if the whole city came out to meet you with parades and fanfares, it would still fall flat!

He stepped back, out of the way of a group of Spaceforce men—tall in black leather, booted blasters concealing their menace behind snug holsters—with stars blazing on their sleeves. The sun was just a fraction off the meridian—huge, red-orange, with little ragged fiery clouds hanging high in the thin sky. The saw-toothed mountains behind the spaceport cast their shadows over the Trade City, but the peaks lay bathed in the sullen light. Memory searched for landmarks along the peaks. Kerwin's eyes fixed on the horizon, he stumbled over a cargo bale, and a good-natured voice said "Star-gazing, Redhead?"

Kerwin brought himself back to the spaceport, with a wrench almost physical. "I've seen enough stars to last me awhile," he said. "I was thinking that the air smells good."

The man at his side grinned. "That's one comfort. I spent one tour of duty on a world where the air was high-sulphur content. Perfectly healthy, or so the Medics said, but I went around feeling as if someone had thrown a whole case of rotten eggs at me."

He joined Kerwin on the concrete platform. "What's it like—being home again?"

"I don't know yet," said Kerwin, but he looked at the newcomer with something like affection. Johnny Ellers was small and stocky and going bald on top, a tough little man in the black leather of a professional spaceman. Two dozen stars blazed in a riot of color on his sleeve; a star for every world where he had seen service. Kerwin, only a two-star man so far, had found Ellers a fund of information about almost every planet and every subject under the sun—any sun.

"We'd better move along," Ellers said. The process crew

was already swarming over the ship, readying it for skylift again within a few hours. Favorable orbits waited for no man. The spaceport was already jammed with cargo trucks, work-hands, buzzing machinery, fuel trucks, and instructions were being yelled in fifty languages and dialects. Kerwin looked around, getting his bearings. Beyond the spaceport gates lay the Trade City, the Terran Headquarters building—and Darkover. He wanted to run toward it, but he checked himself, moving with Ellers into the line that was forming, to verify their identities and assignments. He gave up a finger-print and signed a card verifying that he was who he said he was, received an identity certificate, and moved on.

"Where to?" asked Ellers, joining him again.

"I don't know," Kerwin said slowly, "I suppose I'd better report to the HQ for assignment." He had no formal plans beyond this moment, and he wasn't sure he wanted Ellers butting in and taking over. Much as he liked Ellers, he would have preferred to get re-acquainted with Darkover on his own.

Ellers chuckled. "Report? Hell, you know better than that. You're no greenie, still bug-eyed about his first off-planet assignment! Tomorrow morning is time enough for the red tape. For tonight—" he waved an expansive hand toward the spaceport gates, "Wine, women and song—not necessarily in that order."

Kerwin hesitated, and Ellers urged "Come on! I know the Trade City like the back of my hand. You've got to fit yourself out—and I know all the markets. If you do your shopping at the tourist traps, you can spend six months' pay without half trying!"

That was true. The Big Ships were still too weight-con-scious to permit transshipping of clothing and personal gear. It was cheaper to dispose of everything when you transferred, and buy a new outfit when you landed, than to take it along and pay the weight allowances. So that every spaceport in the Terran Empire was surrounded with a ring of shops, good, bad and indifferent, all the way from luxury fashion centers to second-hand rag markets.

"And I know all the high spots too. You haven't lived till

you've tried Darkovan *shallan*. You know, back in the mountains they tell some funny stories about that stuff, especially its effect on women. One time I remember—"

Kerwin let Ellers lead, listening with half an ear to the little man's story, which was already taking a familiar turn. To hear Ellers talk, he had had so many women, on so many worlds, that Kerwin sometimes wondered vaguely how he'd had time in between to get into space. The heroines of the stories ranged all the way from a Sirian bird-woman, with great blue wings and a cloak of down, to a princess of Arcturus IV surrounded by the handmaidens who are bound to her with links of living pseudoflesh till the day she dies.

The spaceport gates opened into a great square, surrounding a monument raised on high steps, and a little park with trees. Kerwin looked at the trees, their violet leaves trembling in the wind, and swallowed.

Once he had known the Trade City fairly well. It had grown some since then—and it had shrunk. The looming skyscraper of Terran HQ, once awesome, was now just a big building. The ring of shops around the square was deeper. He did not remember having seen, as a child, the loom of the massive, neon-fronted Sky Harbor Hotel. He sighed, trying to sort out the memories.

They crossed the square, and turned into a street paved with hewn blocks of stone, so immense in size that it paralyzed his imagination to guess who or what had laid down those vast slabs. The street lay quiet and empty; Kerwin supposed that most of the Terran population had gone to see the starship touch down, and at this hour few Darkovans would be on the street. The real city still lay out of sight, out of hearing—out of reach. He sighed again, and followed Ellers toward the string of spaceport shops.

"We can get a decent outfit in here."

It was a Darkovan shop, which meant that it spilled out halfway along the street and there was no clear distinction between outside and in, between the merchandise for sale and the owner's belongings. But this much concession had been made to custom of the alien Terrans, that some of the

11

goods for sale were on racks and tables. As Kerwin passed beneath the outer arch, his nostrils dilated in recognition of a breath of the familiar; a whiff of scented smoke, the incense that perfumes every Darkovan home from gutter to palace. They hadn't used it, not officially, in the Spacemen's Orphanage in the Trade City; but some of the nurses and matrons were Darkovan, and the resinous fumes had clung to their hair and clothing. Ellers wrinkled his nose, but Kerwin smiled.

The shopkeeper, a little withered man in a yellow shirt and breeches, turned and murmured an idle formula: *"S'dia, shaya."* (You lend me grace.) Without thinking about it, Kerwin murmured *"Z'par servu,"* and Ellers stared.

"I didn't know you spoke the lingo. Thought you left here when you were only a kid!"

"I only speak the city dialect." The Darkovan was turning to a colorful rack of cloaks, jerkins, silken vests, and Kerwin, exasperated with himself, added curtly in Terran Standard, "No. Earthmen's clothing."

He concentrated on picking out a few changes of clothing —shirts, underwear, shaving things, just what he could get along with for a few days, until he found out what the job and the climate would demand. But while the shopkeeper was making up the parcels, Ellers drifted to a table near the entry-way.

"What sort of outfit is this, Kerwin? I've never seen anyone on Darkover wear one, have you?"

Kerwin joined his friend at the table. A tangle of odd garments, all more or less worn, were flung at random there; Ellers held up an oddly patterned knee-length cloak. Kerwin looked it over, then nodded.

"They wear them back in the mountains," he said, "or at least, they used to. They're warm, and they're comfortable for riding, but even when I was a youngster, they were going out of fashion." He took the cloak from Ellers. It was made of soft suede-like leather dyed a deep russet hue, and as flexible as silk. It was embroidered with metallic threads— gold, gleaming copper—at throat and hem, and was lined with soft dark fur.

"It looks as if it had been made for a prince," commented Ellers in an undertone. "Look at that embroidery!"

But Kerwin was concerned with something more practical. "What it looks is warm," he said. "Just feel that fur." He settled it over his shoulders. It felt very soft and rich. Ellers stepped back, regarding him with consternation.

"Good lord, are you going native already? You aren't going to wear that thing around the Trade City, are you?"

Kerwin laughed heartily. "I should say not! I was thinking it would be nice to wear around my room. If the bachelor quarters in the HQ are anything like the ones on my last assignment, they're damn stingy with the heat! And it gets fairly cold here, as I remember." He took off the cloak and folded it over his arm. But in spite of his practical words, he knew he was rationalizing. He wanted the thing because he liked the looks of it. It was the first thing that had taken his fancy on his return to Darkover, he wanted it, and—well, he was going to have it.

"That kind of money would have kept you happily drunk for a week," Ellers mourned as they came out on the street again. Kerwin chuckled. "Cheer up! Fur isn't a luxury on a planet like this, it's a good investment. And I've still got enough in my pocket for the first round of drinks. Where can we get them?"

They got them in a wine-shop on the outer edge of the sector; it was clear of tourists, although a few of the workhands from the spaceport were mingled with the Darkovans crowded around the bar or sprawled on the long couches along the walls. They were all giving their attention to the serious business of drinking, talking, or gambling with what looked like dominoes or small cut-crystal prisms.

A few of the Darkovans glanced up as the two Earthmen threaded their way through the crowd and sat down at a table. Ellers had cheered up by the time a plump, dark-haired girl came to take their order. He gave the girl a pinch on her round thigh, ordered wine in the spaceport jargon, and, hauling the Darkovan cloak across the table to feel the fur, launched into a long tale about how he had found a

13

particular fur blanket particularly worthwhile on a cold planet of Lyra.

"The nights up there are about seven days long, and the people there just shut down all their work until the sun comes up again and melts off the ice. I tell you, that babe and I just crawled inside that fur blanket and never put our noses outside . . ."

Kerwin applied himself to his drink, losing the thread of the story—not that it mattered, for Ellers' stories were all alike anyhow. A man sitting at one of the tables alone, over a half-emptied goblet, looked up, met Kerwin's eyes, and suddenly got up—so quickly that he upset his chair. He started to come toward the table where they were sitting; then he saw Ellers, whose back had been turned to him, stopped short and took a step backward, seeming both confused and surprised.

But at that moment Ellers, reaching a lull in his story, looked round and grinned.

"Ragan, you old so-and-so! Might have known I'd find you here! Come and have a drink!"

Ragan hesitated, and it seemed, to Kerwin, that the man flicked an uneasy glance Kerwin's way.

"Ah, come on," Ellers urged. "Want you to meet a pal of mine. Jeff Kerwin."

Ragan sat down. Kerwin couldn't make out what the man was. He was small and swart, with a lithe sunburnt outdoor look and calloused hands; he might have been an undersized mountain Darkovan, or an Earthman wearing Darkovan clothes. He spoke Terran Standard as well as either of the Earthmen, asking Ellers about the trip out, and when the second round of drinks came he insisted on paying for them, but he kept looking at Kerwin sidewise, when he thought he wouldn't be noticing.

Kerwin demanded at last, "What is it? You acted like it was me you recognized, when you started over here."

Ragan nodded. "Right. I didn't know Ellers was in yet. But then I saw him with you, and saw you wearing—" he gestured at Kerwin's Terran clothing. "So I knew you couldn't be the person I thought you were. I don't know you, do I?" he added, with a puzzled frown.

Kerwin surveyed him curiously. Could Ragan be one of the kids from the Spaceman's Orphanage? He was a little younger than Kerwin. "I don't think so," Kerwin said at last.

"But you're not Terran, are you?"

The memory of a clerk's sneer—"One of *those* . . ."—rushed briefly through Kerwin's mind; but he shoved it aside.

"My father was. I was born here."

Ragan nodded again. "So was I. I do liaison work for the Trade City when they have to hire Darkovans—guides, mountaineers, that sort of thing."

Kerwin was still trying to decide whether the man had a Darkovan accent. He finally put the question. "Are you Darkovan?"

Ragan shrugged, and the bitterness in his eyes was really appalling. "Who knows?"

He lifted his glass, and drank. Kerwin followed suit, sensing that he would be drunk fairly soon. It didn't seem to matter. Ragan was staring again and that didn't seem to matter either.

Kerwin thought, *In one way, maybe our cases are similar. My mother might have been Darkovan. She might have been anything. My father was in the Space service—that's the one fixed link I've got with reality. But who and what am I, apart from that?*

"At least he cared enough to get Empire citizenship for you," Ragan said bitterly, and Kerwin realized that he must have been actually saying all this out loud. "Mine didn't even care that much."

"Listen, you two," Ellers interrupted, with an air of injury, "this is supposed to be a celebration! Drink up!"

But Ragan leaned his chin in his hands, staring across the table at Kerwin. "So you came here, partly, to locate your parents—your people?"

"To find out something about them," Kerwin amended.

"Has it occurred to you," Ragan said slowly, "that you might be better off not knowing?"

Kerwin had thought of that. He'd been all the way through

that and come out the other side. "I don't care if my mother was a woman of the streets," he said. "I want to *know* it."

To be sure which sun claims me, which world. Darkovan or Terran?

"Have you any clues?" Ragan asked.

Kerwin fumbled, with fingers made clumsy by drink, at his pocket. "Only this. At the orphanage they told me it was around my neck."

"Oh, nuts," interrupted Ellers rudely. "So you'll show it to them, and they'll recognize that you are the long-lost son and heir to the Lord High Muckety-Muck in his castle, and you'll live happily ever after." He made an indescribable sound of derision.

Ragan held out his hand; Kerwin dropped the small blue crystal into it. Although the fine chain was of silvery metal, the stone itself seemed unremarkable, and Kerwin had always thought of it as a cheap trinket, something a poor girl might treasure.

Ragan looked at it, his eyes narrowing. "You know what this is, of course?"

"A gem stone of some sort, I thought."

"No," he said. "It's a matrix jewel."

"A—which?"

Ragan repeated, elaborating. "A psychokinetic crystal. Not much of one. Low-level. But they don't just lie around in the streets, you know."

"I'm lost," said Ellers, stretching out his hand for the little crystal. "I've heard of them, but I never saw one before."

Ragan kept it in his hand, saying, "Watch." He tilted his glass to drink the last few drops, then turned it bottom-up and laid the crystal on the stem. His face took on an intent, concentrated stare; abruptly there was a small blue flash, a sizzling sound, and the rigid slim stem of the goblet melted, sagged sidewise, and bent into a puddle of glass. Ellers gasped and swore; Kerwin passed his hand over his eyes. The goblet still sat there, bowl-down with the wilted stem. There was a Terran artist, once, Kerwin remembered, who painted things like limp watches and fur teacups. The goblet, stem lolling to one side, looked just as surrealistic.

Ragan handed him back the crystal, and Kerwin demanded "Could I do that? Could anybody?"

Ragan nodded. "With a little practice. This is the kind they put in children's toys, or suitcase locks. They haven't enough power to do anything serious. It's a little bigger than the ones we usually see in the Terran Zone, though. Maybe a Darkovan could do more with it, but it won't produce more than a few grams of energy at any one time."

Ellers, sobering briefly, stared at Kerwin. He muttered "A matrix jewel! Sure, I know—the big secret of Darkover. The Terrans have been trying to beg, buy or steal some real information about them for fifty years. They'll bring little ones into the Trade City, and trade them off for drugs, lenses, luxury goods. They transform energy directly, without external fuels or fission by-products. But they're so small. And although we know there must be bigger ones, no Terran has ever seen or heard of them."

"You've already lost me," Kerwin said, feeling bewildered. "What did you call them?"

"Psychokinetic," Ragan told him. "I don't know how they work, but you concentrate on them, and they can move small objects, concentrate intense heat, or—well, other things. It takes training to handle them, I understand—all but the very simple ones, like this." He frowned as Kerwin picked up the crystal again. "You didn't know?"

Kerwin shook his head. "I never thought about it having any use. It was just a trinket."

"Does that mean his mother was Darkovan?" Ellers asked.

"Not necessarily. My father could have bought or found it." Kerwin slipped it into his pocket, and Ragan said, "It represents a sizable small fortune, you know. Take care of it. That may be why your father never mentioned it to the people at the Spacemen's Orphanage—afraid that if they knew what it was, they'd take it away from you. The authorities at HQ would probably give a lot to get their hands on one like that."

Kerwin touched the crystal in his pocket. Childish, he supposed, to be so sure from infancy that this was some possession of his mother's, some key perhaps to his hidden and obscured memories. Seeing Ragan's eyes on him, he laughed uneasily and signaled to the Darkovan girl to bring more wine.

"Of course," he said with heavy irony, "I was hoping it was that amulet which would prove I was the long-lost son of the High Something-or-other of Darkover. Now all my illusions have been shattered."

He raised the wine glass to his lips. As he did so, his eyes fell on the wineglass whose stem Ragan had melted. Was he drunker than he thought?

The wine glass stood upright on an unbroken stem. And there was nothing whatever wrong with it.

CHAPTER TWO

THREE DRINKS later, Ragan excused himself, saying he had a commission at the HQ and had to report on it before he could get paid. When he had gone, Kerwin scowled impatiently at Ellers, who had matched him drink for drink. This wasn't the way he had wanted to spend his first night on the planet whose image he'd carried in his mind so long. He didn't quite know what he did want, but it wasn't just to sit all night in a spaceport bar and get drunk.

"Look, Ellers—"

Only a gentle snore answered him. Ellers had slid down in his seat, out cold.

The plump Darkovan girl came with refills—Kerwin had lost track of how many—and looked at Ellers with a professional mixture of disappointment and resignation. Then, bending to pour, she brushed artfully against Kerwin. Her loose robe was unpinned at the throat so that he could see the valley between her breasts, and the familiar sweet smell of incense clung to her clothing and her hair. A thread of awareness plucked, like a string, deep in him, but then he looked again and saw her eyes hard and shallow, and the music of her voice frayed at the edges when she crooned, "You like what you see, big man?"

She spoke brokenly, Terran Standard, not the musical tongue of her world.

"You like Lomie, big man? You come 'long with me. I nice and warm, you see. . . ."

There was a flat taste in Kerwin's mouth that wasn't just the aftertaste of the wine. Terran, or Darkovan, the girls of the spaceport bars were all the same.

"You come? You come?"

Without quite realizing it, Kerwin grabbed the edge of the table and heaved himself up, the bench going over with a crash behind him. He towered over her, glaring through the dim and smoky light, and words in a language long forgotten came from his lips.

"Be gone with you, daughter of a mountain goat, and cover your shame elsewhere, not by lying with men from worlds that despise your own!"

The girl gasped; cowered backward, one convulsive hand clutching her robe about her bare breasts, and bent almost to the ground. She swallowed, wet her lips and whispered *"Z'servu, shaya,"* and, unexpectedly, sobbing, she whirled and fled. The sob and the scent of musky hair lingered and were gone.

Kerwin clung, swaying, to the edge of the table. *God, how drunk can you get? What the devil was that stuff I was spouting?*

He was bewildered at himself. Where did he get off, scaring the poor girl out of her wits? He was no more virtuous than the next, what Puritan remnant had prompted him to rise up in wrath and demolish her like that? And holy mackerel, what language had he been speaking anyhow? Terran Standard? Not likely. The city jargon? He could not remember. Only the emotion remained; the form of the words had vanished.

What the hell had gotten into him? He glanced at Ellers, now completely unconscious, and thought; I'd better get out of here while I can still navigate.

He bent and shook Ellers, but Ellers didn't even mumble. Darkovan drinks are powerful stuff, and Ellers had drunk as much as Ragan and Kerwin together. He did this in every

19

spaceport. Kerwin shrugged, lifted up Ellers' feet to the chair he himself had vacated, and turned unsteadily toward the door of the wine shop.

Air. Fresh air. That was what he wanted. Then he'd better get back to the HQ. At least, in the Terran Zone, he knew how to behave.

The sun, bleared and angry-looking, lay low over the street. Shadows of deep mauve and indigo folded the huddled houses in a friendly gloom. There were people in the streets now; Darkovans in their colorful silken shirts and breeches, women muffled to the eyebrows in fur, and once, gliding along, a tall form invisible beneath a hood and mantle of shining gray metallic rings; but the mantled form was not human.

And even as he paused, looking up at the flaming sky, the sun sank with a rush and the swift dark came swooping across the sky—dark like great soft wings, folding to blot out the brilliance—the fast-dropping night that gave this world its name. Leaping out in a blaze of sudden glare came the crown of vast white stars, and the two smaller moons, like rose rubies set asymetrically in the band of the stars.

Kerwin stood in the street, staring upward, his eyes wet, unashamed of the sudden tears that had started to them. It was not illusion, then. He was home again. He had seen the dark over the red sky, the blaze of the crown. He stood there until, with the sudden cooling of the air, the thick nightly mist gathered and the blaze of stars dimmed. Then, slowly, he walked on. The tall beacon of the Terran HQ gave him his bearings, but he moved almost reluctantly in that direction.

He was thinking of the Darkovan girl he had rejected so unexpectedly, and so strangely. She had been warm and lissome, and what more could a man want for a welcome home?

He felt strangely restless, at loose ends. Home? A home meant people. He hadn't been at home on Earth; his grandparents hadn't wanted him, only a second chance with his father. In space? Ellers, perhaps, was the closest friend he had, and what was Ellers? A bum of the spaceports. A planet hopper. Kerwin felt the sudden hunger for roots, for people, for what he had never known. The words he had said, self-deriding, to Ellers, returned to haunt him; *I was hoping I was the son. . . .*

Yes, that was the dream that had lured him back to Darkover, the fantasy that he would find a place where he belonged. Why else had he left the last world, Wolf? There had been plenty of work, plenty of women, plenty of rough and ready companionship. But all the time, driving him, had been that restless compulsion, to get home again; to get back to Darkover.

And now that he was back, now that he'd seen the stars and the swift dark of his dreams, would all the rest be anticlimax? Would he find that his mother was just a spaceport girl like the one who had rubbed against him tonight? His father—well, as Ragan had pointed out, at least his father had cared enough to get Empire citizenship for him.

Well, he'd follow through on the mystery. He'd trace his mother, and find out why his father had abandoned him, and why and where he had died. And then . . .

The nocturnal mist had condensed now, and a thin fine icy rain was beginning to fall; it had been so warm during the day that Kerwin had almost forgotten the way in which night, at this season, blots out stars and hot moons in sleety mist. He shivered and walked faster.

At the edge of the square that opened on the spaceport, there was a line of small cafés and restaurants; he walked into one at random. It huddled behind thick walls and thicker curtains, and seemed to be, like the bar, neither Darkovan nor yet all Terran. There were professional spacemen in uniform but there were Darkovans too. In the dim lights, faces were all a blur, and he didn't look for any of the men from the *Southern Crown.* The place smelled of food, Darkovan food, and made his mouth water. That was what he needed; he was hungry.

He sat down at a counter and ordered, and when the food came he sank his teeth in it with pleasure. Not far away, two Darkovans, rather better dressed than average, with gaily colored cloaks and high boots, jeweled belts and short ornate knives stuck into them, were idling over their food. One had a blazing red head of hair, which made Kerwin raise his eyebrows; Darkovans were a swarthy race, and his own red hair had made him an object of curiosity and stares when, as a child, he'd gone out on the streets even in the Trade City. In the orphanage they'd called him *Tallo*, Redhead, a name the Darkovan nurses had been at such pains to suppress that even then it had surprised him. He had collected the notion somehow—though the Darkovan nurses were forbidden to talk about native superstition to the children—that red hair was unlucky or taboo.

On Earth—perhaps because red hair was so common—the memory had dimmed. But that would explain Ragan, too. Obviously, if redheads were that scarce, then you'd assume—seeing red hair from a distance—that it was probably the one you knew.

A loudspeaker on the wall hiccupped noisily, then a metallic voice remarked, "Attention, please. All HQ personnel with planes on the field report to Division B. All surface travel will be canceled; repeat, will be canceled. The *Southern Crown* will lift on schedule, and all private aircraft on the field must be moved, repeat . . ."

One of the men near the front said a brief, expressive word or two, picked up his gold-lace cap and tramped out into the rain. A blast of bitter cold blew into the room, and the Darkovan nearest Kerwin said to his companion *"Esa so vhalle Terranan acqualle. . . ."* and chuckled.

The other glanced past him at Kerwin and said something even more insulting in the dialect of the city Darkovans.

Kerwin felt himself trembling. He had always been childishly sensitive to insults. On Earth he had been an alien, a freak, a Darkovan; here on Darkover, suddenly, he felt himself a Terran. And the events of the day hadn't been calculated to make his disposition sweeter. But he controlled his rage, only saying—to the empty stool at his left, "The rain can only drown the mud-rabbit if he hasn't the wits to keep his mouth shut."

The Darkovan pushed his stool back and swung round, upsetting his drink in the process. The thin crash, and the

bleat of the waiter, drew all eyes to them, and Kerwin slid
off his own stool, warily. But inside he was watching himself
in dismay. Was he going to make two scenes, in two bars, and
would this rip-rousing welcome to Darkover end up by getting
him hauled off to the local equivalent of the hoosegow for
being drunk and disorderly?

Then the man's companion grabbed his elbow. The Darkovan's eyes traveled slowly upward, rested on Kerwin's red
hair—now clearly illumined by the small lamp in a bracket
above—and he said, with a little gulp.

"Com'yn!"

Kerwin wondered just what in the hell *that* meant.

The fighter's eyes darted to his companion's face, found
no encouragement there. He shuffled his feet uncertainly,
then drew back, one big arm going up to cover his face,
and stammered something. He barged across the room, avoiding tables like a sleepwalker, and plunged out into the rain.

Kerwin became conscious that everyone was staring at him;
but he managed to meet the eyes of the waiter long enough
to drive him away. He sat down and picked up his cup,
which contained the local equivalent of coffee—a caffeine-
rich beverage tasting roughly like bitter chocolate—and
sipped. It was cold.

The remaining Darkovan, the redheaded one, got up,
came over and sat down beside Jeff Kerwin on the empty
stool.

"Who in the hell are you?"

He spoke the spaceport jargon; but he spoke it badly,
forming each word with care. Kerwin set his cup down
wearily.

"Evil-Eye Fleegle, a very ancient God," he said, "and I
feel every millennium of it. Go away, or I'll whammy you
like I did your pal."

The redhead grinned—a mocking, unfriendly grin. He was
about Kerwin's age. "He's no friend of mine," he said, "but
you obviously aren't what you look like. You were the most
surprised man in the place when he ran off like that. He
thought you were one of my relatives."

Kerwin said politely, "Did your mother come from Ireland?

23

No, thank you. I come from a long line of Arcturian lizard-people." He picked up the coffeelike stuff and buried himself in it again. He felt the redhead's puzzled gaze on him again. Then the man turned away, muttering *Terranan* in that tone that made the single word into a deadly insult.

Now that it was too late, Kerwin wished he had answered more politely; he had a tardy impulse to go after the man and demand an explanation. But the sure knowledge that this would only mean a new rebuff, prevented him. Feeling frustrated, he put some coins down on the bar and went out into the icy sleet again.

The stars had gone. It was dark and cold, with a howling wind, and he fought his way along, shivering in his thin shirt. Why hadn't he bought some warm clothes? Hell—he had! A little peculiar-looking, maybe, but warm enough until he got out of this wind. With stiff fingers he fumbled the strings of the bundle and got out the fur-lined cloak. He settled it over his shoulders with a shrug, and drew it close around him.

It felt warm and pleasant, the soft supple leather keeping out the wind, the fur closing round him like a caress. The brightly lighted lobby of the Sky Harbor hotel reminded him that he had not yet reported to HQ, nor been assigned to quarters; he'd need a place to sleep. He had half decided to ask if there were rooms available here; he walked across the lobby toward the clerk.

The clerk, busily sorting the day's records, barely glanced at him. "You go through there," he said curtly, and returned to his book.

Kerwin, startled—had the Civil Service made accommodations ahead?—started to protest, then shrugged, and went through the indicated door.

It was a large room, with a long table at the center, long strangely-shaped sofas and divans scattered about the room, and a large fire burning at one end. On one wall a glass pane opened on black night, making the glass a mirror, and Kerwin could see himself—a big man, with red hair standing awry from the rain, and a lonely and introspective face, the face of an adventurer who has for some reason been cheated out of adventure. High around his throat was the embroidered collar of the Darkovan cloak; he had forgotten it. The sight of his own face rising above the unfamiliar dress arrested him, with a strange surge of—memory?

Obviously that was the answer; the clerk, seeing him in this Darkovan garb, had simply taken him for someone else. In fact, that would explain it all. He had a double, or near-double on Darkover in the Trade City, some redhead about his size and coloring, and that fooled people, on a quick look.

He remembered the word the brawler had said; *"Com'yn."* Was that the name of his double? He repeated it to himself. *Com'yn.* It seemed to knock at a concealed door in his thoughts. . . .

"You're here early, *com'ii,*" said a girl's voice behind him, and Kerwin turned, and saw her.

He thought at first she was a Terran girl, because of the red-gold hair clustered atop her small head. She was slight and slim, dressed in an open cloak, and underneath, a simple dress that clung to small neat curves of breast and hip. Staring at a Darkovan girl, in a public place, is insolence punishable by death—if any of the girl's relatives are around, and care to take offense—but she returned his gaze frankly, smiling. And so, even on second thoughts, Kerwin decided she was a Terran girl.

"How did you get here? I thought we had all decided to come together," she said.

Kerwin felt his face heating, and not from the fire. "I'm sorry," he said, "I didn't realize this was a private room. I was directed here—probably by mistake. I'll leave at once."

Now she stared at him, her smile fading. "What are you thinking of? We have far too many things to discuss—" She stopped, and said, "But you—have I made a mistake?"

"Somebody's made one," Kerwin said, but his voice trailed away on the last words. She wasn't speaking Terran Standard, and she wasn't speaking the dialect of the Trade City. She was speaking in a language he had never heard before—yet he understood her, and for a moment the dialect had seemed so familiar that he hadn't even noticed that they were speaking a strange language.

Her mouth dropped open and she said quickly, "Aldones! Who are you?"

He started to say his name; then the red imp of anger, held in abeyance for a moment because he was talking to a beautiful girl, deviled him again. This was the second time tonight. That double of his must be quite a fellow.

Kerwin said curtly, "Don't you know me yet? I'm your big brother Bill, the black sheep of the family, and I ran away to space when I was six months old, and I've been held captive by pirates ever since. Find out in the next installment."

She shook her head uncomprehendingly, and he realized that language and satire would mean nothing to her. Then she said, in that language he understood if he didn't try to concentrate on it too closely, "But aren't you one of us? From the Hidden City, perhaps? Who are you?"

Kerwin scowled impatiently, too annoyed to carry the game any further. He almost wished that the man she had mistaken him for would walk in so that he could punch him in the face.

"Look, you're mistaking me for someone else, girl. I don't know anything about your Hidden City—it's hidden too far away or something. What planet is it on? You're not Darkovan, are you?"

If she had looked startled before, now she appeared thunderstruck. "And yet you understand me! Listen here," she began again, and once again she was speaking the language of the spaceports, "I think we must have this clearly understood. There's something strange here. Where can we talk together?"

"We're doing fine, here and now," Kerwin said. "I may be new to Darkover, but not that new. I know Darkover law pretty well, and I'm not crazy about having an intent-to-murder filed on me before I've been here twenty four hours, in case you have some touchy male relatives. If you *are* Darkovan."

The small pixie face screwed up in a puzzled little smile.

"I can't believe it. You really don't know who I am. But you don't have to worry about that."

"I'm the worrying kind," Kerwin said dryly. "Just for the fun of it, tell me your name and who you thought I was, and then I'll be leaving you to your—rendezvous."

"But you can't," she said. Kerwin couldn't understand the look on her face. She looked shocked, as if he had said he had only an hour to live. He seemed to have a strange ability, tonight, of innocently scaring people half to death. This was the second time. If that double of his actually did turn up, Kerwin was about ready to punch him in the face, just on general principles!

She said, "Please don't go. If Kennard were here—"

"Tani!" A low, harsh voice broke into their thoughts, and a man came into the room. Kerwin wondered as he turned, so mad had the world become, whether he'd see a mirror image of himself; but he didn't. Like the girl, the newcomer was tall, fair-skinned, with thick reddish-gold hair. Kerwin detested him on sight, even in the split second before he recognized the redhead from the bar.

The Darkovan took in the scene at a glance and his features took on the stamp of scandalized conventionality. The girl said "Auster, I only wanted—"

"A *Terranan!*"

"I thought he was one of us."

The Darkovan favored Kerwin with an angry glance. "He's an Arcturian crocodile-man—he told me so himself." Then he spoke to the girl, a rush of words in the same dialect the girl had spoken, Kerwin thought, but so fast and blurred that he could not follow. He didn't need to; the tone of the voice told Kerwin all he needed to know. The redhead was very mad.

A deeper, mellower voice interrupted, "Come, Auster, it's not as bad as all that. Taniquel, don't tease him." A second man came into the room; and he was yet another of the redheads. But his red hair was dashed with long streaks of gray; a burly man this, stooped and feeling the frosts of middle age. His eyes were almost hidden behind ridged brows so thick as to approximate deformity. "I'm Kennard," he said, "third in the Arilinn Tower. Which Nest are you from? Who's your Keeper?"

Kerwin was sure he had said "Keeper."

"They usually let me out without one," he told the man, dryly.

Auster said in spaceport jargon, quickly and mockingly, "You missed, Kennard. Our friend is a—a crocodile from Arcturus, or so he claims. Obviously he's a Terran."

Kennard exclaimed, "But that's impossible!"

Kerwin decided the scene was becoming much, much too intense. "To my great regret," he said, and realized to his surprise that the courteous formula was perfectly true, "I am a citizen of Terra. But I spent my early years on Darkover, and I learned to think of it as my home. Now if I have intruded or offended, I am sorry. Good night, and farewell."

Auster muttered something that sounded like "Crawling chicken!"

Kennard said, "Wait." Kerwin, already out the door, paused at the man's persuasive tone. "If you have a little time, I'd like to talk with you."

Kerwin, glancing at the girl Taniquel, almost yielded. But one look at Auster decided him. "Thank you," he said pleasantly, "I'm already late. Sorry for intruding on your party."

Auster spat out a mouthful of words, and Kennard gave in gracefully. He bowed. "May the moons light you to your door."

The girl Taniquel raised her hand to her mouth and stood there sobered and stricken, gazing at Kerwin with her big golden eyes. He hesitated again, on an impulse to demand an explanation; but he had gone too far to back down and keep any dignity at all.

He said, "Good night," and felt the door swing heavily shut between himself and the redheads, with a curious sense of defeat and apprehension.

The icy rain had dissolved into a stinging mist. Kerwin pulled the cloak about him, and only then did he realize that he was still wearing it. Good lord, he thought, no wonder the girl looked funny when I said I was Terran. I must cut a damn crazy figure.

In the dark, glazed-cold streets, the thick swirling mist cut off any sign of moon or stars. It had an odd deep-purple color, a curious heady smell. The lights of the Terran HQ burned like a tree of yellow glare through the swirls, and Kerwin knew that there he would find warmth and familiar things, shelter and a known place; Ellers had probably already returned, after waking and finding him gone.

Whoever people took him for, it wouldn't hurt to go looking around a little. Good lord, this was his own world. He had been born here. He had lived here. He was no naïve Terran spaceman, warned not to leave the tourist quarter. He knew the city—or had once—and the language. All right, so Terrans weren't welcome in the old Town, he wouldn't go as Terran! Wasn't it a Terran who had said, "Give me a child until he is seven, and anyone who wants him can have him afterward?" That grim old saint had had the right idea, then. By that kind of reckoning, Kerwin was Darkovan. He always would be. And now he was home again, and he was going to get a look round, at least!

The streets were thinly populated by a few people in cloaks and furs, head-down against the bitter biting wind. A little dwarfed creature pattered by, giving Kerwin one swift upward glance from green eyes that glowed in the dark but had unmistakable human intelligence behind them; and almost without realizing it, Kerwin's hand moved in a warding-off gesture, for the *kyrri* were strange creatures who fed on electrical energy and gave off protective electrostatic fields which could give an unwary stranger near-fatal shocks.

A shivering girl, hugging an inadequate fur smock around her, gave Kerwin a hopeful glance and murmured to him, not in spaceport jargon, but in the old tongue of the city, which he had spoken before he could lisp two words of nursery Terran (How did he know that, suddenly?) and he hesitated, caught by her sad eyes and the contrast with the girl in the spaceport bar; but then her eyes fell on his red hair; she murmured unintelligibly and fled.

He walked through the square slowly, savoring the unfamiliar smells and sounds. He stopped by a stall where an old woman was selling fried fish, which she dropped to sizzle in a bowl of clear green oil, boiling without apparent flame. She looked up, and with voluble words in a dialect too thick for understanding, handed him the fish, laid on a green leaf. He wondered vaguely where the green leaves came from. He laid down some coins, and she looked at him, frightened, and backed away. In her babble he caught again the puzzling word *Com'yn*.

The devil! There it was again; he was scaring people! He might as well go back to the spaceport. Maybe it was this rig-out he was wearing? He'd take it off, but in Terran clothes—well, it wasn't safe to go wandering around alone!

He admitted it to himself now. He had had just some such imposture in mind when he bought the cloak. . . .

But too many people were staring. He turned, taking the road back, getting his bearings by the spaceport tower. It was very late; the streets were glazed with ice, and in this quarter, deserted.

He heard a step behind him—a slow, somehow purposeful step—and turned. A man was approaching him on soft feet, almost noiseless; cloaked and mantled, no sign of his face visible. Kerwin drew back to let him pass.

This was a mistake. With a cry, the mantled figure which was not a man sprang at him, with a great leap from almost twelve feet away. Kerwin felt a searing pain; then the top of his head exploded, and from far away he seemed to hear a voice, crying out strange words:

"Say to the son of the barbarian that he shall return no more to the plains of Arilinn! The Tower is broken and the Golden Bell is avenged!"

That didn't make sense. Kerwin felt himself falling, and knew no more.

CHAPTER THREE

IT WAS raining.

There was gray light in his face, and someone was crying out, a long, keening wail.

"Ai, ai, ai! Ai, *Com'yn!*"

He was taken up, and his head exploded again, and Jeff Kerwin slid back into unconsciousness.

Suddenly a bright, white light seemed to shine into the innermost recesses of his brain. He felt someone touching his head, which hurt like hell and grunted, "Easy! Take it easy!" and someone took the light out of his eyes.

He was lying in an antiseptic white room in an antiseptic white bed, and a man in a white smock and cap was bending over him. He wore the caduceus insignia of a Terran Medic.

"All right now?"

Kerwin started to nod, but his head exploded again and he thought better of it. The doctor handed him a small paper cup of red liquid; it burned his mouth and stung all the way down, but his head stopped hurting.

"What happened?" he asked.

Johnny Ellers put his head around the door; his eyes looked bloodshot. "You ask that? *I* pass out—but it's you that gets slugged and rolled! The greenest kid from Earth, on his first off-planet assignment, ought to know better than that."

"Lucky you have a hard head," the doctor said, reprovingly, "you might have been killed!"

Had he dreamed the whole thing then? Had he simply been robbed and rolled in the old town, and dreamed all the rest—his bizarre wanderings in the Darkovan cloak, the people who took him for someone else? Wishful thinking, based on his desire to belong?

Had he dreamed the girl Taniquel, and her golden eyes?

"What day is it?"

"Same day, the morning after the night before," Ellers said.

"Where did this happen?"

"I don't know. Evidently someone found you, got scared, carted you to the edge of the spaceport square and left you there, about dawn." The doctor moved away.

Kerwin decided it was too much of a puzzle to think about now. He turned over and went back to sleep. Ragan, the

31

girl in the wine-shop, the redheaded aristocrats, spun in his mind as he drifted away; if he'd started out by thinking that this return was an anticlimax to his dreams, at least he'd now had enough adventure to last him fifty years.

No satirical daemon whispered in his ear that he hadn't even started yet.

It was a considerably sobered Jeff Kerwin who reported to the Traffic Office the next morning. The Legate regarded him without enthusiasm.

"I need Medics and technicians, and they send me communications men! Hell, I know it's not your fault. Darkover isn't a popular place, and they have to send me what they can get. I hear you actually requested to be transferred here, which means I may be able to keep you—usually what I get are apprentices who transfer out as soon as they have seniority to request transfer. Well, that's something, I suppose. I hear you got yourself bashed up a bit, wandering around alone. That's not smart, here."

Kerwin, under a little questioning, related his adventure, but left out, for some reason, the three redheads in the Sky Harbor Hotel. He wasn't sure why, unless it was the thought of the girl.

"Just why were you so interested, Kerwin?"

"I was born here, sir," he said doggedly. If they were going to discriminate against him because of that, he wanted to know it now. But the Legate only looked thoughtful.

"You may be very fortunate," he said. "Darkover is a strange place. I didn't volunteer, you know. I got in with the wrong political crowd. At least you won't consider it exile. And if you actually like the place, you may have quite a career ahead of you. Normally, no one stays longer than they have to."

"I don't quite know why I came," Kerwin said thoughtfully. "Except—what little I remember as a child. It was—almost a compulsion."

The Legate sighed. "The longing for the smell of your own air, the color of your own sun to your eyes," he said. "I know, lad. I've been out in the galaxy for forty years; I've seen dozens of worlds. But I want to die on Terra." He reached out to Kerwin with an almost embarrassing intensity. "Stay here if you're happy, son. *'Though stars like flowers be thickly sown, no world of stars can match your own. . . .'* " he broke off. "Who were your parents anyway?"

Kerwin thought of the girls in the spaceport café, and then tried not to think of them. At least my father had cared enough to leave me in the Spacemen's Orphanage, not to be dragged up like young Ragan, around the sector—*How did I know that?*

"Kerwin," mused the Legate. "I seem to know the name. Records would have it on file, if he had married here." He didn't suggest the alternatives. "Or the Orphanage might have records. They're fairly careful about who they take in there. Ordinary foundlings get turned over to the Hierarchs of the City. And then, you were sent back to Earth; that's *very* rare. Normally you'd have been kept here and given work at the Legation—mapping worker, interpreter, something like that. Possibly your mother was one of the Terran nurses or medical personnel here."

"I've wondered if I had Darkovan blood—"

"I doubt that. Your hair. We Terrans have a lot of redheads—adrenal types go in for the adventurous life. I've never seen a Darkovan with red hair."

Kerwin started to say, "I've seen three," and could not. Literally he could not speak the words; it was like a fist at his throat. Instead he listened to the Legate talking about Darkover.

"It's a funny place," he said again. "We hold scraps of it by compact, for trade, just as we do elsewhere. You know the routine. We leave governments alone, usually. After the people of the various planets have seen our technology and what we have to give, they start to get tired of living under hierarchies or monarchies, and start to demand what we can give them. They demand to come into the Empire of their own accord. It's almost a mathematical formula. You can predict the thing. But Darkover doesn't. We don't quite know why."

He struck his clenched fist on his desk. "They say we just

don't have a damned thing they want! Oh, they trade with us, sometimes—give platinum, or gold, or matrix crystals—you know what they are?—for things like cameras and luxury goods and medical supplies. But they don't show the faintest interest in setting up industry or commercial exchange with us."

The Darkovans, according to the Legate, were ruled by a caste who lived in seclusion; incorruptible and unapproachable. Few of them ever came into the cities. They were a mystery, a riddle.

"In fact, the only thing we ever had that they wanted was horses. Horses! Somebody brought in a few dozen of them, a couple of hundred years ago, and the Hasturs bought them all. They run wild on the outer steppes—damned backward planet! The people took to them, but they wouldn't take to surface vehicles. They say they don't like building roads. They buy a few planes now and then—"

He leaned his chin on his hands, sighing again. "It's a crazy place. I can't figure it out. Who knows? Maybe you'll do it after me."

When he got off work, Kerwin went through the more respectable end of the Trade City, and toward the Spacemen's Orphanage. He remembered every step of the way. It rose before him, a white cool building, strange among the pale trees, the Terran star-and-rocket blazoned over the door; the outer hall was empty, but through an open door he saw a small group of boys, working industriously around a globe. Sounds came from the back of the building, the high cheery sounds of children playing; he could hear no words, only calls and cries muted by intervening walls.

In the big lobby-office which had been the terror of his childhood, Kerwin waited until a lady in quiet dress, Darkovan fashion—loose robe, furred jacket over all—came out and inquired with calm friendliness what she could do for him.

When he told her his errand, she held out her hand cordially. "So you were one of our boys? I think you must have been before my time. Your name is?"

34

"Jeffry Kèrwin, Jr."

Her forehead ridged in a polite effort at concentration. "I may have seen the name in records. When did you leave? At twelve? Oh, that is unusual. Mostly our boys stay until eighteen. Then, after testing, the HQ finds them work."

"I was sent to my grandparents on Earth."

"Well, we have records on all of our children. If your parents are known—" she hesitated. "Of course, we try to get complete records on everyone, but it's possible that one parent's name is not listed, if your father chose—"

"You mean, if my mother was one of the bar-girls, don't you?"

She nodded, looking ruffled at this plain speaking. "If you'll wait a minute." She went into a little side office. Through the open door he caught a glimpse of machines, and a trim girl in uniform. After a moment, the lady came back looking puzzled and a little annoyed. She said curtly, "I can't imagine what you are talking about, Mr. Kerwin. There is no record here, at all, of you. In fact, we never heard of you."

Kerwin stared, in amazement. "You're kidding. I lived here until I was twelve."

She shook her head. "I'm sorry. We have no record at all of anyone called Kerwin. Any other name?"

He said, puzzled, "I don't know how it could be."

"Furthermore, we have no records of any of our boys being sent to Terra. That would be—quite unlikely."

Kerwin took a step forward. He loomed over the woman, menacing, a big man, furious. "Who are you trying to kid? I *lived* here—twelve years! I *was* sent to Earth! Damn it, I can prove it.!"

She shrank away. "Please—"

"Look," Kerwin said reluctantly, apologetically, "I'm sorry, I don't mean to be—could the name be misfiled, misplaced, misspelled?"

"Of course, if you had been registered here under another name."

"No, damn it," Kerwin shouted, "they called me *Kerwin*.

I learned to write my name—in the schoolroom right in there."

"I'm sorry, we have no record of anyone at all called Kerwin," she said coldly. "But if you wish—" she beckoned him through the enclosure. "If it will convince you," she said coldly, "here."

She took his fingerprints; slid the card into the machine. He watched the great silent steel face of the machine. Scanning, selecting on the computer banks; fingerprints did not change. Somewhere in there would be the record of a kid called Jeff Kerwin—the kid his classmates had called *Tallo*, which was Darkovan for Red.

IBM speeds are recorded in milliseconds; there is none of the humming and clicking which laymen associate with monster machines. With uncanny speed a card was released. Kerwin reached down and snatched it up before the woman could give it to him, but as he turned it over his assurance that she was lying drained away and he felt some cold terror paralyze his stomach. In the characterless capitals of mechanical printing it read: "NO RECORD OF SUBJECT."

She took the card from Kerwin's lax fingers.

"You cannot accuse a machine of lying," she said coldly. "Now, please, I'll have to ask you to leave." Her tone said, clearer than words, that unless he did, someone would come and put him out.

Kerwin clawed desperately at the counter edge. He felt as if he had stepped into some cold and reeling expanse of space. He said, shocked and desperate, "Am I—crazy? Is there another Spacemen's Orphanage on Darkover?"

She stared at him until a sort of pity took the place of anger. "No, Mr. Kerwin. Why don't you try the HQ center, Floor Eight? Maybe they could help you, if there is a mistake."

Kerwin swallowed hard and went. Floor Eight. Medic and Psych.

She thought he was crazy.

Was he?

He stumbled down the steps into the cold air, his feet numb. They were lying, *lying....*

No. That was what every paranoid thought; they, some mysterious and elusive *they*, were lying.

But damn it, damn it, he thought desperately, clutching at reality, *I lived here.* I used to sleep in that dormitory with the windows up there.

He felt like going up to see if the JAK he had carved into the tallath-wood frame was still there. But he abandoned the plan. The way his luck was running, he'd run into a batch of the children and be accused of being a potential child molester, or something like that. But he turned and looked back at the white walls where he had spent his childhood— *or had he?*

Kerwin clasped his hands at his temples, trying to search out memory, but he could only remember a bare dark hall, a sky, a man in a deep-hooded cloak who strode arrogantly down a corridor, flaming hair shining in the sun . . . and then he was in the spacemen's orphanage, playing, studying, eating and sleeping in a cluster of kids wearing blue pants and white shirts. When he was nine he had had a crush on one of the nurses, a slim Darkovan girl named—what? Maruca. She moved softly in flat-heeled slippers, her white robes moving with fluid grace, and her voice was gentle and low. *She tousled my hair and once when I had a fever she came to sit on my bed and stroked my forehead, singing to me her soft songs in a strange lilting contralto.* When he was eleven he'd bloodied the nose of a boy called Hjalmar for calling him *Tallo*, and they'd been pulled apart, kicking and spitting and clawing, still yelling gutter insults at each other, by the gray-haired man who taught mathematics to the Third Group. And just a few weeks before they had bundled him, scared and shaking and listless from the drugs, aboard the starship, there had been a girl named Ivy; he had hoarded his allotment of sweets for her, and they had held hands shyly, and smiled under the falling leaves, and once awkwardly he had kissed her, but she turned her face away so that he had kissed only a mouthful of fine, soft, sweet-scented hair.

No, they couldn't tell him he was crazy. He'd do what the woman said; he'd go to the HQ. Not Medic and

Psych, but Records. They had a record there of everyone who had ever been in the Terran Empire service. Everyone.

They would know.

The man in Records sounded a little startled when Kerwin asked for a check, and Kerwin couldn't exactly blame him. After all, you don't usually walk up and ask for your records. Most people know who they are. Kerwin fumbled for an excuse.

"I never knew who my mother was. I thought it might be on record here. . . ."

The man took his fingerprint and punched buttons disinterestedly. After a time his mechanical printer began giving off information and Kerwin leaned forward to read it, first with satisfaction because evidently it was a full record, then with growing disbelief:

"KERWIN, JEFFERSON ANDREW. WHITE. MALE. CITIZEN, Terra. HOME, Mount Denver. SECTOR, Two. STATUS, single. HAIR, red. EYES, gray. COLORING, fair. EMPLOYMENT HISTORY, hired at age nineteen, apprentice communications department. PERFORMANCE, satisfactory. PERSONALITY, withdrawn. POTENTIAL, high.

"Requested transfer at age 22. Sent as warranted communications officer certificate Magaera. PERFORMANCE, excellent. PERSONALITY, withdrawn. POTENTIAL, rated very high. No entanglements. No demerits. Promotions regular and rapid. Requested transfer after two years. Sent to Phi Coronis IV, planet Wolf. Communications rating expert. PERFORMANCE, excellent. PERSONALITY, adequate, but considered unstable in view of requests for transfer. POTENTIAL, exceptionally high. No marriages. No recorded liaisons. No communicable diseases. Requested transfer to Darkover for personal reasons—unknown. Request approved and granted. PERSONALITY APPRAISAL, Kerwin is excellent. Valuable. Displays personality defects. RATING, extra high. POTENTIAL, excellent."

Kerwin frowned. "That's not the record I want."

"That's your official transcript, Mr. Kerwin. It's all we've got on you."

Kerwin bit his lip. "Look," he said. "I was born on Darkover, don't you keep birth records?"

The clerk frowned. "The print goes through the whole scanning bank," he said, "but I can try you under *pass rights*, if you went as an orphan. I'll try birth records, too."

He punched buttons for several minutes, figures appeared briefly and disappeared, then he shook his head.

"These are the only birth records we have under Kerwin," he said, and tore off the printed paper, handing it to Kerwin. Kerwin scanned it, chewing his lip, frowning in growing puzzlement.

"KERWIN, EVELYN JANIS. Female. Parents, Rupert Kerwin and native woman known as Mally. Died age six months."

"KERWIN, ARTHUR. Male. Parents Rupert Kerwin and unknown mother. School in Trade City."

"KERWIN, HENDERSON. Male. Negro. Died age 45 of radiation burns on Satellite Two."

"Those are all the births or deaths we have under Kerwin,"

he said. "And no pass rights for orphans since—" He consulted another panel briefly, "a girl named Teddy Kerlayne was sent to Magaera, twelve years ago. That's not you."

With fading hopes, Kerwin asked, "Who's this Rupert Kerwin?"

"I know him. Came out here about eight years ago from the Ridge. Married a Darkovan woman—has a kid."

Kerwin mechanically shredded the paper into bits. "Try one more thing," he said at last, desperately. "Try my father."

He shrugged. "Buddy, you sure are hard to convince." But he started punching buttons, staring at the glassed-in surface where the cards first appeared before the facsimiles were printed. Abruptly he started, and Kerwin saw his face change. Then he said, civilly enough, "Sorry sir, we have no records of anyone called Kerwin."

39

Kerwin snapped, "You're lying. There's got to be! Or what are you gawping about? Move your hand and let me see!"

The clerk said blandly, "As you wish," but he had punched a button first and the screen was blank. Fury and frustration surged up in Kerwin, like a cresting wave. "Are you trying to tell me I don't exist?"

"Look," the clerk said wearily, "you can erase an entry in a ledger, but you show me anyone who can tamper with the memory banks of the Terran HQ computers, and I'll show you a cross between a man and a crystoped. According to official records, you came to Darkover for the first time the day before yesterday. Now go see a psych, and quit bugging me."

Lies, Kerwin thought, lies. They couldn't tell him he didn't exist, or that his memories were delusions. Somehow, for some reason, they were all lying.

A computer, too?"

Yes, damn it, a computer too.

Kerwin reached into his pocket; extended a folded bill.

The clerk glanced up, almost frightened. For a moment greed and fear wavered in his face. Finally he said softly, "All right, sir. But if the banks are being monitored, it's my job."

Kerwin watched the programming this time. The machine burped slowly to itself, and a red light flashed. The clerk said, softly, "Shunting circuit."

Then, in the depths of the little screen, red-neon letters flashed into view.

"Requested information is in closed files, for which priority circuit must be presented."

The letters flashed on and off with hypnotic intensity. Finally Kerwin shook his head, motioning, and the screen stared blank and enigmatic.

"Well?" the clerk said softly.

"At least that proves I *had* a father," he said. Now he was sure, at least, that there *was* a mystery; he wasn't just flailing, blindly, against a wall. It might even explain why there had been no record at the Spacemen's orphanage.

But how and why were questions Kerwin still could not answer. He turned and went out, resolve slowly hardening in him.

He had been drawn back to Darkover, only to find a greater mystery waiting for him. Somehow, somewhere, he would find the answer to all the questions. Maybe this was why he had come.

CHAPTER FOUR

HE LET IT alone for the next few days. He had to; breaking in on a new job, however simple the job was, and however similar to the one on his last planet, demanded all his attention. It was a highly specialized branch of Communications—the testing, calibrating, and occasional repair of the intercom equipment both in the HQ building itself and from point to point in the Terran Zone. It was time consuming and tedious rather than difficult, and he often found himself wondering why they bothered to bring Terran personnel in from outside, rather than training local technicians. But when he put the question to one of his associates, his friend only shrugged:

"Darkovans won't take the training. They don't have a technical turn of mind—no good with this sort of thing." He indicated the immense bank of machinery they were inspecting. "Just naturally that way, I guess."

Kerwin snorted brief, unamused laughter. "You mean something inborn—some difference in the quality of their minds?"

The other man glanced at him warily, realizing that he had trodden on a sore place. "You're Darkovan? But you were brought up by Terrans—you take machinery and technology for granted. As far as I know, they don't have anything resembling it—never have had." He scowled. "And they don't want it, either."

Kerwin thought about that, sometimes, lying in his bunk in the bachelor quarters of the HQ building, or sitting over a solitary drink in one of the spaceport bars. The Legate had mentioned that point—that the Darkovans were immune to the lure of Terran technology, and had kept out of the mainstream of Empire culture and trade. Barbarians, beneath the veneer of civilization? Or—something less obvious, more mysterious?

During his off-duty hours, sometimes, he strolled down into the Old Town; but he did not wear the Darkovan cloak again, and he made sure that his headgear covered the red head. He was giving himself time to work it through, to be sure what his next move would be. If there was a next move.

Item: the orphanage had no record of a boy named Jefferson Andrew Kerwin, sent to Terran grandparents at the age of twelve.

Item: the main computer banks at the HQ refused to disclose any information about Jefferson Andrew Kerwin, Sr.

Kerwin was debating what these two facts might have in common—added to the fact that the Terran HQ computer was evidently set in such a way as to give the casual inquirer no information whatever—not even that such a person as his father had ever existed.

If he could find someone he had known at the orphanage, presumably that would be proof, of a sort. Proof at least that his memories of a life there were real—

They were real. He *had* to start from there, because there was no other place to start. If he began doubting his own memories, he might as well open the door right now to chaos, utter and entire. So he would go on the assumption that his memory was real, and that for some reason or other, the records were being withheld.

During the third week he became aware that he had seen the man Ragan just a little too frequently for coincidence. At first he thought nothing of it. In the spaceport café, when he saw Ragan at a far table each time he entered, he nodded a casual greeting and that was that. After all, the place was public, and there were doubtless many steady customers and habitués. He was well on the way to being one himself, by now.

But when an emergency failure in the spaceport dispatch office kept him on duty overtime, one evening, and he saw Ragan in his usual place at well past the usual hour, he began to notice it. So far, it was just a hunch; but he began to shift his mealtimes and eat at odd hours—and four times out of five he saw the swart Darkovan there. Then he shifted to another café, and did his drinking in another bar, for a day or two; and by now he was sure that he was being shadowed by the man. No, shadowed was the wrong word; it was too open for that. Ragan was making no effort to keep out of Kerwin's sight. He was too clever to try to force himself on Kerwin as an acquaintance—but he was putting himself in Kerwin's path and Kerwin had the curious hunch that he wanted to be charged with it; questioned about it.

But why? He thought it through, long and slowly. If Ragan was playing a waiting game, perhaps it was tied in somehow with the other oddities. If he held aloof, and seemed not to notice, maybe they—whoever "they" were—would be forced to show a little more of their hand.

But nothing happened, except that he settled down to the routine of his new job and his new life. In the Terran Zone, life was very much like life in the Terran Zone of any other Empire planet. But he was very conscious of the world beyond that world. It called to him, with a strange hunger. He found himself straining his ears, in the mixed society of the spaceport bars, for scraps of Darkovan conversation; absentmindedly heard himself answer one too many casual questions in Darkovan. And sometimes at night he would take the enigmatic blue crystal from its place around his neck and stare into its strange cold depths, as if by wanting it fiercely he could bring back the confused memories to which it now seemed a key. But it lay in his palm, a cold stone, lifeless, giving back no answer to the pounding questions in him. And then he would thrust it back into his pocket and walk restlessly down to one of the spaceport bars for a drink, again, straining ears and nose for a whiff of something beyond . . .

It was three full weeks before the waiting suddenly

snapped in him. He spun around from the bar on impulse, not giving himself time to consider what he would do or say, and strode toward the corner table where the little Darkovan, Ragan, sat over a triangular cup of some dark liquid. He jerked out a chair with his foot and lowered himself into it, glowering across the ill-lighted table at Ragan.

"Don't look surprised," he said roughly. "You've been on my tail long enough." He fingered, in his pocket, the edges of the crystal; drew it out, slapped it on the table between them. "You told me about this, the other night—or was I drunker than I think? I've got the notion you have something more to say. Say it."

Ragan's lean, ferret face looked wary and guarded. "I didn't tell you anything that any Darkovan couldn't have told you. Almost anyone would have recognized it."

"Just the same, I want to know more about it."

Ragan touched it with the tip of a finger. He said, "What do you want to know? How to use it?"

Briefly, Kerwin considered that. No; at present, at least, he had no use for such tricks as Ragan had done with the crystal, to melt glasses or—whatever else it might do. "Mostly I'm curious to know where it came from—and why I happened to have one."

"Some assignment," Ragan said dryly. "There are only a few thousand of them, I should imagine." But his eyes were narrowed, not casual at all, although his voice was elaborately casual. "Some of the people at the Terran HQ have been experimenting with the small ones. You could probably get a sizable bonus, or something, by turning this one over to them for experimental purposes."

"No!" Kerwin heard himself speak the negative before he even knew he had rejected the idea.

"But why come to me?" Ragan asked.

"Because lately I've stumbled over you every time I turn around—and I don't think it's because you're charmed with my company. You know something about this business, or you want me to think so. First of all—you might tell me who you thought I was, that night. Not just you—everybody who saw me, mistook me for *somebody*. That same night I got slugged and rolled in an alley, presumably because I looked like that other person."

Ragan's mouth dropped open; Kerwin could not doubt that he was, quite genuinely, startled.

"No, Kerwin. If anything, that would have protected you. With almost anybody."

"But who . . ."

Ragan chewed his lip; then, resolutely, shook his head. "It's a messy business, and I don't want to get mixed up in it. I'll tell you this much—it's because of your red hair. If you were brought up on Darkover, you must know that red hair's taboo here."

Kerwin nodded, and Ragan went on. "It's—limited to Darkovans of a particular high caste. Of course, you may get it from the Terran side." He stopped again, his eyes shifting uneasily from side to side. "Frankly, if I were you, I'd be on the first ship out from Darkover, and I wouldn't stop till I was halfway across the Galaxy. That's my advice—dead sober."

Kerwin said, with a bleak smile, "Maybe I like it better when you're drunk," and signaled to the waiter for refills. "Listen, Ragan," he said forcefully, when the waiter had gone, "if I have to, I'll put on Darkovan clothes and go down in the Old Town—"

"And get your throat cut?"

"You just said red hair would protect me. No. I'll go down in the Old Town, and stop everybody I meet on the street, and ask them who they think I am, or who I look like. And sooner or later I'll find *somebody* to tell me."

"You don't know what you're monkeying with."

"And I won't, unless you tell me."

"Stubborn damned fool," Ragan said. "Well, it's your neck. What do you expect *me* to do? And what's in it for me?"

Now Kerwin felt on safer ground. He would have distrusted it, if the shrewd Darkovan had offered to help him.

"Damned if I know, but there must be something you want from me, or you wouldn't have spent so much time hanging around waiting for me to ask you questions. Money? You know how much a Communications man makes with

the Empire. Enough to live on, but no big rakeoffs. I expect—" his mouth twisted, "that you'll be expecting some
pickings whatever happens. And that you have a good
reason to expect them. Start with this." He picked up the
matrix crystal on its chain. "How do I find out about it?"

"There are a couple of licensed matrix mechanics even in
the Terran Zone," Ragan said indifferently.

"There are?" Kerwin was taken aback. "I thought it was
secret—"

"Not the small ones. Even the Terrans can handle those."

Kerwin frowned at the crystal in his hand. "I don't quite
understand. What, exactly, *is* a matrix? What would a
matrix mechanic do?"

Ragan laughed mirthlessly. "If you or I knew the answer
to that, we could write our own tickets, Kerwin. Oh, I can
tell you the simpler things. For instance, in the Terran Zone,
say you have legal papers and they're so important you don't
even feel safe about trusting them to your bank's safe-deposit
vault. Or say you have valuable jewels. You go to a matrix
mechanic, buy one of the smaller matrixes—provided you can
afford it—and get him to key it in, telepathically, to the
pattern of your own thoughts; your own brain-waves, if
you prefer. Then nothing else in the universe will ever open
that box—*nothing*—except your own wish to open it. But
when you want it open, you use the pattern they taught
you, visualize it against the crystal, and whoops—the box
is open. No key, no combination to remember—just the lines
of force that hold it shut, fall apart and there you are."

Kerwin whistled. "What a gadget! Come to think of it, I
can imagine some pretty dangerous uses of something like
that."

"Right," Ragan said dryly. "For instance, when concentration on a crystal can shift small amounts of energy, it
can—let's say—raise the heat in a thermostat so that some
important piece of machinery doesn't function. Say you're an
unscrupulous businessman trying to put your competitors
out of control. You hire a matrix mechanic to sabotage him,
break all his electric circuits, and you can prove that you
never went near the place. Which is why matrix mechanics

are licensed, supervised, and checked by the authorities, both Terran and Darkovan."

Kerwin thought that over. "Then if somebody in the Terran Zone is trying to block every attempt I make to find out—"

"I thought you'd see that. What you want, my friend, appears to be a fortune teller."

Kerwin chuckled, unexpectedly. "Maybe that's exactly what I *do* want. Well, there are telepaths and psychics on Darkover, I understand!"

Ragan said "There's one woman who works undercover. She used to be a matrix mech, a long time ago. She might, possibly, be able to help you." He fumbled in his pocket for a scrap of paper; scribbled briefly on it. "I've got contacts," he said, "in the Darkovan town. It's how I make my living. It'll cost you."

"And you?"

Ragan's brief, dry chuckle cut the silence. "For a name and address? You bought me a drink," he said, "and maybe I have a score to settle against another redhead. Good luck, *Tallo*." He raised his hand at Jeff, and went. Kerwin sat, scowling, into the untouched second drink. He didn't trust Ragan's altruism, and he couldn't help wondering if he was simply playing the other man's game—if he was being steered. He studied the address, realizing that it was in an unsavory part of town. He wasn't anxious to go there in Terran clothing—in fact, he wasn't anxious to go there at all, if there was an alternative.

In the end, he decided to take Ragan's advice, but with a difference. He checked the City Records in Thendara, and found the names of three licensed matrix mechanics. All were listed in respectable areas of the city, and all advertised themselves as bonded and legally responsible, which, Kerwin supposed, was a way of showing that they operated in the open and under the law.

He chose one at random. It was in the Darkovan quarter of the city, but quite different from the area he had explored after dark, the night of his arrival. The address lay in a district of wide, high houses, their translucent walls spilling light in all directions, with here and there a park, a public building of some sort, or a small shop. Horses and pack animals moved quietly in the street, which was smooth, grassy and well-kept without paving. In an empty square, men were working on a building whose walls rose gaunt and half-completed; men laying stone with mortar, moving great sheets of glass swathed in what looked like bundled pinkish straw. In a small market, women were bargaining for food or chatting, children clinging to their skirts.

Primitive? It was very different from the Terran Zone. The very commonplace minutiae of everyday life was some-how reassuring. They had talked so much about a barbarian culture. It was true that these people had no rocket-cars, no great roadways and skyscrapers, no spaceports. Nor did they have steel factories, nor dark mines filled with robot machineries. . . .

Kerwin chuckled, dryly, to himself. He was turning into a sentimentalist; idealizing the backward world which rejected the Empire nearby. He was theorizing without data. He glanced again at the address he had copied from Records, located the modest house, and went up the steps.

The door stood open leading into a quiet office, Darkovan style, with pale draperies shielding translucent walls, and low seats and benches. A woman, standing near the doorway, turned as Kerwin came in, and a man, at the back of the office, came quickly to join her. They were both tall and stately, dressed well in Darkovan fashion, fair-skinned, with gray eyes; and an air of quiet poise and authority. But they seemed a little taken aback, and one of them—the man—breathed "Com'yn," almost inaudibly.

Kerwin had halfway expected that.

"*Vai dom*," said the man, "you lend us grace. How may we serve you?"

But before Kerwin could answer, the woman curled her lip with swift disdain.

"*Terranan*," she said, with flat hostility. "What do you want?"

The man's face mirrored the change in hers. They were enough alike to be brother and sister, and Kerwin noted, in the fluid light, that although both were dark of hair and gray-eyed, there were pale reddish glints in the hair of both; highlights, hardly noticeable. But they did not have anything like the red hair and the aristocratic bearing of the three redheads he had seen in the Sky Harbor Hotel that night.

Kerwin said, uneasy under their focused stare, "I understand you accept commissions from Terrans as well."

The woman shrugged. "At times," she said. "What do you want?"

Kerwin extended the matrix to them. "I want information."

The woman frowned, motioned it away, went to a bench and picked up a length of something sparkly, like silk. Shrouding her hand with the stuff, she took the crystal from Jeff's fingers, scanned and studied it briefly. The man looked over her shoulder. Finally the woman said, "How did you come by this?"

Kerwin repeated the story. With another small shrug, the woman led the way to a low desk, topped with a thick, wavy glass plate. She sat down, the matrix before her, studied it for several moments, picked up a hand lens and looked through it, her face withdrawn and thoughtful.

Lights began to wink briefly in the glass which looked irregular and opaque. The woman frowned over the crystal, her face brightening and darkening with the light.

"I can tell you this," she said, without looking up, "it's not registered here in Thendara."

"The pattern's not quite—" the man bent over the woman's shoulder. Swathing his hand in a fold of the silk stuff, he took up the crystal from the woman. "I think it is—"

He broke off. He looked from the crystal to Kerwin and back again to the crystal. He said to his wife, "Do you suppose he knows what he has here?"

"Probably not," she said. "He comes from off-world, I can sense it."

Kerwin wondered with a little annoyance if they were going to keep right on talking past him.

They were not speaking the language of the spaceport, nor yet the pure dialect of Thendara. With a little shock, he realized that again he was hearing the language the three

49

redheads had used—that language whose form he somehow knew without being able to recall a single word—

The woman raised her head, speaking the mixed language of the spaceport town again, and said quietly, "Do you know anything at all about this?"

Kerwin shook his head. Then, as if compelled under the stern gray gaze of the woman, he said reluctantly, "Two names—" and he remembered them again as from a dream; *Tell the barbarian he will come no more to the plains of—*

"Arilinn," he said slowly. "The Golden Bell."

The woman suddenly shuddered. He saw her poise somehow split and crack. Hastily, she stood up; the man extended the crystal to Kerwin as if their movements were synchronized.

"It is not for us to meddle in the affairs of the *vai leroni*," the woman said, flatly. "We can tell you nothing."

Kerwin stared. "But you know something—you can't—"

The man shook his head. His face was blank, unreadable. "Go," he said. "I am sorry. We cannot help you. We know nothing."

"What are the *vai leroni?* What—"

But the two faces, so much alike, so distant and arrogant, were closed and impassive—and full of dread.

"It is not for us," the woman repeated.

Kerwin felt as if he would explode with frustration. He put out his hand in a futile, pleading gesture. The man stepped quickly back, avoiding the touch, the woman withdrawing fastidiously.

"My God, you can't leave it like that," Kerwin demanded, "If you know something, you've got to tell me!"

"This much—" the woman's face softened slightly. "This much I will tell. I thought that"—she pointed to the crystal—"had been destroyed. Since they saw fit to leave it with you, they may some day see fit to give you an explanation. But if I were you, I would not wait for it."

"Enough." The man touched her arm. "Go," he said. "You are not welcome here. Not in our house, not in our city, not in our world. We have no quarrel with you—yet. But go."

There was no appeal. Kerwin went.

Somehow he had halfway expected this. Another door slammed in his face. But he could not drop it here, even if he had wanted to; even if he had been—as he was beginning to be—frightened.

One more avenue remained.

He took the precaution of covering his hair, and although he didn't wear the Darkovan cloak, he carefully left off the insignia of the Service. When he went into the Old Town he might have been anything—Terran or Darkovan.

The address Ragan had given him was a small stone cottage in a crumbling slum; there was no bell, and after he knocked, he stood there, waiting a long time. He had half resolved to turn away again when steps sounded inside, and the door swung open. A woman stood in the doorway holding the door frame with an unsteady hand.

She was small and colorless, verging on middle age, non-descriptly clad; and she looked at Kerwin with dreary indifference, seeming to focus her eyes with some difficulty.

"Did you want something?" she asked, not caring.

"A man named Ragan sent me. He said you were a matrix technician."

"There are enough of them," the woman said, without interest. "Why come to me? They wiped me out, years ago. Oh, yes, I still do some work. But it'll cost you. If it was legal, you wouldn't be here."

"What I want's not illegal, as far as I know. But maybe it's impossible."

A faint spark of interest flickered behind the dull eyes. "Come in." She stepped aside, motioning him into the room with a gesture. Inside, the place was clean enough, but had an odd, pungent-familiar smell. Herbs were burning in a brazier; the woman went and stirred the fire, sending up fresh clouds of the aromatic smoke, and when she turned her eyes were more alert.

Kerwin thought he had never seen so colorless a person. Her hair, which was coiled loose on her neck, was a faded gray, the same sleazy gray as her faded smock; she walked wearily, stooping a little as if in pain. Lowering herself carefully into a chair, she gestured him with a tired, abrupt motion of her head to sit on a stool before her.

"Now. You wanted—What do you want, *Terranan?*"

"How did you—"

Her pale lips moved in a faint stretching, not quite a smile. "Your Darkovan is perfect," she said, "but remember what I am. There is another world in your walk and your speech. Don't waste your time and mine with lies, *Terranan.*"

Kerwin brushed back his headgear, nodding. At least she hadn't mistaken him for his mysterious double somewhere. Maybe, Kerwin thought, if I level with her, she'll level with me.

He laid down the matrix crystal.

"I was born on Darkover," he said, "although I grew up on Terra. My father was a Terran. I came back here with the idea of finding out more about myself. I thought it would be a very simple matter."

"And it's not? Even with this?" She leaned forward and took the crystal. Unlike the other mechanics, she held it in her bare hands. The hands were beautiful, younger than the rest of her, smooth and supple.

"A pretty toy," she said. "Oh, yes, and more. Given to you that they might trace—Tell me about it."

Feeling suddenly secure, Kerwin spoke of the events of the last few days, including being mistaken for someone else, the attack in the street, the failure to find his name on record at the Orphanage, and finally the refusal of the matrix mechanics to tell him anything. She listened, very still, her eyes fixed on him.

"The Golden Bell is avenged. . . ." she repeated the words musingly in Darkovan, making two words of the name, *Clein Doree;* then spoke it again, "Oh, yes, Cleindori was beautiful. Long, long they sought her in the hills beyond the Kadarin—"

She rose, and from a cupboard she took something wrapped in silks; before her, on the table, she laid a small wicker frame. Carefully, untwisting the silk without touching the thing wrapped in it, she laid it in the frame. It was a crystal, like his but larger, with blue starfire glints inside.

The woman shaded her eyes with her hand and looked at the crystal; winced, closed her eyes and looked up at Kerwin through narrowed lids.

"You aren't what you seem," she murmured, slurring her speech strangely. "You came here for happiness, but you will find something else—You will find the thing you desire, and you will destroy it, but you will save it too. . . ."

Kerwin frowned and said rudely, "I didn't come here to have my fortune told."

She seemed not to hear, muttering almost incoherently. It was dark in the room, except for the dim glow of the brazier, and very cold. Impatient, Kerwin stirred; she made an imperative gesture and he sank back, surprised at the authority with which she moved. This muttering old witch, what was she doing?

The crystal on the table, his own crystal, glowed and shimmered. The crystal in the wicker frame, between the woman's cupped hands, began slowly to glow with blue fire. The light in the room seemed to center, to pour from that blue center. Kerwin sat there a long time, while the woman stared into the crystal and murmured to herself. Finally it occured to Kerwin that the woman was in a trance; if she was a genuine clairvoyant, she might answer his questions.

"Who am I?" he asked.

"You are the one who was sent," she said, low and thickly. "It was a trap that missed its firing. They didn't know, the proud Com'yn. Do you remember the place in Thendara? Cleindori—"

The lights in the crystal seemed to coagulate suddenly into a brilliant flash of flame. Kerwin flinched, as it knifed through his eyes; but he could not move. And then a scene rose before his eyes, clear and distinct, as if printed indelibly on the inside of his lashes:

Two men and two women, all of them in Darkovan clothing, were seated around a table on which lay a crystal not unlike the one before him now. One of the women, very frail, very fair, was bending over it, holding the edges of the table with a tense, intent grip; her face, framed in pale reddish-blonde hair, had an eerie, haunting familiarity. *Where had he*

53

seen her before? The men and the other woman, who was like enough to be her sister, watched as if spellbound while the cold fires played round her gripped hands; then one of the men, a small swart man with a jeweled collar around his throat, suddenly wrenched the woman's hands from the crystal; the blue fires died and the frail woman sank back, shaking, leaning heavily on the man's arm. The scene swept away; Kerwin saw moving clouds, a thin fine rain falling. . . . A man strode through a high-pillared corridor, a man in a jeweled cloak, tall and arrogant; Kerwin gasped as he recognized the dream-face of his vague memories.

The scene narrowed again to a high-walled chamber. The woman was there, and both the men. Kerwin seemed to see these things from a strange perspective, horror and sudden dread making him tremble. He seemed to focus suddenly on a closed door, a turning door-handle that opened slowly, slowly, then was suddenly flung back and two dark forms appeared against the light—

Kerwin screamed. It was not his own voice, but the voice of a child, thin and terrible and terrifying, a wordless shriek of panic. He slumped forward across the table, the scene dark before his eyes, remembered screams ringing and ringing on and on in his ears long after his cry had jolted him up to consciousness again.

Dazed, he straightened and passed his hand slowly across his eyes. His hand came away wet with sweat—or tears. Confused, he shook his head. He was not in that high-walled room filled with vague shapes of terror. He stood in the small stone-sided room of the cottage, and the woman across the table had collapsed forward, her body lying across the wicker frame, spilling the crystal on the floor. There was no blue light in the crystal now. Kerwin looked down at the woman with puzzlement and something like anger. For the pictures had meant nothing to him, nothing. Were they an old memory? *Why had he screamed?* He felt cautiously of his throat, which felt odd and raw. His voice felt frayed.

"What the hell was that all about?"

The woman neither stirred nor spoke. Kerwin scowled;

drunk, drugged? Not gently, he reached out to lay hold on her shoulder, shaking it insistently.

With a nightmarish slow grace, the woman slid down; toppled sideways to the floor. Swearing, Kerwin vaulted the table, knelt at her side. But before he moved, he already knew the truth.

The woman was dead.

CHAPTER FIVE

FOR A moment, caught in nightmarish disbelief, Kerwin stood and stared. His throat still hurt, and he felt a ragged hysteria gripping at him.

All the doors keep closing in my face.

He looked down at the dead woman, with almost an ache of pity. He had dragged her into this—and she was dead. This unknown, unlovely woman—he didn't even know her name!—and he had involved her in the mysterious fate that seemed to be tracking him. Futilely, he bent and felt at her pulse again. Maybe she was only stunned, maybe he should sprinkle her face with water or—

No. She was dead, all right.

Gingerly, Kerwin picked up his own matrix on its long chain; put it into his pocket. He hesitated, cast a glance at the other matrix lying in the wicker frame. Something strange about it caught his eyes.

The light was gone from the blue stone. Lifeless and dead, it lay in the cradle; lusterless, opaque.

Had it died when the woman died? *Or had it been somehow destroyed by that same mysterious force?*

What made me think of that?

Jeff Kerwin got a grip on himself. He looked once more at the dead woman, almost apologetically, and then, turning away, he called the police.

They came, green-clad, cross-belted Darkovans of the City Guard—the equivalent of metropolitan police in all Darkovan cities. They were not at all happy to see a Terran there, and showed it. Reluctantly, with rigid politeness, they allowed him the legal privilege of summoning a Terran consul before questioning, a privilege Kerwin would just as soon have waived. He wasn't at all eager for the HQ to know that he had been making inquiries down here.

They asked him questions, and then they didn't like the answers. Somehow he managed to keep from mentioning his own matrix, or even why he had been there to consult the woman—though he was sure they drew their own conclusions about that. But in the end, because there wasn't a mark on her, and because a Terran medic and a Darkovan one both gave their independent opinion that she had died of a sudden heart attack, they let him go, and escorted him formally to the edge of the Terran Zone, and said goodbye to him with a certain grim finality behind their politeness. He got the impression that if he was found in that part of the city again, they wouldn't be responsible for what happened.

So that was that. He had pursued a narrowing trail into a blind alley, and it had slammed shut in his face.

He thought, then, that he had seen the worst of it, when the blind alley led to a dead end and a dead woman. Alone in his quarters, pacing the floor like a caged animal, he reviewed it again and again, trying to puzzle some sense out of the confusion.

Damn it, there was purpose behind it. Someone, something, was *determined* that he should not trace down his own past—and would stop at nothing, not even murder, to insure it.

The man and woman, refusing to help him, had said, "It is not for us to meddle in the affairs of the *vai leroni.*" The words were unfamiliar to him; he tried to puzzle out their component parts, and finally went and hunted out a dictionary. *Vai,* of course, was a title of honor; *vai dom* meant *worthy lord. Leroni* he found under *leronis* (mountain dialect); "probably derived from *laran,* meaning power or inheritance right; a sorceress." He frowned. A *vai leronis,* then, would be a woman possessing unusual powers of some sort, presumably in a high position of honor. But why should he be thought to be entangled in the affairs of the *vai leroni,* whoever they were?

He was still, vainly, trying to puzzle it out when he went

on duty again; and all the time he tested connections in a faulty intercom circuit, the words were ringing strangely in his mind.

His first night on Darkover. The three strange redheads in the Sky Harbor Hotel, and the girl with the pixie face, who had hailed him as *com'ii*—friend, that is, in the sense of being equal, a member of a clan or family of equivalent social status. By analogy, *Com'yn* would be The Equals, possibly even The Aristocrats.

An intercom buzzer on the wall struck through his pre-occupation; ill-naturedly, he growled into it. Then he blinked and braced, for the face of the Legate was full in the screen, and he looked very grim indeed.

"Kerwin? Arrange for relief and get yourself up to Administration—on the double!"

Somewhat puzzled, Kerwin did as ordered, riding the elevator to the high glass-walled penthouse which was the Legate's staff quarters. As he waited outside by the reception desk, he stiffened, seeing the Legate's office door open. Two men in the green cross-belted uniform of City Guardsmen, Darkovans, emerged, with another man whose rich dress and short jeweled cloak betokened Darkovan aristocracy. All three of them looked straight through Kerwin, and the man felt a sudden twinge of apprehension, a little nagging hunch that the worst was yet to come.

"Kerwin? The Legate will see you now."

Kerwin went into the office. The Legate scowled at him, and this time did not ask him to sit down.

"So it's the Darkovan," he said, not kindly. "I might have known it would be you. What the devil have you been getting yourself into now?"

He didn't wait for Kerwin's answer.

"You were warned," he said. "You got yourself into trouble before you'd been here twenty four hours. Slugged and rolled for wandering around in the Old Town in Darkovan clothes. That wasn't enough for you. You had to go prying, looking for trouble."

Kerwin opened his mouth to answer; the Legate fore-stalled him. "I called your attention, before, to the situation on Darkover. We live here under an uneasy truce at best; and such as it is, we have an agreement with the Darkovans, and if we want them to enforce their side, we have to keep our side of the agreement. Which includes keeping nosey tourists out of the Darkovan sector."

The injustice of that made Jeff's blood boil. "Look here, sir—" he began hotly.

"Save it," the Legate said. "You got me just curious enough to investigate that cock-and-bull story you told us about having been born here. According to Records, the whole thing seems to have been made up out of whole cloth. There's no record of a Jeff Kerwin anywhere." He smiled, grimly. "Except the one I'm looking at right now."

"That's a lie!" Kerwin burst out.

Then he stopped himself. It was like a fist at his throat. He had seen the red warning signal flash for a priority circuit, with his own eyes. But the man who had been bribed to show him, had made it clear; *it's as much as my job's worth.* Could he involve an innocent bystander in his own troubles? As long as he knew—

The Legate was scowling at him. "This is no world for snoops and troublemakers," he said. "I warned you once, remember. I understand you've been doing some pretty extensive nosing around." Suddenly his voice was hard and furious. "I've had an official complaint, about you," he said, "straight from the City authorities here."

Kerwin drew breath, trying to present his case calmly and reasonably. "Sir," he said, "if I made this whole thing up out of thin air, why would my nosing around bother anybody?" He made an eloquent gesture. "Sir, can't you see that if anything, this proves my story—that there's something going on, something awfully damned funny?"

The Legate scowled and shook his head. "All it proves to me is that you're a nut with a persecution complex," he said. "You've got some idea that everybody's against you, or that we're all in some sort of plot to keep you from finding out what you want to know—is that it?"

Kerwin said "It sounds so damned logical when you put it that way, doesn't it?"

"Okay," the Legate said, "just tell me why anybody should bother plotting against you. Against one small-time civil servant on Darkover, son of—as you claim—an ordinary spaceman in the service? Just tell me why you'd be that important? Then ask yourself who's got delusions of grandeur?"

Kerwin made a helpless gesture. What could he say to that? After all, what *proof* did he have?

Why would the woman at the orphanage lie about it? They said, themselves, that they were anxious to maintain contact with "their boys."

Had he placed too much faith in a vague dreamish memory, in a chance resemblance—in a meeting with three redheads, which now seemed like a dream? Had he built the whole thing up from wishful thinking? Johnny Ellers' scoffing voice, that first night in the bar:

You want to be the long-lost son of the Lord High Something-or-other.

With a long sigh, he let the memory go, and the dream.

"All right, sir," he said, very meekly for him. "I'll let it go. Maybe you're right. Maybe I made too much of it. I won't—"

"You won't have a chance," the Legate said coldly. "You won't be here."

"I—" Something struck, sudden and knife-cold, at Kerwin's heart. "I won't be here?"

Grimly, the Legate nodded. "The City Masters have put you on the list of *persona non grata*," he said. "We have a sort of agreement with them. And even if they didn't—well, the official Empire policy is to take a dim view of anybody who gets too mixed up in native affairs."

Kerwin felt as if he had been pole-axed. He stood there, motionless, almost feeling the blood drain from his face, leaving him cold and lifeless. "What do you mean?"

"I mean that I've put you down for transfer," the Legate said. "You can call it that if you want to. In plain words, what it amounts to is this: you've stuck your nose into too many corners of Darkover, and we're committed to making damned sure you don't do it again. So you're fired, Kerwin.

I've signed your transfer application, and I'm afraid you're going to have to be on the next ship out of here."

Kerwin opened his mouth. He shut it again. He steadied himself against the edge of the desk, feeling as if he might fall over if he didn't. "You mean I'm being deported? Kicked off Darkover?"

"That's about it," confirmed the man. "In practice, of course, it's not that bad. You have a clear record, and I'll give you a clean-sheet recommendation. Within limits, you can have any assignment you want in your field, anywhere there's a vacancy. See the board downstairs about that."

Jeff Kerwin said, through a queer thickening lump, "But sir, Darkover—" and stopped. It was his home. It was the only place he'd ever wanted to be.

The Legate shook his head, as if he read Kerwin's thoughts. He looked tired, worn; an old man, a weary man, struggling with a world too complex for him, a world he never made. I'm sorry, son," he said, almost kindly, "I guess I know how you feel. But I've got a job to do, and not such a lot of leeway about how I do it. That's the way it is. You're going to be on the next ship out of here—and you won't be cleared to come back." He stood up. "I'm sorry," he said, and offered his hand, which Kerwin did not touch. The Legate's face hardened. He said "You're relieved from duty until you go. Inside of forty-eight hours, I want a formal transfer request filed for you, and I want you to stay in your quarters from now until then. We can handle this thing decently, or"— his jaw was grim—"I can have you locked up in quarters, if you'd prefer it."

Numbly, Kerwin shook his head and went.

So he had lost, then—lost entirely. It had been too big for him, the mystery he faced. He had run up against something entirely beyond him.

Or was he a dreamer, a fool with delusions of grandeur, of persecution—compensating for his orphan childhood with dreams of something greater than he knew?

He went restlessly to the window, staring at the red sun dipping toward the hills. *The bloody sun*. As the swift dark came rushing from the hills, he stood with his fists clenched, staring into the sky, the condensing mist. *Darkover—the end of Darkover for me. The world I fought for—and it's kicking me out again. I worked and schemed to get back here*—why? *And all I get is frustration, closed doors, death. . . .*

I had known since childhood that Terra had nothing for me. Now Darkover is exiling me too, saying in effect, we have no place for you.

But why?

Kerwin thrust his hand into his pocket, as if compelled, and drew forth the matrix crystal. Somehow, somehow, this was the key to the riddle and the mystery. He stared at it as if it held in its cold depths all the answers that had been denied to him elsewhere.

He drew the curtains against the blackness outside, the dim lights of the spaceport below, and set the crystal on the table. He paused, hesitant, suddenly seeing in his mind's eye the face of a woman sprawled in unlovely death—

The man Ragan had used this crystal and it hadn't hurt him.

Feeling vaguely foolish, he set the crystal up and shaded his eyes, looking into it. Nothing happened. Damn it, maybe there was some special knack to concentrating on it. Maybe he should have hunted up Ragan and forced or persuaded him to teach him, Kerwin, how to use—

He stared at the crystal intently, and for a moment it seemed that a pale dim light flashed within; but it vanished and Kerwin shook his head, foggily. He had a crick in his neck and his eyes were playing tricks—that was all. He'd heard of people who could do the old trick of "Crystal gazing," a form of self-hypnosis. This was evidently the same thing. . . .

He blinked; but the light didn't go away.

It crept, a small faint pinpoint moved faintly. It—*flared.* Kerwin jumped; it was like a red-hot wire touching him, but he still couldn't identify what had made it. He heard, faint and very far off, a voice—calling his name?

Dizzily, he shook his head, gripping the edge of the table with his fists. His head hurt.

He heard speech, speech that was just random syllables to him; a low murmuring voice that went on and on, just below the threshold of awareness, like a running, whispering stream flowing over sharp stones.

Kerwin, Kerwin . . .

It's the one.

You cannot fight it now.

If he is to be any good to us, he will find his way. That much of a test I insist upon.

A barbarian, a Terranan . . .

It sounded strangely like the redhead in the Sky Harbor Hotel, but when Kerwin whirled, there was no one in the room and the strange voices—voices?—were gone. He leaned forward, staring at the crystal.

And then he saw the girl.

From the glint of reddish hair, for a moment, he thought she was the pixie-face called Taniquel by the two Darkovan aristocrats. But immediately he saw that his eyes, and the glint of that red-gleaming hair, had misled him. This girl was tall and slight, and her hair was more gold than red, and her face was round, childish, unmarred; she looked at him from the crystal, wide dreamy gray eyes that seemed to look, unfocused, into space.

"I have faith in you," she said, or at least the words seemed to reverberate inside his head, "and we have need of you. Come."

Kerwin's hands clenched on the table. "Where! *Where?* he half shouted.

But the crystal was dead, lifeless, and the girl had faded. . . . He heard his own cry echo, foolishly, on empty walls.

Had never been there. Dizzily, Kerwin wiped his forehead. He had been mad, dreaming? Had his wishful thinking tried to give him an answer?

And now there was nothing left to do but dispose of his gear, pack for space, and leave Darkover, never to return. Leave his dreams behind, and the last of his youth. Leave behind all those vague memories. Make a new life, a smaller life somehow, bounded by the *Keep Out* sign of the old, dead, inchoate hopes and longings—accept his loneliness, make a life with bitterness and resignation.

And then something rose up inside Jeff Kerwin, something that was not the meek Terran civil servant suddenly stood up on its hind legs and pawed the ground, and said, cold and clear and unmistakably—no.

That wasn't the way. The *Terranan could never force him* to go. As for the City Authorities—*who in the hell did they think they were?*

The voice from the crystal—dream or illusion? No, Kerwin thought; the voice of his own mind, flatly rejecting the Terran commands. This was his own world, and he'd be damned if they were going to force him off it.

It seemed to come from something deep inside him, like a long-buried other self. Kerwin watched himself, with a certain blank puzzlement, as he moved around the room. He glanced at his gear, discarded most of it; thrust half a dozen minor keepsakes into a pocket, left the rest where they were. He put the matrix carefully into a pocket. Then he reached into a wardrobe for the Darkovan cloak he had bought the first night on Darkover, drew it around his shoulders, and fastened it there. He glanced briefly in a mirror, nodded abstractedly, satisfied. Without a backward glance, he walked out of his quarters, the thought dimly skittering across the surface of his mind that he would never see them again.

He paused at the door. A clear and unmistakable inner voice said *No, not now. Wait.*

Not understanding, but riding the hunch—what else was there to do?—he sat down and waited. He felt, oddly, not impatient at all. The waiting had the same wary, certain feeling of a cat watching a mouse hole; a secureness, a—a *rightness.* He sat quietly, half-whistling a tuneless little note to himself, over and over, his hands clasped. He did not feel restless. Half an hour, an hour, an hour and a half went by; his back began to feel cramped, and he shifted, automatically, to relieve it, but went on waiting. . . .

Now.

The strange hunch was working again. Kerwin stood up, automatically fingering the matrix in his pocket, and passed out the door into the deserted corridor. As he walked softly along the corridor, he found himself wondering if there would be a pickup order out for him, if he should be missed from his quarters. He supposed so. Curiously, he had no plans except the vague one of refusing to obey the deportation order. This meant he must somehow get out of the Terran Zone unobserved. What would come after, he did not know— and, strangely, did not care.

He turned aside from the main corridors where he was apt to meet acquaintances in the Service—the Darkovan cloak he was wearing might have caused questions—and went toward a little-used service elevator in a distant wing. As it swooped downward, he told himself that he ought, at least, to take off the cloak until he was out of the Terran Zone. He put up a hand to unfasten it.

No.

Clear, unmistakable, the negative warning in his mind. Puzzled, Kerwin dropped his hand.

He emerged into a narrow walkway and paused, trying to orient himself. This part of the building was not familiar to him. He turned toward one end and went on. There was a door at the end of the walkway; he pushed it open and emerged into a crowded lobby. What looked like a shift of maintenance workers in their uniforms were milling around, getting ready to go on duty; a few spacemen were standing around talking, and a group of Darkovans, city men in their loose colorful dress, were making their way through the crowd toward the outer gates. Kerwin, at first taken aback by the crowds, quickly realized that no one paid any attention to him. Slowly, unobtrusively, he made his way through the jostling people, flinching slightly—he hated crowds— and managed to join the fringes of the group of Darkovans. None of them took the slightest notice of him. He supposed they were one of the city committees that helped administer the spaceport zone. They formed a random stream in the crowd, going in their own special direction, and Kerwin, at the edge of the group but not in it, streamed along with them. They came to the door of the HQ and moved into the street. Kerwin let himself be borne on their stream.

They passed through the gateway that led out of the enclosure; the Spaceforce guards there gave them—and Kerwin—only the most cursory of glances.

Outside the gate, the group began to break up into twos and threes, talking, lingering. One of the men turned at random toward Kerwin, polite non-recognition and inquiry written on his face, eyebrows raised. Kerwin murmured a polite phrase, turned quickly and walked away from them toward the Old Town.

Lying as it was in the lee of the high escarpment above spaceport and Terran Zone, it was already shadowed with dimness. The wind blew chill, and Jeff Kerwin shivered a little in the warm cloak. Where was he going?

He hesitated at the corner of the street where once he had faced Ragan down. Should he seek out the place and try to see if the little man could be useful to him?

Again the clear, unmistakable *no* from that inner mentor. Kerwin hesitated a moment; was he imagining things, rationalizing? Well, it didn't seem to matter much, one way or the other. Somewhat grimly, he looked back toward the fading glow of the HQ building; then turned his back on it, and it was like the slamming of a mental door. That was the end of that. *Don't look back; you've cut yourself adrift. Foolhardy? Maybe. But if so, you're stuck with it.*

In this new rootlessness, it hardly mattered which way he went; he might as well follow his hunch all the way through. A strange peace seemed to descend over him at this decision; quickly, he turned his back on the known street and began to walk in the opposite direction.

He had never come so far into the Old Town; not even on that day when he sought the matrix mechanic, that day which had ended in her death. Down here, the buildings were old, built of great blocks of bleached stone, the streets wide and windswept, rising and falling now and again with low wide flights of steps. At this hour, there were few people in the streets: now and again there was some solitary walker folded in a long cloak, and once a veiled woman appeared in a curtained chair carried on the shoulders of four men, and moving noiselessly in the lee of the building, a gliding, silver-mantled nonhuman regarded him with un-involved malice. A group of boys, street gamins in ragged smocks, barefoot, moved toward him as if to pester him for alms; suddenly they drew back. *The red hair again?*

The swift dark was thickening, and the night mist had condensed into the thin, fine rain, when Kerwin became aware that he was hopelessly lost. He had been walking at random, turning corners with that strange, almost dreamish nonchalance as if it didn't matter which way he went. He stopped at a great open square, shaking his head, slowly coming up to normal consciousness. *Good God, he thought, where am I? And where am I going? I can't wander around in the rain all night, even if I am wearing a Darkovan cloak over my Terran clothes. I should have started looking for—well, for a place to hide out for a while. Or I should have tried to get out of the city.*

He looked around, orienting himself almost dazedly. Maybe he had done the wrong thing, maybe he should even try to find his way back to the HQ and take whatever was coming to him. From where he was, he couldn't even guess in what direction it lay. And the curious hunch that had been guiding him, all this way, seemed to have petered out and gone.

He stood at the corner of an open square. Down along one side was a street of little shops. Down the other, a line of old buildings, leaning at crazy angles to the street, presented blank dim-lit faces to the rain. Kerwin mopped his wet face with a wet sleeve, staring through the sleety mist at the other edge of the square, where behind a low wall a building rose toward the dark rainy sky. Inside, there were lights and, through translucent wall-spaces, moving forms. Drawn some-how magnetically to the lights, Kerwin crossed the square and stood there staring, fighting the invisible pull. *Good God, he thought again, what am I doing? I can't just walk in there. Have I really gone crazy?*

No. Impossible. I can't do it.

What's got into me? Why do I even think of it?

He realized that even as he told himself not to be a fool, his steps carried him—almost automatically—toward the wall, toward the gate in the wall. He swung it back. He passed through; stopped.

You're being a God-awful damned fool, Kerwin. Get out—turn around and get out before you get yourself into something you really can't handle. Not just being slugged in an alley somewhere.

Slowly, step by slow step, he went up the sleet-slipperied steps toward the lighted door.

Too late to draw back now. Might as well brazen it out.

He grasped the handle—carved metal, it was, in the form of a phoenix—and twisted it slowly. The door opened. He stepped inside and stood blinking in a brilliantly lighted hall, the rain still cold on his face against the sudden warmth and light.

Miles away, back in the Terran Zone, a man had gone to a telephone and requested a priority circuit to speak with the Terran Legate.

"Your bird's flown," he reported, and the Legate's face on the screen was composed and almost smug. "I thought so. Push him hard enough and they'll make a move. I knew they would."

"You sound awfully sure, sir. Maybe he just walked out on his own."

The Legate shook his head. "I doubt it."

"You want him tailed?"

The answer was immediate. "No! Hell, no! Let him go, no strings. These people are nobody's fools. No, it's their move; we just—wait."

"We've been doing that for twenty years," the man grumbled, and, slowly, the Legate nodded. "Right. We'll wait for twenty more, if we have to. But somehow I think it won't be that long. The catalyst's working now. Wait and see."

In the Terran Zone, a screen went blank. After a while the Legate pushed another button and called for a closed, priority file marked KERWIN.

He looked satisfied.

CHAPTER SIX

KERWIN STOOD, blinking against the warmth and light of the spacious hallway. He brushed rain from his face, listening to the sound of the diminishing storm. For a moment it was all he could hear. Then a bright tinkle of laughter broke the silence.

"I've won," said a girlish voice. "I told you so."

A curtain parted at the end of the long hall. Framed by the folds, a girl stood there; a small pert girl with upswept red-gold hair and a pixie-pretty face. She stood and laughed at him; the laughter melted suddenly and she said, "It's him!"

Behind her, in the curtained archway, two men appeared, and Kerwin wondered if he had wandered into some daydream—or nightmare! They were the three redheads from the Sky Harbor Hotel; the pretty girl Taniquel, the feline and arrogant Auster; the thick-set, urbane Kennard. Kennard said, now, "Of course he's the one. Hadn't you guessed that, Taniquel?"

Auster glowered and said nothing.

Kennard gently moved Taniquel out of his way and came toward Kerwin, who stood bewildered, wondering if he ought to apologize for his intrusion.

Kennard stopped, a step or two from Kerwin. "You've proved a point for us, anyway. Welcome—welcome home."

Auster said something angry, curling his mouth in a sarcastic smile.

Kerwin shook his head. He said, "I don't understand any of this."

"Tell me," Kennard countered, "how did you happen to come here?"

Kerwin said, too baffled for anything but the truth, "I don't know. Hunch, I guess."

"No," Kennard said gravely, "it was a test. And you passed it."

"A test? For what?" Kerwin demanded. Suddenly he was

both angry and apprehensive. Ever since he landed on Darkover, someone had been pushing him around. Now, when he had made what he thought was an independent move to break away, he wound up—here!

"I suppose I ought to be grateful. Right now, what I want is an explanation. What do you mean a test?"

"A test," Kennard said, "to see if you had inherited *laran*— the Com'yn telepathic gift, if you'd rather. Your father was a Terran, yes. Your mother was a woman of the Com'yn; Cleindori Aillard."

There was a sudden silence, while the incredible word *Com'yn* rolled in the resonant chamber.

"Yes," Kennard repeated, "we are Com'yn. Remember, we mistook you for one of ourselves that night. We were not so wrong as we thought."

Auster interrupted with something more that was unintelligible to Kerwin. It was strange how clearly he could understand Taniquel and Kennard, and hardly a word of Auster's speech.

"Cleindori—died," Kennard said, "and you were taken away—by night and by stealth. We tried to trace Cleindori's child; but before that, they had already sent you to Terra. Then, a few weeks ago, one of the Keepers touched you on a matrix screen."

"What?"

"I can't explain now. Any more than I can explain Auster's stupidity when he met you that night in the bar, except that he'd been drinking."

Again Auster exploded in unintelligible gibberish, and Kennard motioned him to silence. "Sharra's chains, Auster, save your breath, he's not getting a word of it." He turned back to Kerwin. "You passed the first test; you have *laran*." Kerwin remembered that the word referred to telepathic powers. "It's never been done before, but—these are strange days. You might be useful to us. For our part, we offer you a chance to stay on Darkover; I gather that's what you want."

Dazed, still off balance, Kerwin could do nothing but stare.

Well, he had followed his hunch. If it had led him from

the frying pan into the fire, he had only himself to thank. *I don't know where I'm going*, he thought, *but here I am.*

A little airship, buffeted by the treacherous winds and currents of flowing atmosphere above the crags and ridges of the mountains, fled westward through the thin reddening dawn; the first glimmers of the Bloody Sun were turning the sky to fire. They had glided out of the storm area, but the rough terrain, a dizzy distance below, was softened by layers of gray mist.

In the cramped pilot-cabin, Jeff Kerwin sat with folded legs in the low seat that hadn't been designed for the normal seated postures of an Earthman, watching Auster manipulate the unseen controls of the ship. He would not have chosen to share the cabin with Auster, but there was barely room for Taniquel and Kennard in the rear cabin, and he had not been consulted about his preferences.

He was still baffled and somewhat confused at the rapidity with which events had moved. He did understand, now, that he had been guided to them by telepathic instructions, received at least partly through the matrix he had—he didn't understand how, but he had been assured that it wasn't necessary to understand, just yet.

Almost at once they had hurried him to a small private landing field and put him aboard this plane—somehow he had been remotely surprised to know that the Darkovans made use of aircraft—saying that they had a very long way to go.

The telepathic guiding of Kerwin to them had been, he gathered, in the nature of a test; to see if he possessed a sufficient quantity, or quality, of that mysterious *laran* to be of any use to them. What use, Kerwin wasn't sure; but he was not frightened. They seemed—not exactly friendly, but somehow—well, they accepted him, much in the same way his grandparents had. Like family; that was it. Even when Kennard had brusquely cut off his questions with a rough, "Later, later," there had been no offense.

The ship had no visible instruments except a small calibrator. This Auster had adjusted when they first entered the ship, apologizing curtly for the discomfort—an unpleasant vibration that made Kerwin's teeth ache and his ears strain for a half-heard whining sound—that this caused. The adjustment was absolutely necessary, Auster told him in a few grudging words, to compensate for the presence of an undeveloped telepath within the ship.

Since then Auster had barely leaned forward, now and then, from his folded-up, kneeling posture, Darkovan fashion, stirring a hand languidly as if making a signal to some unseen watcher. Or, thought Kerwin, as if he were shooing away flies. He watched, half-fascinated and half-repelled. He asked, once, what power moved the ship—in Cahuenga, the city dialect—and Auster had replied, curtly, "Matrix crystal." This had made Kerwin purse his lips in a soundless whistle. He had not even remotely guessed that the power of these thought-sensitive crystals could be great enough to move even a small ship!

It wasn't psi power alone. He was sure of that. There had been telepaths and other parapsychs in plenty, on the other planets where Kerwin had served, but their powers were limited. Kerwin guessed, from what Ragan had told him and what little he had seen, that matrix mechanics was one of those sciences which Terrans lumped roughly together under the name of *the non-causative sciences*: cyrillics, electromentry, psychokinetics—found on nonhuman worlds. And Kerwin knew no more of these than any Terran knew.

It was easy enough to see that this ship had once been a Terran airlaunch—the lines were unmistakable, though the insignia had been painted out—with the cerberum drives removed and the interior furnishings remodeled to suit the Darkovan purchasers.

Kerwin was plainly and unequivocally scared. And yet, through his fear, there was a curious, relaxed sense of satisfaction. He had never thought of himself as Terran, except by accident of birth. Darkover had been his home, and this justified his lifelong dream, his strange scrap of memory that he really belonged there; that he was in actuality a member of their highest nobility, the Com'yn, recovered from his involuntary exile.

71

Memory of his one long talk with the Legate floated in his mind, disjointed scraps of conversation. *Trying for four generations to beg, borrow or steal something about matrix mechanics. . . . The Com'yn, not only incorruptible but unapproachable. . . .*

The Com'yn—this much he knew—were neither kings, nobility, priesthood, oligarchy, or anything even roughly analogous. And they had signed no treaty with Terra. The compact between the two worlds was a tenuous thing at best. . . . The Com'yn were seldom seen outside the fastnesses of their own hidden habitations. Kerwin had had, with his own eyes, a taste of the fantastic, or rather fanatic awe and reverence with which Darkover treated these redheaded noblemen. And if Darkover resented the nebulous, but undisputable rule of the Com'yn, the Terrans at least knew nothing about it.

Kerwin tried cautiously to unkink his cramped legs without kicking out a bulkhead. "How much further is this city of yours?" he asked Auster.

The man did not deign to glance at him. He was very thin, with a suggestion of the feline in his shoulders and the curl of his mouth; even his voice had a sibilance not unlike a purr. "We do not speak the Cahuenga here," he said tersely, "and I can't understand you, nor you me, in any other tongue, with the telepathic damper adjusted." He made a gesture toward the small calibrator.

"What's wrong with Cahuenga? You can speak it all right— I heard you, in the Terran Zone."

"We are capable of learning any known human tongue," said Auster, with that unconscious arrogance that irritated Kerwin. "But the concepts of our world are expressible only in the nexus of our own semantic symbology—and I have no desire to converse in crocodile with a half-breed on trivial matters."

Kerwin clamped his lips tight. *Double that for me, bud,* he thought, *and cram that telepathic damper up your chimney.* He'd like nothing better than to boot Auster out of the ship and see if the man could talk the birds into catching him. He'd never met a man quite so easy to dislike as Auster,

72

and he hoped he wouldn't have to associate with him much after this.

The sun was just touching the rim of the mountains when Auster stirred slightly, his satirical face relaxing a little, and pointed to a location between twin peaks of the mountains.

"It lies there," he said, "the plain of Arilinn, and the Hidden City of the Com'yn."

Kerwin moved his cramped shoulders and twisted his aching neck to look downward at this, the city of his forefathers. To him it looked pretty much like any other city, a pattern of lights, buildings, cleared spaces. The little craft slanted downward, in response to one of those shoo-fly motions of Auster's thin hands, and Kerwin made a wild grab to recover his balance, leaned, and involuntarily fell against Auster's arm.

He was wholly unprepared for Auster's reaction. The man forgot the operation of the ship, and with a great sweep of his arm, jerked backward, his elbow thrusting out to knock Kerwin away from him, hard. His forearm struck Kerwin a hard blow across the mouth, and he spat out a mouthful of unintelligible syllables; the cabin lurched, swerved. Behind them, in the rear cabin, the girl Taniquel screamed shrilly; Auster, recovering himself with a start, made swift controlling motions.

Kerwin sat rigid. His first impulse—to swat Auster in the teeth and be damned to the consequences—died unacted. He held himself in his seat by an act of will, clenching his fists on the seat-arm until he felt it split and crack between his fingers. He said in Cahuenga, "Fly the damn ship, you. If you're spoiling for a fight, wait till we get landed, and it will be my pleasure."

Kennard's head appeared in the narrow doorway between control and rear cabins. He said something in that dialect Kerwin couldn't understand, and Auster snarled, "Let him keep his crocodile's paws to himself then!"

Kennard said conciliatingly to them both, "Kerwin, you perhaps did not know that any random movement in the cabin can throw the ship off course." There was barely room for him to stand erect in the door; he looked at Kerwin thoughtfully, then shrugged. "We'll be landing in a minute, anyway."

The little ship landed smoothly. In a gray dimness of morning mist, lights were winking around the field. There was a faint, pungent trace of smoke in the air somewhere. Auster unfastened a door, and a swart Darkovan in a red jerkin and breeches threw up a short ladder. He said, in one of the Darkovan languages Kerwin knew well, "Welcome back, *vai dom'yn*," and stepped back, throwing up one hand in a gesture vaguely like a salute, not obsequious, but courtly and courteous. Auster stepped from the ship, gestured Kerwin to follow, and the man repeated the salute for him.

Kennard came down the ladder, fumbling with his feet for each separate rung, and it occurred to Kerwin that Kennard was older than he looked, or else was lame in some previously unnoticed fashion. He gave Taniquel his hand as she scrambled down the ladder, while other men in red and brown and yellow clothing came and surrounded the ship.

Taniquel looked up at Kerwin, then shook her head. "You've got blood on your mouth," she said. "Have you and Auster been fighting already?" Her own mouth quirked up in that pixie malice, and she tilted her head a little to one side, the better to observe their effect on the men. Auster glowered. Kennard said quietly, "An accident, and a misunderstanding."

"*Terranan*," Auster muttered.

"You can't expect him to be anything else," Kennard said. "And whose fault is it that he knows nothing of our taboo? There it lies"—he pointed, drawing Kerwin's gaze with the gesture—"the Tower of Arilinn."

Kerwin looked.

It rose upright, squat, and yet, on closer look, incredibly high, fashioned of some brown and glareless stone. The sight had a queer effect on Kerwin; it seemed to stir a buried memory. He said to Kennard, shakily, "Have I—been here before, sir?"

Kennard shook his head, laying his hand briefly on Kerwin's shoulder—a gesture which surprised Kerwin, in view of the taboo which appeared to surround a random touch here. Kennard withdrew his hand quickly and went on, "It is not the oldest, or the most powerful, of the Com'yn Towers. But our Keepers have worked the Tower Screens for nine hundred and twelve generations."

"And," said Auster behind them, "with the nine hundred and thirteenth, we bring the son of a Terran and a renegade *leronis* here."

Taniquel turned on him, fiercely. "Are you going to question what Elorie said? *You?*"

Auster hung his head. Taniquel came to Kerwin's side. "Now let's get inside, for heaven's sake, and not stand around on the airfield all day!"

Kerwin felt curious eyes on him as they traversed the field. The air felt damp and cold, and it crossed his mind that it would be pleasant to get under a roof, and get warm, and relax. It also crossed his mind that he would very much like a bath, and a drink, and some supper—hell—breakfast? They must have come a good third of the way around Darkover, and his time sense was out of whack, because here the sun was just coming up.

"All in good time," Kennard said. Kerwin jumped, then realized he'd have to get used to that trick Kennard had of reading his thoughts. "First, I'm afraid, you'll have to meet the others of the Arilinn Tower. Naturally they're anxious to know all about you."

Kerwin raised his hand and wiped blood from his face. He wished they'd let him clean up before thrusting him into the presence of strangers. He had not yet learned that telepaths seldom looked hard at the outward appearance of a man. He walked, at their side, across the bricked-in quadrangle of a building that looked like a barracks, a long passageway barred with a wooden gate, from which an unmistakable, familiar smell told him that horses were stabled somewhere. Only as they approached the Tower did he become aware that the clean sweep of its architecture was marred by this cluster of low buildings at its foot. They went across two more courtyards, and finally reached an archway carved of bluish stone, in which there shimmered a thin and rainbow haze. Kennard paused momentarily, and said to Kerwin, "No living human, save those of Com'yn blood, have ever passed through this Veil."

Kerwin shrugged. He felt he should be impressed or something, but he was running low on surprise. It occurred to him that he was both tired and hungry. He hadn't slept in forty-eight hours, and it made him nervous to realize that they were all—even Auster—watching to see what he would do. He said irritably, "My hat's fresh out of rabbits, and anyway, you're writing the script. Do we go this way?"

They kept on waiting, so he stepped through the trembling rainbow.

It felt faintly electric, like a thousand pins and needles, and when he looked back the forms of Kennard, Taniquel and Auster looked like shadows. He began to shake, and suddenly he wondered if this elaborate build-up had been preface to a trap, for he stood alone in a tiny, lightless cubicle, only the haze of rainbow showing where he had come in.

Then he relaxed, letting out a breath of foolish relief, as Taniquel stepped through the rainbow; Auster and Kennard followed. Taniquel made signals with her fingers, not unlike those controlling the airship. The cubicle shot upward; Kerwin swayed, caught himself. It shivered; stopped. They stepped through an open archway into a lighted room which opened, in turn, on a green terrace with a view of dawn-lighted mountains.

The room was huge, rising to echoing space; yet paradoxically gave an impression of warmth and intimacy. The floor was laid with old tiles worn uneven, as if they had seen many feet walking on them. At the far end of the room was a fire that smelled of fragrant smoke and incense; something furry and dark, and not human, crouched there, doing something to the fire with a long, oddly-shaped bellows. It had long prehensile pink hands, and as Kerwin came in it turned large pupil-less green eyes on him, fixing him with an intelligent stare of question.

To the right of the fire was a heavy, carven table of some glossy wood, a few scattered chairs, and a dais covered with a heap of cushions, tapestried and woven with phosphorescent threads.

A middle-aged woman rose out of one of the chairs and came toward them. She stopped, a step away from Kerwin, regarding him with a cool intelligent gray stare.

"The barbarian," she said. "Well, he looks it, with blood on his face. Any more fighting, Auster, and I'll send you to the Nevarsin House of Penitence for a full season." She added, consideringly, "In the winter."

Her voice was husky and harsh; there was gray liberally salted in her dark-red hair. Her body was compact and heavy beneath the sedate dark robe she wore; her face humorous, intelligent, wrinkled around the eyes.

"What name did the *Terranan* give him?"

Jeff told the woman his name, and she repeated it, her lip curling slightly. "Jeff Kerwin. That was to be expected. My name is Mesyr Ridenow, and I am your very remote cousin. Don't think I am proud of the relationship. I'm not."

Among telepaths, polite lies would be meaningless, Kerwin thought. *Don't judge their manners by Terran standards.* In spite of her rudeness, there was something about this hefty old Amazon that he liked. He only said, "Perhaps one day I can change your mind, Mother—" the word he actually used was *kiha,* used for any female relative of an older generation.

"Oh, call me Mesyr," she snapped. "I'm not *that* old! And close your face, Auster, the hole in it would swallow a planet. He hasn't any notion that he's being offensive. How would you expect him to have?"

"If I have given offense—"

Mesyr chuckled. "At that, you can call me Mother," she said. "I never go near the matrix screens any more. Not since my cub was old enough to take his place there. My son, Corus."

A long-limbed youngster in his teens, with mahogany curls, gave Kerwin his hand as if the act were a formal gesture of defiance. He grinned quirkily, in a way that reminded Kerwin of Taniquel, and said "You've been out in space?"

"Four times."

"Sounds interesting," said Corus, almost—it seemed—wistfully. "I've never been further than Nevarsin, myself."

Mesyr scowled at Corus and said, "This is Rannirl."

Rannirl was about Kerwin's age, a thin tall competent-looking fellow with a shadow of red beard, calloused hands, sad-eyed and prosaic. He did not offer to shake hands. He bowed formally and said, "So they found you, I didn't expect it. Kennard, I owe you four cases of Ravnet wine."

Kennard said, with a cordial grin, "We'll drink it together next holiday—all of us. I believe you made a wager with Elorie as well? Your passion for a bet will ruin you, some day. And by the way, where is Elorie? She should be on hand to claim the hawk she wagered, if nothing more."

"Here she is," Taniquel said, and they turned toward the door; and then Kerwin realized that the silence in the room was his own imagination. Mesyr and Rannirl and the kid Corus were still talking, and only in his own mind did a silence move around the girl who stood in the doorway. In that instant, as her gray eyes lifted to his, he recognized the face he had seen in the matrix crystal.

She was tall and delicately put together. Copper hair, touched with sunrose gold, lay in straight pale strands around her sun-browned cheeks. Her dress was heavy, and fell in formal folds, pinned at both shoulders with clasps of cruelly heavy-worked metal; both dress and clasps seemed too weighty for her slenderness, as if the slim shoulders drooped under the burden; a child weighted in the robes of a princess. She had the long-legged walk of a child, and a child's full sulky underlip, and her eyes were gray and dreamy; slowly, she raised the long lashes and looked straight at him.

"This is my barbarian, I take it?"

"Yours?" Taniquel lifted her eyebrows at the girl, with a pixie giggle; and the gray-eyed girl said in her softly husky voice, "Mine."

"Don't fight over me," Kerwin said. He couldn't help feeling a little amused.

"Don't flatter yourself," Auster snarled. Elorie slanted her gray eyes at him, and to Kerwin's surprise, Auster lowered his head with the look of a whipped dog. Taniquel tilted her head at Jeff, with that special secret smile, and said, "And this is Elorie Ardais, Keeper of the Arilinn Tower. And now that's really all of us, and you can sit down and have something to eat or drink, and recover your wits."

Kerwin accepted the drink she put into his hand. Kennard lifted his glass slightly and said, with a deprecating grin, "To homecoming," and the others joined in the toast, gathering around him; Taniquel with her kittenish grin, Corus with that odd mixture of curiosity and diffidence, Rannirl with a reserved welcome, Mesyr and Kennard with honest friendliness. Even Auster showed something akin to friendly interest. Only Elorie neither spoke nor smiled, giving Kerwin only a grave glance over the rim of her goblet, touching it with her lips and lowering her lashes to veil her gray eyes from his.

Mesyr set the glass down, firmly.

"That's that. And now—we all stayed up all night to see if they'd find you—I suggest that we all get to bed."

The girl Elorie rubbed her eyes with childish doubled fists and yawned. Auster said, moving to Elorie's side, "You've exhausted yourself again," and glowered at Kerwin. "Exhausted yourself for *him!*" He went on speaking, but again Kerwin couldn't understand the words.

"Come along," Mesyr said, jerking her head matter-of-factly at Kerwin, "Explanations can come later."

One of the nonhumans went before them, bearing a light, as Mesyr led the way through a wide, echoing hallway, up a long flight of mosaic stairs.

"One thing we've plenty of, is room," she said dryly. "So if you don't like this one, look around and find one you do like that's empty. This place was built to hold twenty or thirty, and there are eight of us, with you. Which, of course, is why you're here. One of the *kyrri* will bring you anything you want to eat, and if you want someone to help you dress, and the like, ask him. I'm sorry we have no human servants, but they can't come through the Veil."

Faintly bewildered, Kerwin shook his head in wonder.

"We'll see you at sunset," Mesyr said, and inclining her head in a formal bow, she went away. Kerwin obeyed the gesture of the furry nonhuman, and went into the indicated room.

When he woke, the sun was declining, and one of the soft-footed nonhumans was moving around in the bathroom, drawing water from which came a faint perfume. Remembering Mesyr's words about a meeting at sunset, Kerwin bathed, shaved, ate some of the food the nonhuman offered him, but when the furry creature gestured toward the bed, where he had laid out some Darkovan clothing, Kerwin shook his head and dressed, again, in the black uniform garb of the Terran civil service. He was sourly amused at himself—among Terrans he felt a need to emphasize his Darkovan blood, but here he suddenly felt a compulsion to emphasize his Terran heritage. He thought, *I'm not ashamed of being the son of a Terran; let them call me barbarian, if they like!*

Without a knock, or any word of warning, the girl Elorie came into his room. Kerwin started, taken aback by the intrusion; if she'd come in two minutes earlier, she'd have caught him in his skin, and even though he was nearly dressed, it disconcerted him!

"Barbarian," she said with a low laugh. "Of course I knew. I'm a telepath, remember?"

Flushing to the roots of his hair, Kerwin stooped and put his foot into his other shoe. Obviously, the conventions of life in a telepathic family, or among a group as close-knit as this one seemed to be, would be different from Terran conventions.

"Kennard thought you might get lost, trying to come down to the hall—that's the big room we use downstairs. I came to show you the way."

Elorie was dressed in a filmy gown, embroidered with sprays of star-flowers, and bunches of cherries; she was standing immediately beneath the picture, and the resemblance was immediately apparent. Kerwin looked from the painting to the frail, flame-haired girl. He asked, "Did you sit for your portrait?"

She glanced up, indifferently. "No. That was my father's great-grandmother," she said. "The women of the Com'yn had a passion, in those days, for being painted as legendary characters. I copied the dress from the painting, though. Come along."

She wasn't being very friendly, or even very polite; but she did seem to take him for granted.

At the end of the hallway, about to lead the way down a flight of long stairs, Elorie hesitated and then went to a window where a deep embrasure in the wall looked out over a sunset landscape. She pointed.

"Look. From here you can see just the tip of the mountains at Thendara—if your eyes are trained to look. There is another Com'yn Tower there. There are others, all over Darkover. Though many of them are empty now."

Kerwin strained his eyes, but could only see the green plains, and the faraway, low foothills dying into bluish haze. He said, "Everything is—confusing. I still don't know what the Com'yn is—are. Or what they do. Or what a Keeper is— besides," he said, smiling, "being a very beautiful girl."

Elorie looked at him. Before the leveled, childlike eyes, his own fell; she made him feel that the compliment had been both rude and intrusive.

"It would be easier to explain what we do, than what we are. A Keeper works in the central position of a—a group of matrix technicians. She—well, gathers all the others into the contacts; a sort of central co-ordinator, a telepathic control. The Keeper is always a woman. We spend our entire childhood training for it, and sometimes"—she turned to the window, looking out over the mountains—"we lose our powers after only a few years."

"Lose them? How?"

Elorie shrugged slightly and did not answer. Kerwin was not to realize until a long time later just how much Elorie overestimated his telepathic abilities. That Elorie had never in her life known any man, or for that matter any person, who could not read clearly any thought she did not choose to put into words. Kerwin knew nothing, as yet, of the seclusion of the young Keepers.

"A Keeper must be a woman, and usually the others in the screens are men. Except for the Keepers, the work is too dangerous and difficult for women. We are hoping that you will be able to work very closely with me."

"Sounds like nice work," Kerwin said. Elorie whirled and stared at him, her mouth wide in disbelief. Then, her eyes blazing, her cheeks aflame, she said, "Stop it! *Stop it!*"

Kerwin backed away a step, helplessly. "Take it easy, miss—Miss Elorie. If I've offended you, I'm sorry as the devil, but remember, I don't know how I did it."

Her hands gripped on the rail, so hard that he could see the white knobs of her knuckles. They looked so frail, those white hands. After a moment of silence she tossed her head, with a little impatient movement.

"I was going to answer your questions about the Com'yn. There are exactly seven families of telepaths on Darkover."

Kerwin blurted "I thought the place was *crawling* with telepaths."

Her eyes were cool, watchful. "I don't mean the ability to receive worded thoughts. Everyone has that, to some extent. I mean the whole range of special psychokinetic talents, bred into our caste in the old days; specifically the ability to manipulate a matrix. You know what a matrix is, I take it."

"Vaguely."

"I thought so. It was through Cleindori's matrix that we reached you," Elorie said. "That proved you had *laran*— that you had inherited the mark of our caste. In simplest form, a matrix is a crystal that's sensitive to thought. I could talk about space lattices, and neuro-electronic webs, and kinetic energons, but I'll let Rannirl teach you all that—he's the technician. Matrixes can be as simple as this—" she touched a small crystal which, in total defiance of gravity, seemed to suspend her filmy gown from her throat. "Or they can be enormous, synthetically-made screens with immensely complex interior crystalline structures. They release pure energy from the magnetic field of a planet, and channel it, either as force or matter. Heat, light, kinetic or potential energy, the synthesis of raw materials into usable form—all these potentials can be released through a matrix. You know that thought waves, brain rhythms, are electrical in nature?"

"Vaguely," Kerwin said again.

"Well, thought waves—even those of a telepath—can't affect anything in the material universe. They can't move the weight of a single hair. But the matrix crystals can—I suppose the word is, *amplify* those waves enormously; they act as a catalyst to transform force into form. That's all."

"And the—Keepers?"

"Some matrixes are so complex that one person can't handle them; it takes the union of several concentrated minds, forming a nexus of energy. A Keeper handles the forces. That's all I can tell you," she finished abruptly, and turned, pointing down the stairs. "Straight down that way." She turned and walked away in a filmy flutter of draperies, and Kerwin watched her go, startled. Had he done, again, something to offend her? Or was this some childish whim?

He went down the stairs, finding himself again in the great firelit hall where, this morning at sunrise, they had welcomed him—welcomed him *home?* His home? The room was completely empty. He went in, and dropped into one of the low seats, burying his head in his hands. If somebody didn't explain things fairly soon, he was going to go crazy with frustration!

Kennard, coming in through the curtains with an uneven tread, found him that way. Kerwin looked up at the old man and said helplessly, "I—guess I'm just confused. Sorry. It's all too much to take in at once."

Kennard looked down at him with a curious mixture of compassion and amusement. "Yes. I can see how it would be."

"My head's spinning," Kerwin confessed.

Kennard lowered himself to the mass of cushions, hands clasped behind his head. "Maybe I can clear it up for you."

"Kennard, who am I? And why the devil am I here?"

Kennard ignored the question. After a while he said, "Do you know what I saw, that night in the Sky Harbor?"

"Sorry. Not in the mood for guessing games."

"Remember, I didn't know who you were. You looked like one of us, but of course I knew you weren't. I looked at

83

you—I'm an Alton, and I have one of those screwy, out-of-phase time perceptors—and I saw a little boy, a child, who had never known who he was. Or what he was. I was curious. I wish you'd stayed, that night, and talked to us, when I asked you to."

"I do, too," Kerwin said, slowly. *A child who had never known who or what he was.* "I grew up, all right, but I left myself somewhere."

"Maybe you'll find yourself here." Kennard got slowly to his feet. Kerwin rose too, noting that the older man deftly avoided touching him. Kennard smiled.

"You're wondering why?"

"No, I hate—people jostling me. I've never gotten along with most people—and I feel like hell in a crowd."

"Telepath, marginal—and, I suspect, empath," Kennard said. "You pick up enough to feel that any physical contact is distasteful."

Kerwin chuckled. "Not *any* kind."

Kennard's brows moved in sardonic amusement. "Distasteful except as a deliberate gesture of affection. Right?"

Kerwin nodded, thinking back over the rare personal encounters of his life.

"You're—how old? Twenty-six, twenty-seven? Hell of a long time to live outside your proper element!"

"Proper element hell," Kerwin retorted. "Show me where I fit into this mess, will you?"

"I'll try," Kennard said, locking his knobby fingers meditatively. "I think Elorie told you that there are seven families of telepaths on Darkover. The Hasturs, the Ridenow, the Ardais, the Elhalyn, the Altons—my family—and the Aillard—yours."

"That's only six," Jeff said, counting.

"We don't discuss the Aldarans," Kennard's face was suddenly grim. "They sold our world to the Terrans. It's a long story, and a shameful one. I couldn't tell it now, even if I had the time, which I don't. Anyway, it's nothing to do with you. But—with only six telepath families—have you any idea how inbred we are?"

"You mean that normally you marry only within your caste? Telepaths?"

"Not entirely. Not deliberately," Kennard said. "But being a telepath, and being isolated with others of our own kind, in the Tower circles—it's like a drug," his voice was not quite steady. "It completely spoils you for—for contact with outsiders. You—you get lost in it, and when you come up for air, as it were, you find you can't breathe ordinary air any more. You find you can't stand having outsiders around, people who—who jostle against your mind. People who aren't in sympathy with all your—feelings, and needs, and desires. Non-telepaths. They feel like barbarians, or like strange animals—"

He was staring into space, over Kerwin's head. Abruptly, with a little shiver, he recalled himself.

"Anyway. We're inbred mentally, even more than we are physically, just because of that—inability to tolerate outsiders. Outbreeding might save us, if we could do it—but most of us can't." For a moment Kerwin thought he was going to say something more, but he didn't. "So we seem to be dying out. Fewer and fewer of us, in each generation, inherit *laran*, or Gifts." He spoke briskly now, without a trace of the bitter remoteness. "There are two lines of thought within the Com'yn. One faction felt that we should—cling to our old ways while we could, resist every change, until we died and it didn't matter any more. The others felt that since change was inevitable, we should make terms we can tolerate, before we have intolerable ones forced on us. We wanted to find out the truth about matrix science. These people felt that outsiders could be—*should* be—developed and trained to work in any way that a Com'yn telepath could do. They were in power in the Council for only a few years; but during those years, a generation ago, the matrix mechanics came into being as a profession. We found out that ordinary people, with only a little telepathic ability, could be trained in the use of simple matrixes."

"I've met a couple."

"You've got to remember," Kennard said, "this was complicated by a lot of intense, very emotional attitudes. It was almost a religion. At one time the Com'yn were almost a priesthood. The Keepers, especially, were objects of religious fanaticism that amounted to worship. Even now—well, that's neither here nor there. So we come to where you fit into the story.

"Thirty years ago—I was quite young then—there was a Keeper whose name was Cleindori Aillard, The Golden Bell. She was from one of the highest families on Darkover, and a member of the Council in her own right. She was my foster-sister. I was fond of her." Briefly, Kennard paused, and his face grew bitter again.

"Cleindori was a Keeper. That meant she was a pledged virgin, as well as a *vai leronis*. But Cleindori believed that all these things were superstition. She was—I suppose you'd call her a reformer at heart. She fought bitterly against the new Council, and their order that the Com'yn should keep its secrecy and its semi-religious status. She broke the taboos again and again. And at last she ran away from Arilinn. With an Earthman."

Jeff had begun to suspect this, but it was still a shock.

"Jeff Kerwin. My father?"

"Yes," Kennard said. "It is why Auster hates you, why some people think your very existence is a sacrilege. Auster has a particular reason for his bitterness. Cleindori did not go alone. The Council called them traitors. Auster, too, was born among the Terrans, and although he does not remember, he too lived in the Spacemen's Orphanage. We managed to get Auster back from them and that's a curious story too," Kennard smiled. "But the Council was very bitter against Cleindori's sacrilege. Your very existence was an offense to them—the child of a Keeper who had broken her sacred vows, and worse than that, with a *Terranan!* It is fortunate for you"—he looked grim again—"that the Terrans sent you to your father's world. There were plenty of fanatics who would have considered themselves merely avenging the dishonor of a *vai leronis* by killing the child of the renegades."

Kerwin found that he was cold. "But if that's the case," he said, "what the devil am I doing here?"

"Times have changed," Kennard said. "We're dying out. There just aren't enough of us any more. Here at Arilinn we have a Keeper who has the full *laran* powers. There are only two or three sub-Keepers on the whole planet, and a couple of little girls growing up, who *might* become Keepers. The fanatics have either died off, or mellowed with old age. Different people are ruling the Council. When you came back to Darkover it didn't take me too long to guess who you must be. And Elorie saw you in the screens and confirmed it. She spoke for you before the Council and so did I. If there was even a remote chance you had inherited *laran*—well, we are in no position to waste the people with those gifts.

"So, we called you and you came. And here you are."

"Here I am. An outsider—"

"Not really," Kennard said, "or you couldn't have passed the Veil. You've probably guessed that we don't like having non-telepaths around. It's painful, especially when we're working. That's why we have no human servants, and why Mesyr stays here and keeps house for us, though she's long past working in the matrixes. The nonhumans are telepathic, and receive from us, but there's no mutual receptivity. As far as we're concerned, speaking in human terms, they're deaf and dumb." He smiled. "I feel at ease with you. That's a good sign."

"He's wishing he felt the same way," said Taniquel, popping her head into the room. "You will. You've lived with barbarians too long, that's all."

"Don't tease, Tani," Kennard said, in indulgent reproof. "He's not used to you, either, which doesn't mean he's necessarily a barbarian. Get us a drink, and stop making mischief. We'll have enough trouble without you joining in!"

"No drinks yet," said Rannirl, pausing beneath the archway into the room. "Elorie will be down in a minute. We'll wait."

"That means she's decided," Taniquel said. She came over to the cushions and dropped gracefully, catlike, her head against Kennard's knee. She flung out her arms, one of them striking Kerwin; she yawned and crooked it carelessly round his foot, giving it a little, absentminded pat. She let it rest there, with her pixie eyes glinting up, filled with mischief, at Kerwin. He was uncomfortably conscious of the touch.

The girl shifted, restlessly, until she was leaning back

between Kennard and Kerwin, an arm across the lap of each. Kennard patted Taniquel's arm, affectionately, but Kerwin drew uneasily away. Was the girl just an outrageous tease? Or—was she simply naïve, relaxing childlike among men she found as neutral as if they were all her brothers? Once again, as when Elorie had walked unannounced into his room, Kerwin felt troubled. Damn it, the etiquette of a telepath group was still a mystery to him!

Elorie, Auster, Mesyr and the boy Corus came into the big hall. Auster's glare instantly sought out Kerwin, and Taniquel drew herself away.

Corus was standing before a cabinet, hesitating before an array of bottles and flasks. Casually, evidently carrying out a well-established custom, he asked, "What will you drink? Your usual, Kennard—Mesyr? Elorie, I know you never touch anything stronger than *shallan*."

"She will tonight," Kennard said. "We'll have some *kirian*."

Corus turned for confirmation; he seemed startled. Elorie nodded. Taniquel rose and went to help Corus, filling low goblets from a curiously shaped flask. She brought a glass to Kerwin, not asking if he wanted it.

The liquid was pale and aromatic. Kerwin glanced at it and felt that they were watching him. Damn it, he was getting tired of that performance! He set the goblet, without tasting it, down on the floor.

Kennard laughed. Auster said something Kerwin didn't catch. Elorie watched, smiling faintly, raising her own glass to her lips and taking a slight sip. Taniquel giggled.

"Zandru's hells," Kennard exploded, "this is too serious for jokes! I understand that you like your fun, Tani, but just the same—" He accepted a glass from Corus, turning to Kerwin, with a sigh. "I seem to be cast in the role of schoolmaster too damned much of the time. This stuff—" he indicated the glass, "is *kirian*. It's not exactly a drug or a stimulant, but it does lower the threshhold of perception, and raise the level of sensitivity to telepathic reception. You don't have to drink it unless you want it, but it helps." He sipped his own, briefly, and went on "Now that you're here, and you've had a chance to rest a bit, it's fairly important to us to find out just how much of a telepath you are and how much training you'll need in order to work with us. All that. So we're going to test you, half a dozen ways. Hence—" he drank another sip, "*kirian*."

Kerwin shrugged and picked up the glass. The liquid had a sting and a curious volatile smell; it seemed to evaporate on his tongue almost before he could taste it. It wasn't his idea of a good way to get drunk. It was more like inhaling fumes than like drinking anything. Four or five sips finished the glass. The flavor was vaguely lemony.

"Now what happens?" To his surprise, his tongue was curiously thick; he had some trouble framing the words, and after he spoke he was not sure what language he had been speaking; but Rannirl turned toward him, and said "Nothing to worry about."

"I don't know why this is necessary," Taniquel said. "He's already been tested for *laran*. As for the rest—"

Kerwin looked down at the girl, curled up close beside his knee. Her eyes were bright, sympathetic, alert on his own; her face upturned to his. He could have bent down and kissed her.

He did.

Taniquel leaned against him, smiling, her cheek resting against his. Then she raised her head and murmured, "First test, mark him positive on your scoreboard, Kennard. High degree of response."

Kerwin stared, startled, at his own arms around Taniquel; then laughed and relaxed, suddenly not worrying about it. If the girl was going to object, she'd have done it already; but he sensed that for some reason she was pleased. Auster exploded into a mouthful of unintelligible syllables, and Mesyr shook her head reprovingly at Taniquel. "Child, this is too serious a matter for your teasing."

"I wasn't," Taniquel said, smiling. "I was perfectly serious, even if my methods may strike you as unorthodox." She rested her cheek against Kerwin's arm. Suddenly, surprisingly, Kerwin felt a lump in his throat, and for the first time in years, tears stung his eyes. Taniquel, not smiling now, cradled his hand against her cheek. She said softly, "Can you think of a better test for an empath? If he didn't belong here, no harm was done, for he wouldn't receive from me; if he did—then he deserves it." He felt her soft lips touch his rough hand.

Kerwin felt an almost overwhelming emotion. The completeness of that small gesture was somehow more meaningful to him than anything any woman had ever done in his whole life. He felt that it was a perfect acceptance of him, as a man and as a person, that he and Taniquel had somehow become more intimate than lovers. The others had suddenly ceased to exist. Without hesitation, he drew the girl to his lap and she leaned her head against his shoulder, tenderly, comfortingly, a gesture of reassurance and warmth unlike anything he could remember. He raised his eyes, blurred a little, and blinked, embarrassed at this display of emotion; but he saw only understanding and kindness.

Kennard's grim face looked less craggy than usual. "Tani's the expert on empathy. That's settled, anyhow—although it's damned unusual for a man to have it, and I didn't expect it, with your family background. Throwback, I expect. You have Ridenow blood, three or four generations ago."

Taniquel, still clinging to Kerwin, said softly, "How lonely you must have been."

All my life, he thought. *Not belonging.*

But you belong here now.

"Much as I dislike to interrupt this touching display," Auster began. Taniquel, with a resigned little shrug, let go of Kerwin; she was still holding his hand. Auster was speaking, but he had dropped back into that incomprehensible dialect. He came to Kerwin, who shook his head slightly and said in Cahuenga, "I'm sorry, I don't understand you."

Auster turned to Kennard, with a shrug.

Kennard said, "You don't understand him at all?"

"No, and it's damned funny, because I understand you and Taniquel just fine."

Rannirl said, "You've understood most of what I say, haven't you?"

"All but a few words now and then."

"Jeff, answer me quickly, without stopping to think—what language am I speaking?"

Kerwin started to say, Thendara dialect, and then stopped, confused. Kennard nodded, slowly. "That's right," he said. "That's what we noticed first of all about you. I've spoken to you in four different languages tonight, and Rannirl in a fifth, and you've understood them all without thinking about it. But you only get about half of what Auster says, unless he's speaking Cahuenga. You're a telepath, all right. Haven't you always been an exceptionally good linguist?" He nodded, not waiting for Kerwin's answer. "I thought so. You catch the thought, without waiting for the words. But you and Auster just don't operate on the same frequency."

"It may come in time," Elorie said, "as they understand one another better. But we already knew that he has minor ESP, or he wouldn't be here. What else?"

Kennard glanced at Rannirl and said, "You're the technician."

Rannirl asked, "Can you let me see your matrix?"

Kerwin took the crystal out and handed it over to Rannirl. As the man took it in his fingers, however, Kerwin felt a vague, crawling discomfort. Automatically he reached out; almost rudely, he caught it away from Rannirl again. The crawling discomfort faded. He stared, amazed, at his own hands.

Rannirl nodded. "I thought so. He's managed to key himself into it—roughly."

Kerwin said, "That never happened before!"

"Probably it happened while we were guiding you to us," Elorie said, and extended her slim fingers. "May I try, Jeff?"

Bracing himself, Kerwin let Elorie take the crystal. He felt the touch, as if the light hands were actually touching his nerves; but it was not acutely painful. She said, "I'm a Keeper; I can usually key-in to almost anybody. Tani?"

Kerwin felt the discomfort ebb away as Taniquel took the crystal in her hands; she smiled, her arm around Kerwin's waist. "Jeff and I are still in rapport," she said. "That's no fair test. I'll try again later. Corus?" She handed it on.

91

Kerwin flinched, uncontrollably, at the rough prickling sensation all over his body; Corus shuddered as if in pain, and quickly passed the crystal to Kennard. Kennard's touch was not actually painful, but Kerwin was unpleasantly conscious of it. Kennard handed it to Auster.

Auster gasped and dropped the matrix as if it were a live coal. Kerwin twitched and felt Taniquel shiver under his hand, a deep, painful thing. He felt her physically draw away. She picked up the dropped crystal; the pain stopped and Kerwin drew a deep breath. Auster was shaking, white.

"Zandru's hells," he whispered, and his look at Kerwin was not, now, so much of malevolence as of fear. "Kerwin, I swear I didn't do that deliberately."

"He knows that, he knows that," Taniquel soothed; she dropped Jeff's hand and went to Auster, laying an arm round his waist, gently caressing his hand. Kerwin watched, in surprise and sudden, jealous amazement. How could she pull away from close, emotional contact with him and go straight to that—that so-and-so Auster, and start making a fuss over *him*? Jealously intent, he watched Taniquel draw Auster down, watched the lines in Auster's lean face smoothing out, calming.

Elorie picked up the dropped crystal and gave it back to Kerwin. "It's evidently been keyed," she said. "Don't let anyone handle it, now, unless you're fairly sure they're in rapport with you. You could get a painful shock."

Kerwin thrust it into his pocket again. He was still glowering at Taniquel, feeling wrathful and deserted.

Rannirl smiled, a faint sardonic grin. "All that, just to find out what we could have guessed this morning, when we saw you with blood on your face; you and Auster aren't sympathetic to one another."

"They'll have to be," Elorie said tensely. "We can't have that kind of friction here!"

Auster said, his eyes closed, in Cahuenga, "You know my feelings in the matter. But I said I'd abide by the majority decision, and I'll do my best. I meant it."

"Fair enough," Kennard said, and looked round the circle. "A pattern test?" he asked.

"Kerwin grew suddenly apprehensive again. Most of these tests had been simple things, but Kennard looked tense and drawn, and Taniquel was holding Kerwin's hand tight. She said, "If he could key into a matrix without special help, maybe he can get the pattern spontaneously."

"Maybe pigs can fly," Kennard said shortly. "I'll test for the possibility, but I doubt it. Kerwin—" he surveyed the Earthman consideringly for a moment. "Let's have the crystal again. No, don't give it to me." He made a gesture of refusal when Kerwin would have handed it over. "Here, give me your glass, Tani."

He up-ended the crystal goblet. "A simple test, Kerwin. Crystallize it."

"Huh?"

"Make a clear picture in your mind of that glass going to pieces. Careful, don't let it shatter or explode. Use the matrix."

Suddenly Kerwin remembered the man Ragan doing something like this, in the spaceport café. It couldn't be so difficult, if Ragan could do it. He stared intently at the crystal, as if intense concentration could *force* the process from it. He felt a curious stirring in his mind.

"No," said Kennard harshly. "Don't help him, Tani. I know how you feel, but we've got to be sure."

Kerwin stared intently at the crystal and then shook his head.

"Sorry," he muttered, "no can do."

"Try," Taniquel insisted. "Oh, Jeff, it's so simple! Why, Terrans, children, anybody can be taught."

"Taught," Kennard said. "We're wasting time, Taniquel; he *doesn't* have it spontaneously. I'll have to give him the pattern in direct contact."

"What—"

"I'll have to show you how it's done," Kennard said, "and it's non-verbal. I'll have to go straight in. I'm an Alton. That's our special technique—forced rapport." He hesitated; it seemed to Kerwin that they were all looking at him apprehensively.

Kennard said, "Watch my finger." He put it close to Kerwin's nose; Kerwin, startled, wondering if it would disappear or something, and if this were a demonstration of psi power, watched as Kennard slowly drew it back, and . . .

He remembered no more.

He moved his head groggily. He was lying back on the cushions, his head pillowed on Taniquel's lap, Kennard looking down at him with friendly concern, Elorie's face, over his shoulder, aloof. Kerwin whistled. "What—what did you do?"

"Hypnosis, in a sense," Kennard said, "Next time you won't consciously remember this, but it'll be easier." He handed Kerwin the goblet. "Here. Crystallize it."

"I just *tried*—"

Under Kennard's eyes he stared rebelliously at the matrix. Suddenly the goblet before him blurred and took on a strangeness. It was no longer a flat piece of glass; he seemed to be seeing it differently, seeing curious tensions and movements. He was conscious of a strange throb from the crystal, a sort of emotional tension, of equilibrium—

The crystals of the glass lie in a plane. . . .

He perceived the plane; and suddenly, he heard a sharp crack; with a start, the new consciousness blurred and vanished and he stared down, unbelieving, at the goblet lying on the cushions before him, split evenly along a straight line down the center. A few drops of the pale *kirian* lay soaking into the cushions. He squeezed his eyes shut, in disbelief.

Kennard nodded in satisfaction. "Not too bad, for a first attempt," he said. "Although, Zandru, you've got strong barriers! Headache?"

Kerwin started to shake his head no, then realized the answer should be yes. He touched his temples gingerly. Elorie's gray eyes met his, cool and aloof.

"Mental defense," she said, "against intolerable situations. Typical psychosomatic reaction—you say to yourself, *if I'm in pain they'll stop hurting me and let me alone*. We had to stop, to avoid hurting you worse. Pain is the best defense against telepathy. For instance, if anyone tries to pick your mind, the best defense, if you haven't any other, is simply to bite your lip till it bleeds. Damned few telepaths can get through that. I could give you a technical explanation about sympathetic vibrations and nerve cells, but why bother?" She went to the cabinet where the drinks were, shook three flat green tablets from a small vial and put them into his hand, deftly, without touching him.

"Take these, and in an hour it'll be all right."

Kerwin obediently swallowed the pills. He was still staring without belief at the glass, struck asunder along a clean line of cleavage. "Did I really do that?"

Rannirl nodded. "At least," he added dryly, "none of us did—and you can estimate the probabilities of its having split that way by itself."

Kerwin picked up the two halves in his hand. He was trying to formulate some explanation that would satisfy the Terran half of his mind, playing with phrases like subliminal perception of atomic structure—hell, for a minute he had seen the way the thing hung together like a pattern of living tensions and forces. During his school days somewhere he had read that atoms were just whirling aggregates of electrons, that a solid object actually consisted of empty space occupied by forces in stasis. It made him feel dizzy.

Kerwin took up the broken glass, fitted the edges together, staring at it fiercely. Once again, without volition, the sudden perception came; the insight as if seeing beneath the surface, the *awareness*—

The glass lay whole in his hand, the cleaved edges fitting smoothly together, with only a faint notch showing what had been done.

Kennard smiled, as if relieved. "That leaves only one test."

Again Kerwin felt Taniquel's small fingers folding through his own, and he felt it like a pain in him, her fear and dismay. "Is that really necessary, Kennard?" she appealed, "Can't you try—just putting him in the outer circle, and seeing if he can be shocked open that way?"

Elorie gave her a pitying glance. "That almost never works, Tani."

Kerwin began to be afraid again. He had come so well through the other tests, he had begun to be proud of what he was accomplishing.

"What is it? What now? Tani?"

It was Elorie who answered, gently. "What Kennard means is only this; we've got to see where and how you can fit into the Tower circle, the relay—the nexus of power. We know you're a high-level empath, and you've passed the basic tests for PK. But this is the big test—to see how you'll mesh with the rest of us." She turned to Kennard.

"You tested him on patterns. How is he on barrier?"

Kennard said, "Hellish." He explained, to Kerwin. "She means that I forced rapport on you, to give you the matrix pattern there—" he pointed at the broken-and-joined goblet. "Everybody has some natural defense against telepathic invasion—we call it barrier. It's a protective device in telepaths—protective coloration to keep you from broadcasting your private thoughts all over the locality, and from picking up a lot of random telepathic static. Everybody has it. It's a conditioned reflex. Well, when we go into rapport, we have to drop our barriers against each other. And since the barrier *is* a conditioned reflex, you have to learn how to overcome it. Sometimes the barrier won't drop at all, and it has to be forced down, or shocked open. We've got to have some idea of how hard it's going to be to work with you, and how much resistance you have."

Mesyr spoke, for the first time since they had begun, "Tonight? Can't you give him time?"

"Time is what we haven't got," Rannirl said. "Remember we're working against a deadline."

"Rannirl's right," Kennard said. "We brought Kerwin here hoping we could use him—because if we can't, you know as well as I do what's going to happen to us all." He looked bleakly at Kerwin. "We've got to get you in shape to work with us, damned fast—or else."

"We're wasting time," Elorie said, and rose, her pale draperies floating in some intangible drift of air. "Bring him up to the lab."

One by one, they rose; at Taniquel's tug on his hand, Kerwin stood up too. Kennard looked pityingly at Taniquel's hand linked to Kerwin. He said, "I'm sorry, Tani. You know why you can't be part of it." To Kerwin he explained, "Tani's our empath. And in rapport with you. If she was part of this, she'd help you too much—she couldn't stand it otherwise. You stay here, Tani."

Taniquel let go Jeff's hand, and Kerwin felt suddenly cold and scared.

Rannirl said, "Cheer up," and put his arm lightly through Kerwin's. The gesture was reassuring, but the tone wasn't. It was too much like an apology. Kennard motioned, and they went in a close group through the long hall, up a flight of stairs Kerwin had not seen before, and into a small, closed-in room. On two walls were glass and mirrory banks that reflected nothing identifiable, distorting their shapes, and Kerwin saw himself a lean streak of black topped with a brief crimson flame of hair. Elorie turned to them and Kerwin saw that between her cupped palms she held a giant crystal, multifaceted, sparkling with a thousand colors. She looked questioningly around the circle at the others. Kennard nodded. Rannirl followed suit. Auster looked briefly doubtful, but finally shrugged. Young Corus pursed his lips and looked skeptically at Kerwin, but finally said, "I can take it if you think he can."

Elorie looked at Auster, who said something unintelligible to Kerwin. Kennard leaned toward Kerwin and said in a low voice, "As long as you and Auster can't understand each other, we'll have to try and keep you on separate levels."

Elorie said, "I'll take Auster first, and Kerwin last. Kennard, you bring him in." She lowered her head, gazed for a moment at the matrix, and then pointed a slender finger at Auster.

Kerwin, watching, apprehensive, sensitive and sensitized to undercurrents, felt something like a palpable line of force from the delicate girl to Auster; felt something like an electrical *snap* as they dropped into contact.

An overtone of emotion like a sullen flame from Auster, a covered flame burning against the ice . . .

"Corus," Elorie whispered.

Grinning nervously, Corus covered his face with his thin hands, his forehead screwed up into intent concentration. He looked very young. Kerwin, still tentatively feeling out the atmosphere of the room, sensed his curious visualization of hands and wrists suddenly interlocking, like the meshing grip of acrobats in mid-air; none of them moved, Corus's face was hidden behind his hands, but Kerwin caught a brief pictured image of meshed and interlocking hands, wrists, bodies . . .

Kennard murmured in an undertone, "Corus thinks in pictures. Take it easy, now. I'll bring you in." Abruptly his voice thinned, seemed to hum in Kerwin's ears from an immeasurable distance. They were grouped around the matrix now, and for a moment he saw them melt together, a blend of eyes, swooping faces, a single unit. He knew he was hovering on the fringes of the telepathic rapport; it looked to him like a web, gently waving its strands. . . .

Elorie said softly, "Jeff," but it sounded like a scream.

Just let go and slide into contact, it's easy. . . . It was like the instructions he had been given, how to find his way to them. . . . He could tell where they were, but how to become part of the network, he could not guess. He stood helplessly, staring at them, not guessing what he was supposed to do. They seemed to think he knew.

He said "Look, I'm not—"

You can do it, Jeff. You've got the Gift. It was Kennard's voice, and he sounded as if he was pleading.

No use, Ken. He can't quite make it.

The barrier's a conditioned reflex. After twenty years with the Terrans—he'd have gone mad without it.

Kennard, his face wavering oddly in the curious light reflected from the giant crystal—for the room was strangely dark to Jeff, dark and wavering at the edges—turned to Kerwin. His mouth moved before he spoke.

It's going to be rough. Twenty years. It was bad enough for Auster after five.

He moved blurrily through the light in the room, and to Kerwin he seemed to be swimming underwater. He felt Kennard take his hand and draw him forward. Kennard said in a low voice, "Try not to fight it, Kerwin."

Abruptly, like a knife-stab, he felt the touch—indescribable, unbelievable, so alien and indefinable that it could be interpreted only as pain. . . . In a fractional second he knew that this was what Kennard had done before, that this was what could not be borne or remembered. . . .

It was like having his skull bored open with a dentist's drill. Kerwin stood it for about five seconds. Then he felt himself twitch convulsively and heard a scream from a million miles away as he slid into darkness.

When he came out of it this time, he was lying on the floor of the octagon room, and Kennard and Elorie and Auster were standing looking down at him. Dimly somewhere he heard a muffled sound like sobbing and saw, with the fringes of his mind, Corus hunched over, his face buried in his hands.

Kerwin's head was a giant balloon filled with red-hot seething pain. It was so awful he couldn't breathe for a minute, then he felt his lungs expand and a hoarse sound coming from him, unwittingly.

Kennard knelt by him and said gently, "Can you sit up?"

Kerwin made the effort to raise himself, and Auster put out a hand to help him. He looked sick.

Kennard said, "We've all been through it, Jeff. Here, lean on me. Corus, are you all right?"

Corus raised a blotched face, and said, "I—guess so."

Elorie said in a taut voice, "Let's get through it quickly. Neither of them can take much more." She was shaking, but she stretched a hand to Corus; Kerwin felt, like a faint snapping jolt, the meshing of the minds. Auster, then Rannirl, dropped palpably into the swirl. Kennard, still holding Kerwin upright, dropped away and was gone.

Elorie did not speak, but Kerwin felt her whisper like a command.

Come, Jeff-the-barbarian.

With a jolt, like breath crashing from his body, he felt the sudden impact of their meshed minds, as if he had dropped into a facet of the crystal. A pattern flamed, like a giant star of fire in his mind, and he felt himself run round the circle, swirling in and out of contact; Elorie cool, aloof, firmly holding him at the end of a safe lifeline of contact; the gentle sureness of Kennard; a feather-touch from Corus;

99

a brief sullen flare from Auster, like a painful shock; Rannirl, a crisp spark.

"Enough," Kennard said abruptly. Suddenly Kerwin was himself again, and the others were not intangible mind-touches but separate people, standing grouped around him.

Rannirl whistled. "Avarra, what a barrier! If we ever get it all the way down, Kerwin, you'll be one hell of a good mech—*if* we ever do, which I doubt." He looked gloomy.

Kerwin's head was still one fiery mass. He said, "You mean I didn't—"

"We got through partly," Elorie said. She went on speaking, but suddenly the words had no meaning. Kennard glanced swiftly at Kerwin. He said something, but the words were just noise, like static in Jeff's brain. He shook his head, uncomprehendingly.

Kennard said in Cahuenga, "Headache any better?"

"Yeah, sure," Kerwin muttered. It hadn't gone away. If anything, it was worse. Kennard didn't argue. He took Kerwin firmly by the shoulders and put him in a big chair. He said to somebody, "Get Tani up here and hurry."

Kerwin didn't say anything. He was past that now. He was rocking in a giant swing, faster and faster, on a pendulum of dizzy pain. Elorie came and spoke to him, but Kerwin couldn't understand a word of it. Even Kennard's voice was an indistinguishable blur of meaningless syllables. Auster's words rose and fell like a song in some alien language. Then Taniquel was there, a grayish blur seeming to surround her; she fell to her knees beside Kerwin, with a little cry.

Kerwin could hardly see now.

"Jeff! Can you hear me?"

How could he help it, Kerwin thought with the unreason of pain, she was shouting straight in his ear. Damn it, if they'd just leave him alone. . . .

"Jeff, look at me. Please, look at me. Let me—"

"No," he muttered wearily, "no more of this. I've had enough for one night, haven't I?"

"Please! I can't help you unless you let me," Taniquel begged. He felt her hand, hot and painful on his throbbing head; he twitched restlessly, trying to throw it off. It felt like red-hot iron.

Then, slowly, slowly, as if some tense full vein had been tapped, he felt the pain drain away. Moment by moment it receded, until at last he could see the girl clearly again, and heard his breath go out in a harsh wheeze. He sat up, the headache just a dim throb at the base of his brain.

"Good enough," Kennard said softly. "It probably isn't much comfort now. But eventually, you'll work out, Kerwin. I think."

Auster muttered, "It's not worth the trouble!"

Kerwin said, "I heard that," and Auster made a startled movement. Kennard gave a slow, grimly triumphant nod.

"You see," he said. "I told you so. It worked." He drew a long, weary sigh.

Kerwin lurched to his feet and stood there, gripping the chair-back. He had the curious sensation that he had been through a wringer, but he was painfully at peace.

Taniquel was slumped over, gray and exhausted. She said, weakly, raising her head, "Don't worry about it, Jeff. I was just glad I could do something."

Mesyr was standing within the door of the room; she too looked tired, yet somehow satisfied. Corus looked up and smiled, painfully, and it struck Kerwin, with a curious wrench, that the kid had been crying over *his* pain. Even Auster, biting his lip, said, "I've got to give you this: you're one of us. You can't blame me for doubting, but don't hold it against me."

Kennard's arm was around Kerwin's shoulder; Elorie came and stood on tiptoe, and he felt, in amazement, the cool lips brush his cheek with a gossamer touch. Rannirl linked arms with him as they went down the stairs to the hall.

"This time at least we can decide for ourselves what we want to drink," he said, laughing. Kerwin understood, suddenly; he had come through the last ordeal. Taniquel had accepted him before this, but now they had all accepted him with the same completeness. He, who never had belonged anywhere, was suddenly overwhelmed with the knowledge of how deeply he belonged. Taniquel came and sat on the arm of his chair; Mesyr asked if he wanted anything to eat or drink. It was incongruously like a birthday party.

Halfway through the evening he found himself next to Kennard. Sensitized to the man's mood, he heard himself say, "You look happy about this. Auster isn't pleased, but you are. Why?"

"Why isn't Auster, or why am I?" Kennard asked with a droll grin.

"Both."

"Because you're part Terran," Kennard said.

"Which? Auster or you?"

"Both," Kennard replied in his turn, somberly. "If you do become a working part of the Tower circle, then there's a chance the Council will accept *my* sons. You see, I did what Cleindori did. I married a Terran girl—and I have two sons, and it sets a precedent. And Auster isn't too happy about that prospect, either."

Kerwin could have asked a dozen more questions, but he sensed this wasn't the time. It didn't seem to matter. He belonged.

CHAPTER SEVEN

THE DAYS slipped by in Arilinn, and Kerwin soon began to feel as if he had lived there all his life. And yet, in a curious way, he was like a man lost in an enchanted dream; as if all his old dreams and desires had come to life, and he had stepped into them and closed a wall behind him. Never, in any world, had he felt so much at home. Never had he belonged anywhere as he belonged here. It made him almost uneasy to be so happy. He wasn't used to it.

He was beginning to lose track of time, but he thought he had been at Arilinn about three weeks when it occurred to him that he had seen nothing of the city, and one morning he asked Kennard—he was still not certain of his status here—if he could go and explore the city. Kennard stared briefly and said, "Why not?" Then, breaking out of reverie, laughed and said, "Zandru's hells, youngster, you don't need my permission to do anything you please. Go alone, or I'll come along and show you about, or take along one of the *kyrri* to keep you from getting lost. Suit yourself."

Auster turned from the fireplace—they were all in the big hall—and said sourly, "Don't disgrace us by going in those clothes."

Anything Auster said always roused Kerwin's stubborn determination to do exactly that. Rannirl turned and said, with a slight shrug, "You'd be stared at."

"He'll be stared at anyway," Mesyr said.

"Nevertheless. Mesyr, find him some of my things—we're about the same size—for the time being."

Kerwin felt ridiculous when he got into the short laced jerkin, the long loose-sleeved blouse, the tight breeches of Darkovan custom. Rannirl's notions of color were not his, either. If he had to wear Darkovan clothing—and he supposed he looked pretty silly in the black leather of the Empire—he'd suit himself out in something a little less gaudy. At least he needn't, if he chose his own clothing, go around in green and purple!

He hoped.

He was surprised, though, when he glanced in a mirror and discovered how the flamboyant dress suited him; it concealed—or rather, showed to advantage—the unusual height and coloring that had always seemed awkward in Terran clothing. Mesyr warned him about wearing any headgear; the Com'yn, men and women, wore their red heads proudly, and this protected them against accidental injury or insult. On a world of daily violence, like Darkover, a world where street riots were a favorite form of showing high spirits, Kerwin conceded that probably this made good sense.

As he walked in the city—he had chosen to go alone—he was conscious of stares and whispers, but nobody jostled him. It was a strange city to him; he knew only Thendara, where the Terrans had been for so many years. The footgear of a Terran did not suit the Darkovan clothing he was wearing, and on passing a street-shop where boots were displayed, he went inside, on impulse, and asked to see a couple of pairs.

The proprietor seemed so awed and respectful that Kerwin began to wonder if he had committed a breach of proper conduct—evidently the Com'yn seldom went casually into shops—until the bargaining began. Then the man kept trying so hard to shift Kerwin from the modestly-priced boots he looked at, to the most expensive and well-crafted pairs in the shop, that Kerwin lost his diffidence and began to bargain hotly. The shop-keeper kept insisting with a genuine distress that those poor things were not worthy of the High-lord. Kerwin settled, at last, on a pair of riding boots, and one set of the soft indoor boots such as Kennard and Corus wore. He asked, taking out his wallet, "What do I owe you?"

The clerk looked shocked and offended. "You have lent me grace, *vai dom*. I could not accept a price."

"Oh, look here—"

The man said implacably, "I have told you these poor things are unworthy your attention, and I feared you would not accept them, but—"

"Hell's bells," Kerwin muttered, "I bought them, didn't I?" The man looked shocked again. The he gave Kerwin a sharp look and said, "Forgive me, but are you the Com'yn Kerwin-Aillard?"

Recalling the Darkovan custom which gave a child the name of the highest-born parent, Kerwin admitted it.

The man said, firmly and respectfully, but as if he were instructing a feeble-witted child, "It is not the custom to accept payment for anything which a Com'yn condescends to accept, High-lord."

Kerwin gave in gracefully, but he felt embarrassed. How the devil was he going to get the other things he needed? He reflected that the Com'yn had themselves a nice little racket going, but he wasn't larcenous enough to enjoy it. He was used to working for what he got, and paying for it.

He tucked the package under his arm and walked along the street. It felt curiously different and pleasant to walk along a Darkovan street and to be one of them.

This was what I wanted. And I've got it. He thought briefly of Johnny Ellers, but the years he had spent with the Terran Empire seemed like a dream.

Someone spoke his name, and he looked up to see Auster, in green and scarlet, standing before him. The man said, pleasantly for him, "It occurred to me that you might lose your way in the city. I had nothing else to do at this moment. I thought perhaps I might find you in the marketplace."

Kerwin was startled by the friendly gesture, for Auster alone, of all the circle, had been persistently unfriendly. "Thanks," he said. "I didn't lose my way, but I might have wandered a bit. Good of you to come down after me."

Auster shrugged; and suddenly, clearly as if the man had spoken, Jeff Kerwin had a clear, patterned perception:

He's lying. He didn't come down to meet me; he told me that so I wouldn't ask his business here.

He shrugged the thought aside. Auster presumably had his own affairs—*what the hell, maybe he's got a girl here*—and they were none of Kerwin's business; Kerwin couldn't have cared less.

But why did he have to explain to me?

They had fallen into step together, turning their steps back through the marketplace toward the long-lying shadow of the Tower, which lay beyond the city. Auster paused as they were about to leave the marketplace:

"Want to stop and have a drink before we go back?"

He didn't sound overly enthusiastic. Kerwin said, "Thanks, but no. I've been stared at enough for one day."

Auster gave him a quick look, not friendly, but understanding. He said, "You'll get used to it—on one level. On another, it gets worse. The longer you're with your own kind the less you can take outsiders."

They walked for a moment, shoulder to shoulder. Behind him, Kerwin heard a sudden yell.

Auster whirled, giving Kerwin a hard, violent shove. Taken off balance, he slipped, lost his balance and fell, sprawling. At the same moment something hurtled past his ear and struck hard against the wall behind him. A flake of stone ricocheted off, striking Kerwin's cheek and cutting it open.

He stared at Auster, who had stumbled off balance and

slid to his knees. Auster hauled himself to his feet, looking round warily, but the crowd had melted.

"What the hell!"

Auster said, stiffly, "I apologize for—"

Kerwin cut him short. "Forget it. You saved me a nasty bruise." Thoughtfully, he rubbed his cut cheek. "Who threw the damn thing?" He wished he spoke the local dialect better; someone had yelled a word he didn't understand.

"Some malcontent," Auster said, and his eyes were unquiet. "Kerwin, do me a favor."

"Guess I owe you one, at that."

"Don't mention this to the women, or to Kennard. We have enough to worry about, now."

Kerwin nodded. Silently, side by side, they walked up the path toward the Tower. Kerwin didn't feel like talking; he had two facts to chew on. One, Auster, who didn't like him, had moved automatically to save him from somebody's heaved rock; and, two, there was somebody on Darkover who didn't share the local feeling that the Com'yn were inviolate and not-to-be-touched. Suddenly he wished he hadn't given Auster his promise not to mention the incident. He'd have liked to talk it over with Kennard.

When he saw Kennard again, that afternoon, to keep himself from mentioning the rock-throwing, he told him about the shopkeeper and the boots, mentioning his disquiet at the custom. The older man threw back his head and howled with laughter.

"My dear boy, you've given the man free publicity for the next couple of years. The mere fact that a Com'yn, even not an important one, came alone into his street-shop and bargained with him—"

"Nice racket," Kerwin said sourly. He wasn't amused.

"Actually, it makes excellent good sense. We give a good slice of our lives to the people," Kennard said. "We have a talent no one else can imitate. They wouldn't think of letting us have a good excuse to do anything else. So anything we happen to want, we're given. That way we've no excuse to leave the matrixes on the grounds that we can make a better living elsewhere." He looked at the boots, adding "and poor enough merchandise he gave you. It speaks ill for him."

Kerwin laughed suddenly. "No wonder he tried so hard to steer me to a better pair of boots!"

"Seriously, you'd make the man happy by going back and accepting the best pair he has in his shop. Or better yet, commissioning a pair specially made from some design you happen to fancy," Kennard laughed.

Slowly, a picture was beginning to emerge in Kerwin's mind—not a complete picture. He still didn't understand what the Com'yn, actually, *did* that was so important. For all their talk, he couldn't connect the simple tricks with glasses and crystals with the overwhelming importance the Com'yn seemed to have on Darkover.

And there was something else that didn't fit; a rock, thrown at two of the Com'yn—not accidentally in the midst of a crowd, but deliberately, in the light of day. A rock big enough to disable or kill.

He didn't mention it to Kennard—but it didn't fit in.

Ten days later, he got the answer to the first of his questions.

In one of the insulated rooms, supervised by Rannirl, Kerwin was practicing simple force-emission techniques, not dissimilar to the glass-melting trick Ragan had shown him, the first night on Darkover. They had been at it for over an hour, and Kerwin's head was beginning to throb, when Rannirl said suddenly, "Enough for now. Something's going on."

They came out on the landing just as Taniquel darted up the stairs; she almost ran into them, and Rannirl, with big-brotherly kindness, caught and steadied her.

"Careful, *chiya!* What's going on?"

"I don't know," she said, "but Corus was working in the relay net, and told me that he got a message from Thendara. The Hastur is coming to Arilinn."

"So soon," Rannirl murmured. "I hoped we'd have more time!"

Kennard came up the steps toward them, and Kerwin asked, "Is this something to do with me?"

"I don't know. It might be. Hastur gave his consent to bringing you here—though we accepted responsibility."

"Do you suppose—" Kerwin found sudden fear constricting his thoughts. Had he been traced here? The City Masters of Thendara had demanded to have him deported. If the Terrans wanted him back . . .

"Don't worry," Kennard said, "They have no authority to deport you, not now. By Darkovan law, citizenship follows the parent of higher rank, which means you are Darkovan by blood-right, and Com'yn." But he still looked troubled. He started to go up the stairs, but stopped and said edgily, "But, damn it, wear Darkovan clothes!"

As Kerwin got into the somber blue-gray outfit he had chosen in the city, he looked nervously in the mirror. He looked Darkovan—outwardly at least. He felt like one. And yet he had the sense of being still on trial. Did the Arilinn tower really have the power to defy the Terrans?

They gathered, not in the big hall, but in a smaller, more formally arranged chamber high in the Tower, a room brightly lit with prisms suspended from silver chains. The seats were old, curiously carved from some dark wood, and in their midst was a low octagonal table inlaid with patterns in pearl, a seven-pointed star at the center. Kerwin, taking a seat, saw that the names of the Seven Domains were written there, in the odd curling scrips of Carthon.

Neither Kennard nor Elorie was in the room. Kennard, he knew, had gone to the airfield to welcome the expected guest. Kerwin, seeing that one of the seats was higher and more imposing than the rest, supposed that this place was reserved for the awaited personage.

A curtain was drawn back by one of the nonhumans. Kennard said ceremoniously, "Danvan Hastur of Hastur, Regent of the Council, lord of Thendara and Carcosa. Enter, *vai dom*. Welcome to Arilinn."

"You lend me grace," a resonant voice replied, and a man came into the room.

Danvan Hastur of Hastur was not a tall man. Simply clad in gray, with a fur-lined cloak, his hair graying at the temples and his face deeply lined, he seemed at first glance merely an elderly man, a quiet, dignified and scholarly man. But something—the stately straightness of his stance, the firm line of the mouth, the swift sure incisive summing-up of his gray eyes—instantly dispelled that impression. Kerwin knew at once that here was a man of tremendous presence, an enormously powerful personality.

Somehow, he seemed to take up more space in the room than he physically occupied, and his voice filled it to the corners, without being loud. "You lend me grace," he repeated. The clear gray gaze fixed on Kerwin, and he moved toward him; automatically, moved by spontaneous respect, Kerwin rose to his feet.

"Via dom—"

"You are Cleindori's child, the one who was sent to Terra for so many years," he said. He spoke the Thendara language of Kerwin's own childhood. "What name did they give you?"

Jeff told the man his name, and Hastur nodded, thoughtfully. "Well enough. Although you might consider adopting one of the Darkovan names of your clan. *Jeff* has an unnecessarily barbarous sound. Had you thought about it?"

Jeff shook his head.

"Well, please yourself," Hastur said. "I did not mean to suggest that you deny your Terran heritage. I wanted to see you myself, and to be sure about you. Not that Kennard would deceive me, even if he could. But I wanted to make certain for myself that the Terrans had not duped us into accepting an—imposter. But it is true, I can see. You are very, very like your mother, my son." He sighed. "These are strange days. I had not thought I would ever welcome a son of Terra to the Council. Yet I do welcome you." He bowed, a formal bow of recognition. "I dare to hope you may build a bridge for better understanding between your two worlds, Jeff Kerwin-Aillard."

"Strange words for the Regent of Com'yn Council," Auster said from his place, and Hastur gave him a fierce hawk-bright stare before saying, "I deal in realities, Auster. I do not live isolated in Arilinn with my equals and my brothers, but in a city at the very edge of the Terran Zone. I cannot pretend that the ancient days are still with us." He sat down—not in the high throne-like chair, but in the other empty seat.

"Now tell me, my children, how is it with you in Arilinn?"

Kerwin, watching the man, thought: *I'd like to tell him about that heaved rock. He'd know what to make of it. There's no nonsense to this old fellow!*

A bell rang softly somewhere. The curtains were drawn aside by the silk-furred nonhuman, and Elorie came into the room.

Once again her small, stately body seemed weighted with the cruelly heavy ceremonial robes, the golden chains at her waist and throat almost fetter-like with their weight, the clasps at her shoulders like a burden. She seemed a slender, aloof, ethereal girl who scarcely seemed real. She moved to the throne-like chair and took her place in silence. Hastur rose and made a deep bow while Jeff watched, paralyzed. This was the same girl who sat and played with her pet birds in the hall downstairs, the one who quarreled with Taniquel and made silly bets with Rannirl and absentmindedly walked in and out of stranger's rooms! He had not seen her before in her regalia as a Keeper, and it was a shock and a revelation.

"Welcome, in the name of Evanda and Avarra," she said in her soft and throaty voice. "You lend us grace, Lord Hastur."

"Your words brighten the sky, *vai leronis*," Hastur replied, and Elorie took the throne-like central chair.

Kennard said, "It's a long time since you made a visit to Arilinn, Lord Hastur. We are honored, but—if I may speak frankly—we know you didn't come all this way to do us honor, or even for the pleasure of our company. If you please, tell us why you have come."

The old man's face creased in a sudden smile.

"I might have known you'd see through me, Ken," he said. "Though we need you on the council, too, when Arilinn can spare you. Not yet. I came from Thendara because we have a delegation waiting—with the big question."

All of them, except Kerwin, seemed to know what he meant. Rannirl muttered, "So soon?"

"You haven't given us much time, Lord Hastur," Elorie said. "Jeff's making good progress, but—it's slow."

Kerwin leaned forward, his hands gripping at the chair-arm. "What's this all about, why are you all looking at me?"

Hastur said, solemnly, "Because, Jeff Kerwin-Aillard, with you, for the first time in many years, we have a Tower Circle with the full complement of powers. Once again we may be in a position to save the power and prestige of the Com'yn— if you do not fail us. Otherwise—" he spread his hands, "the Terrans will have their entering wedge. The rest will follow, and there won't be any way to stop it. I want you to come and talk to the delegation. What do you say, Elorie? Are you ready to take the chance—for the sake of all the Com'yn on Darkover? Do you trust your Terran barbarian as much as that?"

CHAPTER EIGHT

In the silence that followed, Kerwin felt Elorie's gaze, calm, childlike, resting on him. *Barbarian,* he thought, *Elorie's barbarian. I'm still that to them all. Except, perhaps, to Tani.*

Elorie's face was placid, but Kerwin saw that the frail hands were clenched, as if against trembling, and she looked indecisively from face to face. "Kennard," she appealed at last, "You know him best—"

Kerwin had gotten used to being discussed before his face; in a world of telepaths, there was no sense in trying to conceal it. He fought to maintain his impassive face.

Kennard sighed. "As far as trusting goes, we can trust him, Elorie," he said, "but the risk is yours. We'll all stand by your decision."

"I speak against it," Auster said passionately. "You all know how I feel—you too, Lord Hastur!"

Hastur turned to the younger man, his calm manner contrasting curiously with Auster's tense, knotted face and angry tone. He said, "Is it just blind prejudice against Terrans, Auster? Or have you some reason?"

"Prejudice," Taniquel accused, "and jealousy."

Auster's lean arrogant face was sullen.

"I'll not deny either. It was entirely too easy—to get him from the Terrans. How do we know that the whole thing wasn't concocted for our benefit?"

Kennard asked, "With Cleindori's face written in his own?"

"Cleindori!" As he spoke it, the word was an epithet. "And she a renegade—"

Elorie rose, angry and white. "Cleindori is dead. Let her lie in peace! And Zandru tear with scorpion whips at those who killed her."

"And at her seducer—*and all of his blood!*" Auster flung back.

A set of new, unaccustomed emotions were fighting in Kerwin. It was his father and his unknown mother they were cursing! For the first time, perhaps, in his entire life, he felt a surge of sympathy for his Terran grandparents. Unloving and cold they had seemed, yet they had accepted him as a son. The intense family feeling he felt was something new, and he felt that the urge must escape him to rise and fling a challenge at Auster; words in a long-forgotten tongue were struggling for utterance. He half-rose to his feet.

"Enough!" Hastur's ringing voice, angry and emphatic, compelled them both to silence. "We are not here to rake up the deeds and misdeeds of men and women a quarter of a century dead!"

"The risk is mine—to take or refuse!" Two spots of color burned on Elorie's pale cheeks. "I have never used my authority—" she spread her hands, with a little, helpless gesture. "I am not a witch. I am not superstitious. But for good or ill, authority rests in me, by law, as Keeper of the Arilinn Tower. We will hear the delegation—all of us. There is no more to be said."

She turned toward the door, her small figure stately and unbending. Kerwin, watching her, still racked by that curious surge of emotion, felt himself suddenly one with her disquiet. He knew how much it had hurt Elorie to invoke the ritual authority she hated and knew how little liking Elorie had for the superstitious lore and taboo surrounding her. All at once, this pale, childish girl seemed *real* to him; her calmness merely a mask for passionate convictions, for emotions so controlled that they were like the eye of a hurricane—dead calm.

He felt Elorie's emotions as if they were his own;

So I've done what I swore I'd never do. I've used their conditioned reverence for a Keeper just to force them to do what I want! But I had to, I had to, or we'd have another hundred years of this nonsense. . . .

Riding down in the shaft, between Taniquel and Rannirl, Kerwin was still shaken with the backwash of that contact with Elorie. What had Kennard called him? Empath, gifted with the power of sensing the emotions of others. Now, for the first time, he believed it. Before, he had accepted it intellectually; now he *felt* it.

They went out through the trembling rainbow of the Veil, down into the lower part of the Arilinn Tower, into a hall that Kerwin had never entered before, a long, narrow, silk-hung hall, and two of the crimson-and-yellow-clad guards stood before the doorway. Somewhere a ceremonial gong rang out as they filed into the room.

There were about a dozen men there, prosperous-looking men of middle age, wearing Darkovan dress, in the fashion of the cities. They waited silently for Elorie to take the high, raised central chair and bowed with more perfunctory reverence to the other Com'yn. It was Hastur who spoke.

"You are the men who called yourselves the Pan-Darkovan Syndicate?"

One of the men, a heavy-set and swarthy man with fierce eyes, bowed. "Valdrin of Carthon, at your service, Lord Hastur," he confirmed. "With your permission, I will speak for us all."

"Let me review the situation," said Hastur meditatively. "You have formed a league—"

"To encourage the growth of manufacturing and trade on Darkover," Valdrin of Carthon said. "I hardly need to tell you the politicial situation, with the Terrans and their foothold on our world. The Com'yn and the Council, since the Terrans came, have tried to ignore their presence."

"That is not precisely the situation."

113

"I won't bandy words with you, Lord," said Valdrin, respectfully but impatiently. "The facts are this: in view of our compact with the Terrans, we should work harder than ever to preserve the integrity of Darkover as a world, and as a civilization. Times change. Like it or not, the Terrans are here to stay, and Darkover is being swept into the Empire. We can still confine them to their Trade Cities, but the barrier will crumble in another generation. I've seen it happen on other worlds."

Kerwin remembered what the Legate had said. *We* leave governments alone, but the people see what we have to give, and they start demanding, of their own accord, to come into the Empire. Darkover hasn't, yet—we don't quite know why.

Valdrin of Carthon was saying the same thing, quite passionately:

"In short, Lord Hastur, we protest the decision of Com'yn Council! We want some of the advantages that come with being a functioning part of the Terran Empire. Are we to stay a barbarian state forever?"

Hastur said, "I have seen the Terran civilization, more closely than you. We want none of it."

"Speak for yourselves, then, not for us! Perhaps in the old days there was some justification for the rule of the Seven Domains. In those days, Darkover had its own science, its own technology. But those arts are lost, those powers have died out, and it is time to admit it and replace them with something new!"

Kerwin was beginning to see it clearly. By virtue of their inborn psi powers, once the Com'yn had been rulers—and, in a sense, slaves—of Darkover. They, through the tremendous energy released from the matrixes—the great ones, requiring linked circles of telepaths to release vast amounts of energy from the magnetic field of a planet—had given Darkover her own science. This explained the vast ruins of a past technology, the memories of lost sciences.

But at what cost, in human terms! The men and women possessed of these powers had lived strange, circumscribed lives, guarding their precious powers carefully, spoiled for ordinary human contacts.

114

Kerwin wondered if the natural drift of evolution, in nature, toward the norm and away from the extreme, had been responsible for the waning of these powers? Fewer and fewer were born, Kennard told him, with full measure of what they called *laran*. The science of Darkover had become a forgotten myth and a few psi tricks . . . too little to keep Darkover independent of the Terrans, in these new days that had come upon them.

"We have dealt with the Terrans," Valdrin of Carthon said. "We have won most of the people to our side; the new Council will almost certainly give us permission. In brief, the Terrans have promised that they will lend us technicians, engineers, industrial experts—everything necessary to begin extensive mining and manufacturing operations here. Metals and ores are the key, my lord. Before we have technology we must have machinery; and before we have machinery—"

"You must have mines," Hastur said. "And you must run them with machinery, and some one must make the machinery, and someone must mine the materials to make the machinery. We are not a mechanized civilization, Valdrin."

"More's the pity."

"But," Hastur said quietly, "the people of Darkover are content on their farms and lands, in their cities. We have what industry we need—dairy farming, the milling of grains, the weaving of cloth."

"Transported at horseback pace!"

"And," said Hastur, "no men need to slave at the building of roads, to keep them in condition for monstrous robot vehicles to whizz over at breakneck speed and make our clean air rotten with the spew of their chemical fuels!"

"We have a right to industry—"

"—and to factories? To work done by automatic machinery, leaving men with nothing to do but drug their senses with cheap amusements, and repair machinery? To mines, and people herded together in cities to service these machines, so they have no time to grow and prepare the food they need, and the raising of food turns into another monster factory plan?" Hastur's voice was filled with contempt.

"You cannot hold us back to a barbarian society forever, my lords," Valdrin said.

"And you would make our world into a replica of the Terran Empire?"

"Not that," Valdrin said, "not what you think."

"Do you think our people can fight the Terrans on their own ground? No, Valdrin, the world that accepts the good things of this interstellar Empire, must also accept the evil that comes with it. And yet, perhaps you are right. We cannot bar the way forever, and keep our people poor and simple.

"Perhaps the accusation is just. Once we were more powerful and rich than now. We have slipped back into a Dark Age, it is true. But it is not true that we must go Terra's way. What if the Com'yn could do, again, what legend said they could do? What if energy sources were available again, in the old ways without the endless search for fuels, without the radioactivity that blasted our lands once, before the Compact?"

"It's a good dream," Valdrin said, "but there hasn't even been a competent Keeper, let alone a Com'yn Circle, for years."

"There is now." Hastur turned, with a gesture. "A Com'yn circle complete and ready to demonstrate their power. I ask only this: that you keep free of the Terrans, and their ruinous, dehumanizing methods. Don't accept their technicians and their engineers! And if you must trade with Terra, do it as equals, not as poor protégés being helped up from barbarian status! Our world is older than Terra, and prouder! Don't shame us this way!"

He had appealed to their patriotism and pride, and Kerwin saw it catch fire in the eyes of the delegation, though Valdrin still seemed skeptical. "Can the Com'yn do this?"

"I'll speak for the Com'yn," said Rannirl. "I'm the technician. I know something of your needs. What's your first step?"

"A group of Terran engineers have contracted to make a survey and inventory of natural resources for us," Valdrin said. "Our major needs are for metals—tin, copper, silver, iron, aluminum, tungsten. Then for fuels, sulphur—they have promised us a complete inventory, and will locate with their surveying equipment all the major deposits of natural resources."

Rannirl held up a hand to stop him. "At the same time finding out where they are," he drawled, "and spreading all over Darkover with their infernal machines, instead of staying decently shut up in the Trade Cities."

Valdrin said hotly, "I deplore that just as much as you do! I have no love for the Empire, but if the alternative is to slip backward into a feudal state—"

"There is an alternative," said Rannirl. "We can survey those metal deposits for you, if you like—and *mine* them for you too. And we can do it quicker than the Terrans—and without breaking the Compact!"

Kerwin drew a deep, gasping breath. He should have guessed, when he knew that a matrix crystal could power a Terran airlaunch, the full extent of the Com'yn powers; but he had not guessed at their scope and strength.

Good God, what a concept! And to keep the Terrans out of Darkover . . .

Kerwin had not realized until this moment just how deeply he felt on the question. His years on Terra came back to his mind, the dismay when he saw the Trade City and realized that it was only a little corner of the Empire, his passionate hunger to know his own world and his own people. With the hunger of an exile for his home, he understood Hastur's words.

To keep Darkover as it was, the world he loved! And he was part of it!

Valdrin said, "It sounds good, my lords. But the Com'yn haven't ever been that strong, not in living memory. Oh, my grandfather used to tell of the old days, but now it's a mighty to-do, to get enough iron to shoe a couple of horses!"

Another of the men said, "It sounds good, yes. But these Com'yn may simply be trying to delay things—slow us down until the Terrans lose interest. I think we should deal with Terra now!"

Valdrin conferred briefly with the other men. Finally he said, "Lord Hastur, we want something more than vague talk about the old Com'yn powers. We'll make you an offer. How long would it take you to make this survey for us?"

Rannirl asked, "How long would the Terrans take?"

"Six months, they said."

Rannirl glanced at Kennard, at Elorie. Then he said, "We'll have it for you in six weeks."

"On one condition," Auster broke in, passionately, "that if we do, you give us your word to abandon these dealings with the Terrans!"

Elorie backed him up. "That is only fair. If we prove to you that we can do as much for Darkover as your Terran engineers and scientists, will you be guided by the Council? Our only desire is that Darkover shall continue to be Darkover and not a replica of the Trade City. If we succeed, you will agree to be guided by Com'yn Council in the use of all these things, so that Darkover will not change to a third-rate imitation of an Empire world!"

"That seems fair enough, my lady," Valdrin said, then his voice hardened. "But it's only fair that it should go both ways. If you fail, then Com'yn Council will pledge itself to withdraw all objections, and let us deal with the Terrans as we wish."

The formalities of leave-taking were prolonged and elaborate; Kerwin attended them with half an ear, knowing that he—"Elorie's barbarian"—would be excused for minor lapses.

Something tremendous, then, hung on the success or failure of the Com'yn circle at Arilinn. And that success or failure hung on him—half Terran, newcomer, unskilled at this work! It was a paralyzing responsibility. He felt shaken by the immensity of the obligation that lay on him. Unseen, he slipped away, back through the courtyards, through the shimmering barrier of the Veil.

It was a heavy weight for his unskilled shoulders. *I thought I'd have more time to learn. . . .* He felt young, unlearned, and—remembering the agony of his first experience with the rapports—horribly afraid.

He turned into his room and flung himself down, in silent despair. It wasn't fair, to demand this much of him, so soon! It was too much, to feel that the very fate of the Darkover he knew should depend on his untried powers!

The ghostly scent in the room felt strong to him; in a flash of remote half-recognition, it penetrated the closed place in his memory.

Cleindori. My mother, who broke her vows to the Com'yn, for an Earthman—am I redeeming her fault?

It was not betrayal!

A flash of *something*, recognition, memory, wavered for a moment on the fringes of his memory; for a moment Kerwin *knew*—

It was gone, leaving him dazed, numb.

Taniquel came softly to his side, not speaking; the web of rapport meshed between them, the girl's pixie face was drawn and grieved with his trouble.

"But it's not like that, Jeff," she whispered at last. "We trust you. If you fail—if we fail—it's not your doing alone. Don't you realize—" her voice broke; she clung to him, suddenly, holding him in her arms, and Kerwin, shaken with a new, violent emotion, crushed the girl to him. Their lips met, and Kerwin knew that he had been wanting this since first he saw her, through the rain of a Darkovan night, through the smoke of a Terran room. The woman of his own people, the first to accept him as one of themselves.

"Jeff, don't you know we love you? Don't you know—if we fail, it's not *your* failure, it's *ours?* You won't be to blame. But you won't fail, Jeff, you won't, you won't—"

Her arms sheltered him, and the surge of love and desire in him was something he had never known or guessed.

Here was no easy conquest, no cheap girl from the spaceport's bars, to give him a moment's ease but leave his heart unfed. Here was no encounter to leave the aftertaste of lust in his mind, the strange aftermath of loneliness, sensing the woman's emptiness as deep as his own disillusion.

Taniquel, Taniquel, closer than a lover from that first moment of rapport between them. How was it that he had not known? He shut his eyes, the better to taste this closeness, the touch that was closer than the touch of lips or arms alone. . . .

Taniquel whispered, "I've sensed your—loneliness and

your hunger. But I was afraid to share them—until now. Jeff, Jeff—I've taken your pain to myself, let me share this too."

"But," Kerwin said hoarsely, "I'm not afraid now. I was afraid only because I felt alone."

"And now," she spoke his thoughts, sinking into his arms with a surrender so absolute that he seemed never to have known a woman before, "you'll never be alone again."

CHAPTER NINE

IF JEFF KERWIN had visualized this vast planetary survey of natural resources as some swift, simple work of telepathic magic, he found quickly that he was wrong. The actual rapport work, Kennard told him, would come later; meanwhile there were preparations to be made, and only the Com'yn themselves could make them. It was almost impossible to focus telepathic rapport on any given object or substance unless the object or substance had first been brought into contact with the telepath who would use it. Jeff had imagined that the gathering of materials and the like would be done by outsiders or menials; instead, as the least skilled telepath, he found that he could be dispensed with, in the early stages, and was put to several small technical jobs in the preliminary stages. He knew something of metallurgy from his work in the Terran communications bureau; assisted by Corus, they located samples of various metals and, working in a laboratory which reminded Jeff of an Earth-history conception of an alchemist's study, melted them and, with primitive but unusually effective techniques, reduced them to pure form. He wondered what on earth the Com'yn were going to do with these tiny samples of iron, tin, copper, zinc, lead and antimony.

Working with Corus, Elorie and Rannirl, Kerwin felt his own sensitivity growing. He had no trouble, now, in maintaining stasis in any crystal structure, and was beginning to sense the condition of other substances; one day he found himself sensing the oxidation of the iron in a slowly-rusting doorhinge, and—his first unaided effort—drew out his own matrix and—with a sudden intense effort of concentration—reversed the process.

He still got the splitting headaches when he was among the screens, and the effort was still tremendous, racking, each expenditure of psychic energy leaving him spent and drained, his body demanding enormous quantities of food and sleep. He understood, now, Elorie's childish appetite, which had seemed, at first, only a little-girlish greediness for sweets; he had been amazed, sometimes, seeing so frail and dainty a little girl put away such enormous quantities of food, but now he realized that he was hungry all the time; his body, drained of energy, demanded replacements with ravenous hunger. And at times, when—the day's work completed, or called to a halt because Elorie could tolerate no more of the strain—Kerwin could rest, or when Taniquel had a little time to spend with him, he found he only wanted to fling himself down and rest.

"I'm afraid I'm not a very ardent lover," he apologized, once, feeling half sick with chagrin; Taniquel close to him, loving, willing, but the only desire in his body was an exhausted hunger for sleep. Taniquel laughed softly, bending to kiss him.

"I know," she murmured. "I've been around matrix mechanics all my life, remember? It's always that way when you're building the screens—you have just so much energy, and you can't afford to waste it. Don't worry about it, when this is over we'll have time together—if you still want me."

"*If* I still want you?" Kerwin sat upright, staring down at the girl. Her eyes were closed; her pixie face, pale amid her scattered hair, looked suddenly remote and strange. "What do you mean, Tani?"

"Oh, people change," she said vaguely. "Never mind that now. Here—" she pulled him gently down, her light hands caressing his forehead. "Sleep, darling; you're worn out."

Weary as he was, the words had driven sleep from his mind. How could Taniquel doubt—or was the girl in the grip of some premonition? Since they had been lovers, he had been happy; now, for the first time, a curious disquiet moved in him. A picture of Taniquel, hand in hand with Auster, made him flinch with angry jealousy. What had been between them? He *knew* Taniquel cared for him; in a way he had never known before, they were in harmony. He knew, now, why his casual affairs with women had never gone beneath the surface. The unrecognized, but sensitive telepath facility in him had picked up the fundamental shallowness of the kind of women he had known; without knowing why, he had kicked himself for being an idealist, never satisfied. He could not, like other men, close his eyes to the pretense and the mercenary aspect, and enjoy his own dreams projected on some girl. The relationship with Taniquel had brought a whole new world into focus, his first taste of shared passion, shared emotion. Could she care for him so deeply if she had cared for someone else in that same way?

Many disquiets began to come into focus as he lay awake, his head throbbing. Of course, now it was clear to him. Everyone in the Arilinn Tower had known that he and Taniquel were lovers. A smile from Kennard, a meaningful glance from Mesyr, Corus laughing teasingly at Taniquel—all these took on new significance.

Damn it, there are drawbacks to a telepath society! Like, no privacy!

Suddenly, the thought was embarrassingly present. Telepaths all, were they reading his thoughts, his emotions, what he had — shared — with Taniquel? Sudden, scalding embarrassment flooded him, as if he had had some shameful dream of walking naked in the public square and waked to find it was true. . . .

Taniquel, drowsily holding his hand, jerked awake as if struck by a live wire. Indignation flamed in her face.

"You—you *are* a barbarian," she flared at him. "You— *Terranan!*" Quickly, she was gone, her light footsteps dying away with an angry pattering on the uneven floor, and Kerwin, baffled at her sudden rage, lay awake until dawn, confused and dismayed.

But when they met again she was gentle and affectionate as always, greeting him with her spontaneous embrace. "Forgive me, Jeff. That was unfair of me. It's not for me to blame you, that you've lived among the Terrans. You'll come to understand us better, in time."

And with the reassurance of her arms around him, he could not doubt the sincerity of her feelings.

Thirteen days after Hastur's visit, the matrixes were prepared, and that morning, in the great hall, Elorie told them, "We can start the first locating operation tonight."

Kerwin felt last-minute panic. This would be his first experience in full rapport; previous contacts had been brief, experimental. But this was it.

"Why at night?"

Rannirl answered, "Because, in this hemisphere, most people sleep during the dark hours, and we get less telepathic interference—in radio it would be static. There's telepathic static, too."

"We'll get some sleep during the day," Elorie said. "I want you all fresh and rested for tonight."

Corus winked at Kerwin. "Better give Jeff a sedative, then. He'll lie awake fretting." But there was no malice in his words, and Mesyr looked questioningly at Kerwin;

"If you want something—"

Kerwin shook his head, feeling foolish. They talked a few minutes longer, then Elorie, laughingly saying that she was going to take her own advice, yawned and went up the stairs. One by one, they began to drift away from the fireside. Kerwin, not sleepy in spite of his weariness, remained. *If only Taniquel were with him he could relax.*

"Elorie meant it, youngster," Kennard said, pausing beside him. "Better get some sleep, or tonight will be too much for you." A moment of silence, then his heavy brows went up almost into his hairline. "Oh, it's like *that?*"

"Damn it, I don't—is there no privacy around here?"

"I'm an Alton," Kennard said. "We're the strongest telepaths in the Com'yn. Sorry if it offends you, but let me say something. I told you. I married a Terran woman. I've been among Terrans enough to know that they're damned touchy on some subjects, so don't be offended—"

"Go ahead. I won't be offended."

"Liar," said Kennard, without anger. "But don't blame

Taniquel for leaving you alone just now, when you think you
need her most. I know how you feel—Aldones! How well I
know!" He chuckled, wryly, as if at some private joke. "But
Tani knows, too. When a major matrix operation is in the
works, celibacy is the rule. She knows better than to break
it."

"Why—"

"Why do you think the Keepers are required to be virgins?"

Kerwin hadn't ever thought about it. Suddenly he realized
that it explained Elorie. That was it; that was what set
her apart from Taniquel. A lovely woman—but as sexless as
a little girl. As unconscious of her own beauty and desirability
as any child.

"The ancients would have called it a ritual thing—a
religious matter," Kennard said. "I think that's superstitious
drivel. But there's this much truth to it, you are going to
need every scrap of your nervous energy, and strength, tonight. Taniquel knows that. She's mischievous—but not mali-
cious. Hence, you get some sleep. Alone." He laid his hand
on Kerwin's arm, a kindly, almost a fatherly gesture. "The
trouble is—you're so much a part of us, now, that we forget
you haven't always been here. We take it for granted you'll
know all these things, as we do—without being told. Jeff,
when you came here, we were doubtful about you. But now,
win or lose, you're one of us. True Darkovan—and true
Com'yn. That thought may not be as reassuring as it would
be to have Tani with you," he smiled, "but maybe it will help
a little."

They sent for him at moonrise. The Arilinn Tower felt
strange and still in the deeps of the night, and the matrix
laboratory had that strange, resonating quiet. They gathered,
speaking in hushed voices, feeling the quiet as a live and
palpable thing.

Kerwin felt slack and empty; less like telepathic work than
ever in his life. Kennard moved stiffly, his lameness very
evident, each step seeming to be made with pain; Rannirl
looked sleepy and cross, and Elorie was nervously clenching
and unclenching her frail hands.

Taniquel's fingers touched Kerwin's forehead and he felt

124

the faint feather-touch of her thoughts, the swift sure rapport. "He's all right, Elorie."

To Kerwin, Elorie explained, "Taniquel is an empath, and will keep in rapport with all of us—keep watch over automatic functions. If one of us forgets to breathe, or anything, she'll know it in time to keep us from being too depleted, or damaged."

Auster said, "And I'm the barrier-holder. We all drop our individual barriers for rapport. I put up a telepathic barrier which shields our minds as a group. This keeps out telepathic eavesdropping, and I can sense it if anyone tries to interfere with us. In the old days there were alien forces on Darkover. Some say that there are still. So I throw a barrier around the gestalt formed by our minds, and keep out intruders."

Elorie reached out her hands, motioned to Kennard and Rannirl, and Kerwin, nervously intent, saw and felt them, one by one, drop into place in the growing mesh of rapport. There was the swift image of linking hands, a meshing grip.

Kerwin never knew, for time had ceased to have meaning, how long he whirled and probed and flashed in and out of contact with textures of soil, rock, lava, darting in and out, riding magnetic currents. Again and again he saw Rannirl's perceptions pick him up and ride on the tip of an orange crayon to a strange surface, but at last he felt the whirling slowing down. Fragmented, shattering, he felt Corus (a liquid cooling into a crystal!) drop with an impalpable noise out of the mesh; heard Rannirl slide noiselessly out of some invisible door; felt Elorie open her hand, gently releasing Kennard from the mesh. Pain racked Kerwin, like the pain of breathing water, as he felt himself drop free into dizzy nowhere. Auster made a thick sound of exhaustion, sliding forward in his chair, half insensible. Kerwin blinked, shaking his head, seeing Taniquel sigh wearily and straighten up. Rannirl slumped, a crayon stump still clutched in his fingers. The map was covered with cryptic symbols. Elorie was moving cramped fingers, raising her hands to her face with a sound like a sob of exhaustion.

Taniquel said very softly, "No more. Corus's heart was fluttering, and Jeff was ready to collapse."

Elorie came on unsteady tiptoe to stand behind Rannirl. "Jeff did the structural work," she said softly, "he was there, all the time. He has a good structural sense." She touched the map with a light finger. "These are copper deposits. Kennard has measured the depth. Rannirl marked the place. Corus and Jeff assayed the richness." Suddenly, through her weariness, her eyes were exultant.

"Show me the Terrans, for all their technology, who can do so much!" She stretched, catlike. "Do you realize what we've done?" she demanded. "It worked! All of you—it *worked!* Now are you glad you listened to me? Who's a barbarian now?" With an overpowering burst of glee, she flung her arms childishly around Kerwin and hugged him tight. "Oh, Jeff, I knew we could do it, with you!"

Kerwin felt the surge of her emotion; his arms tightened around the girl, and he drew her to him, kissing her long and hard. It had begun as the merest gesture of brotherly affection, good-natured response to her exuberance; but he sensed the exact moment when it changed, when her lips softened under his.

Then she was standing away from him, her face ghastly, eyes wide in terror. She clasped both hands over her breast, panting, looking at Kerwin with those wide frightened eyes.

"Elorie—"

But it was only a flash of awareness; it closed down and she swayed, tiredly, and leaned hard on Kennard's suddenly-supporting arm. She shut her eyes and covered them childishly with her fists. "I'm—worn out," she whispered. Kerwin, aware again of his own agonizingly cramped muscles, stretched and looked at the sun, flooding in through the window. They had been within the matrix—and in rapport—for fourteen hours!

Rannirl folded the map carefully. "We'll try again, in a few days, with tin, iron, aluminum. It'll be easier next time." He looked past Kerwin, frowning. "Auster, what's the matter with you, man?"

Auster's eyes were fixed on Kerwin with steady, unblinking malevolence. Kerwin thought, *He's not happy that I did it. He wanted me to fail.*
But why?"

CHAPTER TEN

THE DEPRESSION lingered, even after he had slept away the exhaustion. As he made ready to join the others, near sunset, he told himself that he should not let Auster's malevolence spoil this for him. He had come through the acid test of rapport, and it was his triumph. Auster, after all, had never liked him; probably it was no more than that.

And now that the first session was over, he knew there would be a free interval, while they recuperated from the effects. He felt almost light-hearted as he went down the long stairway. He was free again to be with Taniquel. . . .

The others had all wakened before him, and were already in the hall. The very casualness of their greeting warmed him with a sense of belonging; he accepted a glass of *shallan*—the sweet, mildly alcoholic drink he had come to like—and sank down, in his accustomed seat, looking around for Taniquel. She was near the fire with Auster, deep in conversation with him. Troubled, Kerwin tried to catch her eye, and finally succeeded. He made an unobtrusive motion of his head, a signal she knew well, fully expecting her to make some light-hearted excuse to Auster and join him.

However, she only gave him a little, eye-blink of a smile, and lightly shook her head. Startled, rebuffed, he watched her; her hand was lying in Auster's, their heads close together; they seemed quite absorbed; Kerwin watched, his puzzlement and irritation growing. The girl had never seemed so desirable as now, when her laughter, her pixie smile half impish, half tender, were all for Auster. From irritation he proceeded to bewilderment, and resentment. How could she do this to him? Was she nothing but a heartless tease?

As the evening passed, he sank deeper and deeper into dejection. The attempts of Kennard and Rannirl to engage him in conversation fell flat. After a time, assuming that he was still weary, they left him to himself. Corus and Elorie were playing some sort of game with cut-crystal dice; Mesyr was busy with needlework. It was a perfectly calm domestic scene, except for Kerwin's knifelike awareness of Taniquel, resting her head against Auster's shoulder. Rannirl studied some maps; Kennard dozed. A dozen times Kerwin told himself he was a damned fool to sit and watch it, but bewilderment and resentful anger strove in him. Why?

When Auster had risen to refill their glasses, Kerwin rose abruptly; Kennard looked up, startled and alert, as Kerwin crossed the room, bent to take Taniquel by the arm. "Come with me," he said, in a sharp undertone. She looked up, startled and not pleased, but with a quick glance around— she wasn't going to make a scene—she said, "Let's go out on the terrace."

The sunset had long gone, and the mist was condensing into fine rain; Taniquel put up her hands to her cheeks. "It's nice and cool here," she said. "Jeff, what's the matter with you, why have you been staring at me like that all evening?"

"Don't you know?" he flung at her. "Haven't you any heart?"

"Are you *jealous?*" She shook her head, not understanding. Jeff drew her into his arms; she sighed, smiled and kissed him. He seized her by the elbows, saying hoarsely, "I should have known you were just deviling me, but I couldn't stand it, watching you with Auster, before my very eyes." He let out a long sigh, both angry and relieved. But she held herself away, her pixie face wiped clean of merriment. He sensed her anger.

"Jeff, Auster needs me—can't you understand that? Have *you* no feelings? This is your triumph, and his defeat. Can't you see?"

"Are you trying to say you've turned against me?"

"Why should I have turned against you? All I'm saying is that Auster needs me, right now. More than you do." She raised herself on tiptoe, kissing him coaxingly, but he held her roughly at arm's length, some hint of her meaning beginning to reach him.

128

"Are you saying what I think you're saying, Taniquel?"

"What is the *matter* with you? I can't seem to get through to you at all tonight!"

He said, his throat tight, "I—I love you. I thought—"

"Of course I love you," she said impatiently. "I think you're overtired, Jeff, or you wouldn't talk this way. What has it to do with you—that for tonight Auster should need me more than you do?"

His mouth felt dry. "You little bitch!"

Taniquel stepped back as if he had struck her. Her face in the dim light from the doors was dead white.

"And you are a selfish brute," she retorted, "the barbarian Elorie called you! You—you Terrans think women are *property!* Yes, I love you, but not when you behave like this!"

He felt his mouth twitch, painfully. "That kind of love I can buy in the spaceport bars!"

Taniquel's hand went up, hard and stinging, across his face. "You—you," she flared, speechless. "I belong to *myself,* do you hear? Auster was right about you, all along!" She moved past, not touching him, and he heard her steps recede, swift and final, into the Tower.

His face burning, Kerwin did not at once follow. The rain, blowing around the cornice of the Tower, was already crystallizing into snow; he brushed it from his smarting cheek. What had he done? On a numb impulse to hide himself, he went swiftly along the passageway and up the stairs toward his own room; but before he reached it he heard Kennard's uneven step behind him.

"Jeff, what's the matter?"

He did not want to face Kennard's craggy, knowing face just now. He muttered "Still tired. Think I'll get some sleep."

Kennard came around in front of him, barring his way to his room. "Jeff. If you think you can keep it from us—"

"Damn it," Jeff said, his voice cracking, "is there no goddamn privacy in this place at all?"

Kennard slumped and sighed. "Zandru's hells," he muttered. "Look, man, I know. You Terrans—How can I make you understand, Jeff? Taniquel—"

"Forget it," he said curtly. "It's between me and Taniquel. And none of your business."

"It's not between you and Taniquel at all," Kennard said. "It's between you and Auster. Look, do you remember what I told you that first day? Everything that happens here affects us all. Taniquel is an empath. Can't you understand what that means? Can't you understand how she feels when she senses—that sort of need and hunger? She's a woman. Can any woman worth the name feel that in a man, and not—answer it? Feed it? Damn it," he concluded, "if you and Auster understood each other—if you had empathy with him, you'd feel it too—and you'd understand!"

Against his will, Kerwin began to grasp the concept. In a world of wide-open telepaths, among such a closely-knit group as the Tower circle, emotions, needs, hungers did not affect only the one who felt them, but all his associates.

Taniquel, sensing his loneliness and bewilderment, had freely given her love and understanding. Now, when Jeff was triumphant and Auster apparently defeated, it was Auster's pain for which she felt empathy, Auster's loneliness that she desired to soothe. . . .

Human flesh and blood couldn't endure it! Taniquel, Taniquel whom he loved, Taniquel who had given him so much, in the arms of a man he hated!

Kennard's expression was almost one of pity. "It must be very difficult for you. But you spent too much time among the Terrans. You've taken their neurotic codes to yourself. Marriage itself is a recent development on Darkover. What you call monogamy, more recent yet, and it's never been really accepted. I'm not blaming you, Jeff. You are what you are, just as we are what we are. I just wish you weren't so unhappy about it." He went away, wearily, and Jeff caught the overflow of his emotion, his memories . . . Kennard too had married a Terran wife, had known the pain of a man caught between two worlds, had seen his own sons rejected for it . . .

Lying awake, aflame with jealous rage, Kerwin fought a solitary battle, and toward morning he came to grim equilibrium. The girl wasn't worth it. He wasn't going to let Auster wreck things for him. They had to work together, somehow or other.

It was galling to lose out to Auster. But if the girl wanted him, she was welcome to him. She's made her choice and she could stick to it.

It wasn't ideal, but it worked, after a fashion. He was icily remote, and she took her tone from him. Again they began the work of building complex matrix-screens, keying them to verified maps; five days after the first rapport search, they gathered again, and again the mesh of rapport built up, a guarded and infinitely extensive consciousness which searched out fragments of spacetime containing atoms of the particular pattern to make up the metal known as zinc, isolating rich concentrations and deposits, marking them for accessibility and depth. The day before they were to go into a third rapport search, Jeff came in from a solitary ride in the foothills to find Corus waiting for him, looking pale and excited.

"Jeff, Elorie wants us all in the lab, as soon as you can come. Quickly!"

He followed Corus, wondering what had happened. The others were all gathered there already, Rannirl with his map in hand.

"Trouble," he said. "I had word from our clients after I passed this map to them. In three separate places—here, here, here"—he indicated map markings—"the Aldarans have moved in, and filed claim on the lands we marked as rich in copper. You know as well as I do that the Aldarans are pawns of Terra. They're fronting for the Empire, claiming that land in order to set up a Terran-type industrial colony there! How did they know?"

"This has never happened before," said Auster angrily. "The first time Jeff works with us—the front men for Terra move in, not on one, but on three of the claims." His eyes blazed at Jeff. "What did the Terrans offer you to betray us?"

"You're mad!" Jeff said.

"It's just a matter of bad luck," Kennard said.

Auster said, "*One* might be coincidence, and two might be sheer bad luck. But *three?*"

131

"There's one way to settle it," Taniquel said, looking at Jeff and then away again. "He can't lie to an Alton, Kennard."

Jeff knew immediately what she meant, and rage surged through him. "Telepathic examination? I *demand* it," he said, "and then, damn it, I'll make you eat those words, Auster. I'll cram them down your throat with my fists!" He faced Kennard, rage making him oblivious to the usual fear of facing that nightmarish probe. "Go ahead! Find out for yourself!"

Kennard made a disclaiming movement. Elorie said softly "It's the only way now."

Jeff shut his eyes, bracing himself for the painful shock of forced rapport. No matter how often it was done, it was no easier. He stood it for a second or two before the merciful haze swirled up; then he was standing, gripping the table with both hands, hearing his own breath loud in the silence. Kennard was looking back and forth from him to Auster.

"Well," Jeff demanded.

"I have always said we could trust you," Kennard said quietly, "but there is something. Something I do not understand, some blocking of your memory, Jeff."

Auster said, "Could the Terrans have given him some sort of post-hypnotic conditioning? Planted him on us—a time bomb?"

"They couldn't," Elorie said scornfully, but Kennard did not answer. He said, "I can assure you that Jeff is not feeding them information, Auster. There's no guilt in him."

But a cold, bleak horror had suddenly gripped Jeff by the throat.

Ever since arriving on Darkover, he had been pushed around by some mysterious force. The Com'yn—they certainly had not been the ones who destroyed the records on the Terran computer banks, who kept him off balance until he had no place to go. . . .

Had he been planted on the Com'yn—an unconscious spy within their ranks?

"I never heard anything so damnably foolish," Kennard said angrily. "I'd as soon believe it of Elorie or Auster! But if there's this kind of suspicion and friction among us, the

132

Terrans will be the ones who will benefit. Enough of this, now!" He took up the map. "It's more likely that someone among the Aldarans—they have some telepaths—was spying with an unmonitored matrix. A second level barrier can be broken, sometimes, and that's probably what happened. Your barrier may have slipped, Auster. That's all. Call it bad luck, and we'll try again."

CHAPTER ELEVEN

HE TRIED to dismiss the idea from his mind. After all, Kennard on telepathic examination had warranted him clear in that direction. But once roused, the idea persisted, like the nagging pain in a neglected tooth.

Would I even have to know it?

Did the Terrans plant me here?

The Com'yn found me, yes, from Adrilinn. I was so damned glad to be out of the pressure that I didn't even ask questions. Like, why did the computer at the Spacemen's Orphanage have no records of me?

Auster, too, was born among the Terrans.

He went through the days silent and morose, riding solitary in the hills, lying on the bed in his room for hours and trying to think of nothing. He was conscious of Taniquel's eyes watching him whenever he was with the others, feeling her sympathy (*Damned bitch, I don't want her pity!*) and the pain of her awareness. He avoided her when he could. The memory of their little time as lovers cut like a knife. Because it had gone so much deeper than any casual relationship, for him, it could not be casually cut away.

He was vaguely aware that she tried to encounter him alone; he took perverse pleasure in evading her. One morning, however, he met her face to face on the stairs. "Jeff—" she said, putting out a hand to him, "Wait. Don't run away, I want to talk to you."

He shrugged, looking over her head. "What's to say?"

The girl's eyes, once so full of mischief, spilled suddenly. "I can't stand this—the two of us like enemies, and the Tower filled with needle points of jealousy and hate!"

He said, the ice of his resentment giving way before the genuineness of her pain, "I don't like it either, Tani. But it wasn't my doing, remember."

"Why must you—" she broke off, controlling her temper, biting her lip. "I'm sorry you're so unhappy, Jeff. Kennard told me, a little, how you felt."

He said, knifing the words with heavy sarcasm, "Am I unhappy enough for you to come back to me?" He took her, not gently, by the shoulders. "I suppose Auster has you thinking the worst, too—that I'm a spy for Terra?"

She was quiet between his hands, making no move to break away, and her voice held no anger.

"Auster's not lying, either, Jeff. He's only saying what he believes. And if you think he's happy about it, you're very much mistaken."

"I suppose it would break his heart, to drive me away!"

"I don't know, but he doesn't hate you the way you think. Jeff, look at me. Can't you *feel* that I'm telling you the truth?"

That was the hell of it, Jeff thought wearily, they were all telling the truth as they saw it.

Taniquel's shoulders were trembling; somehow the sight of Tani—the mischievous, the carefree—in tears hurt worse than all the suspicions of the others. She neither attacked nor defended, she simply shared his pain. She fell against him, sobbing, clinging helplessly.

"Oh, Jeff, we were so happy when you came—and it means so much to us, to have you here. Oh, if we could only know. If we could only be sure!"

He faced them down that night in the hall, waiting until they were gathered with their evening drinks before rising aggressively, hands clenched behind his back. He spoke Cahuenga, in defiance:

"Auster, you made an accusation and when Kennard probed, and cleared me, you didn't accept the proof. What proof would you demand? What will you accept?"

Auster rose to his feet, slender, graceful, cat-lean and

dangerous. He said, politely, "Com'yn immunity prevents me from dealing with—"

"Com'yn immunity be——!" Jeff used a word straight from the spaceport gutters. "I spent ten years on Terra, and they have an expression there. Put up or shut up. Either tell me what proof you'll accept, and give me a chance to prove it to your satisfaction—or right here and now, brother, take my word that if I hear one damned syllable out of you, or pick up one telepathic syllable out of you, to the effect that I'm in the pay of Terra, or anybody else, I'll beat the living hell out of you!" He stood, fists clenched, and when Auster side-stepped, he moved too, keeping in front of him. "I'm saying it again. Put up or shut up and stay shut."

"He has the right of it," Kennard said. "You can't just keep on sniping, Auster. Prove what you say, or apologize to Jeff, and keep your mouth buttoned afterward. You owe it to all of us. We can't live like this, with half of us snarling at the other half." His face was lined, deeply pained. "We have too much trouble as it is."

Auster glanced at Kerwin. If looks could kill, Kerwin thought, Auster would have no problem. But when he spoke, his voice was smooth.

"Elorie. Can you build a trap matrix?"

"Yes, but I won't," she flared at him. "Do your own dirty work!"

"Kennard can, but he's prejudiced in Jeff's favor."

"I will," Rannirl said. "Not because I'm on your side, Auster. But because if you were left to do it yourself, I know what the result would be. Jeff, do you trust me?"

Kerwin looked at the sad-faced older man and nodded. He wasn't sure what a trap matrix was, but with Rannirl supervising it, he was fairly sure that the trap wouldn't be set for him.

They were finishing the screens one afternoon, and Jeff was holding the pattern, when suddenly he saw the figure in the monitor break and run together, melt into a green streak. Pain suddenly darted through him; he jerked alert and scarcely knowing what he did, he smashed the rapport between Rannirl and Elorie, blanked the screens, and, hardly aware that he had left his seat, caught Elorie's limp body in his arms as she fell. For a panicked moment he thought she was not breathing; then he saw her smoky-dark eyelashes flutter, and she sighed.

"She's been working too hard," Kennard said, rising and covering the crystal structure. "She *will* keep on, even when I beg her to rest."

Rannirl said, "Lucky Jeff caught it in time. He got her out before she blurred the crystalline structure, when she started to go foggy. How did you do it, Jeff?"

"I don't know." Kerwin had acted automatically, as if some warning trigger had filtered into his consciousness. "Luck. Instinct. Who knows?"

Elorie was crying weakly with exhaustion; her face was deathly white, and her sobs shallow as if she no longer had the strength to breathe. Rannirl took her up like a child, and strode out of the lab, flinging back over his shoulder, "Get Tani up here—hurry!"

Kennard said, "Taniquel went with Auster in the airlaunch. I'll try to get through to them, but meanwhile—"

Rannirl pushed in the nearest door with his foot. It was one of the empty rooms. He laid the girl down on a couch covered with dusty tapestry. Jeff stood helplessly in the door. "Anything I can do?"

"You're an empath," Rannirl said.

And abruptly Jeff remembered what Taniquel had done for him that night of testing, when he collapsed with the breaking of his barriers.

"I'll do what I can."

Elorie moved her head from side to side, like a fractious child. "No," she said irritably. "No, let me be. I'm all right." But she had to breathe twice while she said it, and her face was like scraped bone.

"She's always like this," Rannirl said. "Do what you can, Jeff."

He went out, and Jeff came forward, awkwardly dropping by the girl's side.

"I don't know much about it," he said, "but I'll do anything I can to help, Elorie." Remembering how Taniquel had given him strength, he took Elorie's hands in his. They were rigid, cold as ice. He began to chafe them, almost without thought, moulding them to pliancy. He tried to raise and heighten his sensitivity, to be aware of Elorie's weakness. . . .

He felt it like a pain in himself, her strengthless weariness, the ebbing tide of her consciousness . . . the girl was almost unconscious. Cautiously, he reached for rapport, sensing, with that heightened awareness, the limits of her fatigue, seeking to take it upon himself, willing his own strength into her. Gradually, as he knelt there with her hands limp between his own, he felt the life coming back into her exhausted body. It seemed a long time, though it was not more than a few minutes, before Elorie opened her gray eyes and looked at him, her face still pale, the soft and childlike lips still colorless.

"Thank you, Jeff," she whispered. On an impulse stronger, for the moment, than any emotion he had ever known, he held out his arms. The girl came into them, raising her face to his, and then, without surprise, Kerwin felt the swift strange exquisite blending of perceptions as their lips met. He sensed the moment with an intensely heightened dual consciousness, feeling Elorie's warm slight body in his arms, her frailness blended with steel strength, the childlike quality blended with the ageless, calm wisdom of her caste and her order. (*And dimly through these things he sensed and felt with Elorie her awareness, the lassitude and eagerness with which she accepted his kiss, a strange and only half understood wakening in her senses. He shared with the girl her own wonder and surprise at this touch which was not fatherly and impersonal-kindly—shared her shy and shameless surprise at the strength of his man's body, at the sudden rising heat in him . . .*)

"Elorie," he whispered, but it was like a triumphant shout. "My love, my love . . ."

There was a spasmodic, convulsive moment of shattering fear, clawing with anguish at every nerve in him; then the rapport smashed, like a breaking crystal, and Elorie, white to the lips, was straining away from him, fighting like a cat in his arms. "No," she gasped, "No, no—"

Dazed, numb with shock, Kerwin let her go. She scrambled quickly up and away from him, her hands clasped over her breasts, that rose and fell with soundless, anguished sobs. Her eyes held horror, but she was barriered against him again. Her childish mouth moved and worked, soundlessly, her face set with a little girl's grimace against tears. "No," she whispered again at last. "Have you forgotten what I am? Oh, Avarra pity me," she said in a falling, broken gasp, covered her face with her hands and fled from the room, half tripping over a stool, eluding Jeff's automatic step toward her, slipping through the door and her light running steps dying away down the hall. Far away, far up in the Tower, he heard the closing of a door.

He did not see Elorie again for three days. For the first time since he had come to the Tower, she failed to join them in the evening ritual of drinks and companionship; Jeff, from the moment Elorie fled from him, felt cut off and alone; alien among them, a stranger in a world suddenly gone cold and strange.

The others seemed to take Elorie's sudden self-seclusion for granted; Kennard said with a shrug, explaining her to Kerwin, that all Keepers did that now and then. Jeff, holding his barriers firm against involuntary betrayal, said nothing. But Elorie's eyes, dark and luminous with dismay and that sudden, shocking fear, seemed to swim in the darkness, each night, while he lay awake, feeling with an almost tactile memory her kiss on his lips, the feel of her frail and frightened body in his arms.

At first he had only been dazed, numb with the shock of that broken rapport, still weak with the aftermath of Elorie's collapse. He stood there in shock, not understanding, half dismayed, half angry at the girl's surrender and sudden withdrawal.

And then, slowly and painfully, understanding came.

He had broken the strictest law of the Com'yn. A Keeper was a pledged virgin, trained for her work, body and brain given lengthy conditioning for her difficult and dangerous task. To every man on Darkover, Elorie was inviolate—a Keeper, beyond desire, never to be touched by lust or even by the purest love.

He had heard what they said (and worse, felt what they felt) about Cleindori, who had broken this vow. (And with one of the despised Terrans!)

Another man might have defended himself, saying that Elorie had invited his advance, and he had only taken what was offered. But for Kerwin there were no such easy evasions. He had always been aware of Elorie's innocence— the childish way she showed affection to the other men in the Tower. She had had confidence in the taboo which protected her; for them all, she was sexless, like another man or a child.

She had accepted Jeff in the same innocent, unwary way— and he had betrayed the trust!

Worse than this was a terrible fear, knifing at his heart. Kennard had warned him about the dangers of emotion, of the nervous exhaustion he could suffer, counseling him to keep apart from Taniquel during the days immediately before the matrix work. Taniquel! His feeling for her now seemed dreamlike; he had loved her, yes, but only with gratitude for her understanding and her kindness. Nothing like this vast and surging thing that swallowed up his whole consciousness. . . .

The Keepers keyed themselves, body and mind, much more completely into the matrixes they operated. This was why they must be kept apart from emotion. His memory went back to his first night at Arilinn; to Elorie's flustered distress at his compliment, to her words: "We are trained all through childhood for this ability—and sometimes we lose it within a very few years."

And now, perhaps the very fate of Darkover hung upon the strength of the Arilinn Tower, and their work. And the fate of this work they were doing depended on the strength and fortitude of their central and cherished Keeper. Jeff Kerwin, the stranger in their midst, had betrayed their trust and struck through the defenses of their Keeper.

When he reached this point in his thoughts Kerwin buried

his head in his hands and tried to blank out his mind completely. This was worse than Auster's accusation that he was a spy for Terra.

On the morning of the fourth day, he heard Elorie's voice on the stairs. Alone in the night, he had fought his way to a hard-won battle. Nothing lay before him now but renunciation.

He loved Elorie, but his love for her could destroy her as a Keeper, and might endanger the work they were doing for the Darkovans. If they failed, the Pan-Darkovan syndicate would take it as their permission to bring in Terran experts, start the remodeling of Darkovan trade in the Terran pattern.

And would that be so bad, a traitor part of himself whispered. Sooner or later Darkover would fall into the pattern of the empire.

And it would be better so!

Even for Elorie—it's too much, no young girl should have to face this seclusion, this avoidance of all that's good in life. And if we fail, if we fail, then it doesn't matter whether Elorie is a Keeper or not, and she can be mine. . . .

Traitor! He accused himself bitterly. These people took you in, gave you the chance to stay on Darkover, accepted you as one of themselves—

And you'd destroy them!

Whatever happened, Elorie's peace of mind must be safe.

But with the sound of her voice it all came up, boiling, within him again. Oh, God, oh God, Elorie, Elorie . . . He had started toward the door, but he went back blindly and flung himself down across his bed, lying there in blind ache and rebellion. He couldn't face her yet. . . .

Later he heard Rannirl's voice at his door. "Kerwin? Will you come down?"

Armoring himself with all his self-control, Kerwin accompanied Rannirl down the stairs. The Com'yn were gathered before the fire, but he had eyes only for Elorie, once again wearing the filmy gown embroidered with cherries, anchored at her throat with a single crystal that seemed to suspend it there in defiance of the laws of gravity. Her coppery curls were twisted into a band of shimmering white flowers. She raised her head as Kerwin came in, and Kerwin, bracing himself, felt sudden relief and calm, for her smile was gentle, aloof, calm as ever.

Had she felt nothing, then? Had he imagined it all?

Kennard's knowing eyes met Jeff's and the touch of the old man's hand on his elbow was almost fatherly. Some awareness seemed to pass between them, and Jeff guessed, suddenly, the truth. *The Keepers are trained in ways you could hardly guess at.* Somehow, some way, in those three days, Elorie had managed to bring herself back to the old remote calm, the untouched coolness. She smiled at Kerwin, outwardly the same affectionate, accepting smile but he sensed, with that catastrophic awareness of her, the new brittleness and wariness in her calm.

"Auster tells me that his trap-matrix is finished, Jeff. We're going to do a clearing operation tonight, and Auster wants to set the trap. I told them you'd consent."

"Of course," Jeff said, "but what's a trap matrix?"

Elorie made one of her childish faces. "It's a—a filthy perversion of an honest science," she said hotly.

"Not necessarily," Kennard said. "There are different kinds. The Veil outside the Arilinn Tower is one sort. It keeps out everyone not accepted as Com'yn. Auster, what sort is yours?"

"Barrier trap. Someone's picking one of the minds in our circle. Well, if anyone tries to break our barrier tonight, this one will seize and hold him, and give us a good look at him."

"Fair enough," Kerwin said. "Believe me, if anyone's spying, I'm as anxious as you are to find it out!"

Elorie stood up, restlessly. "We'll start, then. I—" she hesitated, bit her lip and said abruptly, "I want some *kirian*." At Kennard's disapproving look she brushed past him and poured the liquid for herself. "Anyone else who doesn't trust himself tonight? Auster? Rannirl? Stop looking at me like that, Tani, I know what I'm doing and what my limits are."

"Elorie. If you're not feeling well enough for it, we can delay the clearing operation for a few days."

"We've delayed for three days already." She raised the glass of *kirian* to her lips, glancing at Jeff when she thought

141

he did not see her, and her pained, lost look struck him to the heart.

She too? He had thought he was hurt that she did not remember; now, knowing the grief it was to her, Kerwin wished, in all sincerity, that Elorie had been unmoved, that his kiss had meant nothing to her. Because now he saw what it had done to her. . . .

Jeff had never seen a trap-matrix before. It looked like a piece of strangely shiny metal, studded with crystal and twisted with little ribbons of gleaming light. Auster's thin lips drew back into a tigerish smile. He said, "Can you still manage the monitor for a minute, Elorie? Give us a picture of who we have here." He pointed a tapered finger at the beautiful, deadly thing in his lap. "I set it for whoever tried to hit our barriers. I sensed it when the trap sprung—and whoever it was, he's very nicely immobilized, and we can get a picture of him on the monitor."

Elorie reached for a handful of the silky-metallic insulating cloth, wrapped her hand in it, and fastidiously, as if she touched something filthy, picked up the trap-matrix. She moved a calibration on the monitor mechanism. A point of pale green light sprang into life, widened and began to grow into a picture. It centered down gradually in the city of Arilinn, and Kerwin's lips pursed in a soundless whistle as he recognized landmark after landmark in the moving eye of the monitor. Then, swiftly, the picture was of a small mean room, almost bare, and the figure of a man, bent in soundless concentration over something in his lap, and motionless as death. Jeff drew a deep breath as the picture in the screen centered down on the face, and then cried out, "*Ragan!*"

It was the little bitter man from the spaceport gutters and bars, the man who had dogged his steps, the man who had shown him how to use the matrix crystal, and guided him in his search.

Ragan.

He should have known.

There was no one else it could have been.

Suddenly, he was swept by a great, calm, icy rage, leaving him cold with fury. Some atavistic thing in him, all Darkovan, swept aside all perception of anything but his fury at being pushed around like this. He said, in the ancient language of the Com'yn which seemed to spring without thought to his tongue,

"*Com'ii, this man's life is mine!* When, how and as I can, I claim his life, one to one, and who takes it before I do, settles with me!"

Auster, braced to fling new challenges and charges, stopped cold, his eyes wide and shocked.

Kennard said, "Com'yn Aillard, as representative of the Council, I hear your claim and allot this life to you, one to one, seek it, or give your own."

Jeff heard the ritual words almost without understanding. His hands literally itched to tear Ragan limb from limb. He said tersely, gesturing the picture off the screen, "Rannirl, can you find that place for me? How long will that thing hold him, Auster?"

Taniquel broke into the silence, her voice shrill. "You can't let him do this! It's suicide! Jeff doesn't even know how to use a sword, and do you—do you think that *sharug* would have honor to fight him fairly, one to one?"

"I'll see to that." Rannirl unbuckled the knife he wore, and held it out to Kerwin.

Kerwin took it, balancing it easily in his hand. There had been a fight or two on other worlds. *There was a roughneck buried* . . . it had been a long time, but the memory was there. And the code of blood-feud, which even a Terran child brought up on Darkover would absorb into the very roots of his being.

Ragan was going to get a damned big surprise. And then he was going to get very, very dead.

CHAPTER TWELVE

THE CITY of Arilinn lay beyond the Veil; the Bloody Sun was rising over the foothills. Jeff walked between Auster and Rannirl, his face drawn, his hand feeling strange and cold

143

on the hilt of his knife. For the first time, he felt almost grateful to Auster.

At this hour the streets were almost deserted; only a few startled onlookers in the street saw the three redheads, moving steadily shoulder to shoulder, armed with knives and ready for a fight—and those who did, suddenly discovered that they had urgent business in several other directions.

Down the long streets they moved, through the market where in a better day Jeff had chosen a pair of boots, and into a crowded and dirty suburb. Auster began to move more cautiously; he said in a low voice, "The trap won't hold him much longer."

Kerwin grinned, a mere stretching of his mouth, "Keep him where he is long enough for me to find him,—and then let him go any time you damn please."

"Here," Rannirl indicated a low-roofed house in a narrow alley, across a dim and littered courtyard. He pointed up a steep, crazy flight of outside stairs to an outside gallery with two rooms opening off it. From the lower floor a girl in a torn skirt and scarf watched them, her mouth a wide O of astonishment; as they turned toward the stairs she clapped her hands over her mouth and fled.

They went softly up the stairs. Auster said "Now!" and his hands moved swiftly, crushing the matrix between them. From inside the room came a long cry of rage and dismay as Kerwin, leaping forward, kicked the door in and burst into the room.

Ragan, still crouched in the held-fast posture of the trap matrix, whirled on them like a trapped cat, knife flashing from the sheath in his boot. He backed off and faced them, the naked steel between them, saying in a low voice, "Three to one, *vai dom'yn?*"

"Just one," Kerwin rasped, getting his own knife out; with his free arm he motioned Rannirl and Auster back, and the next moment reeled under the impact of Ragan's body crashing against his; felt the slash of a point along his forearm as he whipped his knife up. It had only torn his sleeve; he countered with a fast thrust, bearing Ragan off balance; then they were locked into a deadly clinch and he was struggling to keep Ragan's knife from his back.

They swayed, silent, Kerwin's breath coming loud as he jerked away, thrust hard and felt his knife rip leather. It came away red; Ragan grunted, struggled, made a sudden swift step forward—

Auster, watching like cat at a mouse hole, suddenly flung himself forward against them. He knocked Jeff off balance, and Kerwin, hardly believing that this was really happening, felt Ragan's knife rip again along his arm and go in a few inches below the armpit. A numbness, then a burning pain, spread in him; the knife dropped from his right hand; he snatched it with the other hand, fighting Auster's deathgrip on his arm. Auster's lips were drawn back over his teeth, his eyes demented. Jeff Kerwin swore, brutally, "Get away, you—"

Ragan wrenched loose. Rannirl, standing as if paralyzed, suddenly broke free, ran and flung his arms around Auster, braving the naked knife. "Are you mad?" he panted.

There was a crash, the sound of Ragan running down the stairs, the clatter of rubbish kicked loose on the stairs; Auster struck the floor, hard, under Rannirl's body.

Kerwin, dropping his own knife, flung himself on Auster and forced the man's hand back. Auster struggled; then his grip relaxed and he dropped it. There was a long slash on his cheek, and his eye was darkening, blood streaming from his nose where Kerwin's elbow had smashed at him.

Rannirl eased away, looked down at Auster with ill-concealed horror. Auster started to get up, and Jeff made a menacing gesture. "Stay right where you are," he said, and Auster, wiping blood from his face, subsided.

Kerwin walked to the window. Ragan, of course, was gone. He had disappeared somewhere into the labyrinth of streets in Arilinn. There wasn't a chance they'd find him again.

"That's something more I owe you for," he said grimly, walking back to Auster. "Give me one good reason I shouldn't beat your brains out."

Auster shook his head. He looked beaten, exhausted. "Go

ahead, *Terranan*," he said, "pretend we owe you the protection of our codes of honor and blood-feud!"

Rannirl said "Auster. Kennard accepted his challenge, gave him the right—"

"'To murder his accomplice, so we'd never know the truth, and put on a good show for us," Auster said. "Oh, yes, very clever, but you saw he recognized the man, Rannirl. What else could he do but make a great show of killing him? I wanted to take the man alive, so we could get the truth out of him."

He's lying, lying, Jeff thought hopelessly; but doubt had come even into Rannirl's face, as Auster went on, "If you hadn't interfered, Rannirl, we'd have had him!"

"Come on," Kerwin said, wearily, "we might as well get back." Auster had managed to confuse the issue, to twist it. And Ragan was alive. Kerwin felt weary. His arm was beginning to ache where Ragan's knife had gone in.

There were more people in the streets now, and more eyes to stare at the three Com'yn, one with a bloody face and one with his arm roughly pinned up in a sling improvised with the torn sleeve of a shirt. Kerwin felt all the weariness of the night's work descending on him. Auster, too, seemed at the end of his strength. When they reached the Tower, and passed through the Veil, the faint stinging seemed to drain his last energy; without a glance one way or the other, he strode past the hall, up the long stairs, and into his room. He flung the door shut.

In the luxurious bathroom he ripped off sling and shirt, awkwardly raising his arm with a grimace of pain. He stuck his head into the cool fountain of icy water, raised it, dripping, still exhausted but clear-headed. The furry non-human who served him glided into the room and stood aghast, great green pupil-less eyes fixed on him and fuzzy lips parted in consternation; then, with an unintelligible murmur, glided away and returned with bandages, some thick yellow stuff he smeared on the wound, and deftly, with his odd thumbless paws, bound it up.

He had finished when Auster came, unannounced, into

146

the room. Kerwin gestured at Rannirl's knife, which lay on a table.

"If you've had another brainstorm, there's a knife," he said. "If not, get the hell out."

Auster looked pale; blood was still smeared on his face, and he touched his nose as if it hurt.

"I don't blame you for hating me, Kerwin. But I have something to say to you."

Kerwin started to shrug, found that it hurt, and didn't. Auster flinched, asking, "Are you much hurt? Did the *kyrri* make sure there was no poison on the knife?"

Kerwin snorted. "Terrans don't fight that way. That's a Darkovan trick. And it doesn't ring very true—you worrying about it, after doing your damndest to make sure I got knifed."

"I deserve all that, maybe," Auster said. "Believe anything you want to. I only care about one thing—two things—and you're destroying them both. Maybe even now you don't realize, but damn it, it's worse than if you did!"

"Get to the point, Auster, or get out."

"Kennard said there was a block in your memory. I don't accuse you of betraying us on purpose."

"Damned good of you!"

"You *don't* want to betray us," Auster said, his face suddenly cracking and going to pieces, "and you still don't realize what this means! *The Terrans planted you on us!* They sent you here, hoping for just what happened—that we'd accept you, come to depend on you, because you were so obviously one of us—" his voice broke. In consternation, Kerwin realized that there were tears in Auster's eyes and the man was shaking from head to foot. "So we fell for it, Kerwin, and for you, and how the hell can we even hate you for it?"

Kerwin shut his eyes. This was the thought he had kept pushing away.

He had been pushed around from the first moment he landed on Darkover. Who but the Terrans could have done it? And what possible motive could they have had, but this—to keep him off balance, keep him guessing, show him to the Com'yn?

He was an elaborate booby-trap! The Arilinn Com'yn had taken him in, and at any moment, he might blow up in their faces!

Auster took Jeff gently by the shoulders, careful not to disturb his wounded arm. "I wish we'd been better friends. Now you must feel I'm saying this because we haven't been friends."

Kerwin shook his head. Auster's pain and sincerity were unmistakable to anyone with a scrap of telepathic awareness. He said, "No. But what can I do? And what could they hope to achieve?"

Auster's voice was almost inaudible, "I think they hoped that the circle would disintegrate with you in it."

"But now that we've caught the spy, and can catch him again?"

"If it were only that, Kerwin. But there's something else—the thing I've been trying not to see." His face was set and white. *"What have you done to Elorie?"*

Jeff could not answer. His guilt, Auster's fear, were like a miasma in the room. Auster let him go and said earnestly, "Go away, Jeff. For the love of any Gods you had on Terra, go away. I know how you feel, but if it's true, if you care about any of us, go away before you destroy us all. Before it's too late."

He turned and went out, and Kerwin cast himself down, facing it clearly.

Auster was right. He heard like a grim echo the words of the old matrix mechanic, who had paid with her life for showing him a scrap of his own past: *You will find the thing you love, and you will destroy it, but you will save it, too.*

The prophecy had come true. He had found what he loved—and already he had come near to destroying it. Could he save it, if he went away?

Kerwin rose, grim-faced, knowing what he must do.

Slowly, avoiding the mirrors in the luxurious room, he stripped off the suede-leather breeches and laced low ankle-boots. He dressed himself in the black silk-and-leather of the

Terran Empire, that he had laid aside when he came to Arilinn.

He hesitated over the matrix stone, cursing, torn, wanting to fling it out of the window, but at last he put it into his pocket. *It was my mother's. It went with her into exile. It can go with me.*

He hesitated again over the embroidered Darkovan cloak, lined with fur, that had begun this chain of events, but at last he cast it about his shoulders. It was his own, bought with money earned honestly on other worlds, and, sentiment aside, it was a bulwark against the snow and rain of Darkovan night. With two knife wounds there was no sense in getting himself chilled. And—an immensely practical consideration—on the streets of Arilinn, a Terran would show up like a starflower on the bare peaks of the Hellers; it would keep him decently anonymous until he was far away from here.

He went to the door of his room. There was a good smell of hot food somewhere; knife fights, blood feuds, endless telepathic operations within the eerie matrix rings could come and go, but practical Mesyr would plan their dinners, scold the *kyrri* into cooking them as she wished, frown at Rannirl for spoiling his appetite with too much strong wine before eating, sew new ribbons on Taniquel's filmy dresses, chide Corus for flinging his boots in the hall. He heard her cheery calm voice in the distance, and felt the sudden ache of nostalgia and pain. *This was home, this was the only home he had ever known.*

He passed an open door; the drift of Taniquel's fresh, flowery perfume wafted out, and he heard her singing. A brief vision caught him, of her slim, pretty body half-submerged in greenish water, her curls piled atop her head as she scrubbed. Tenderness overwhelmed him; she did not yet know of the result of the knife fight; she had slept away the weariness of the night's work, and as yet had not caught the aftermath from Rannirl or Auster or Kennard. . . .

The thought froze him, suddenly. Very soon now, if not already, the touch of rapport would begin to drift among them, and then they would all know what he planned. He

149

must leave quickly, without lingering on these sentimental farewells, or they would guess what he planned (*Oh, God, if they only would!*) and he would have to face them all again.

He flung the hood over his head and went silently down the stairs, down the shaft, through the prickling Veil that barred them away. Now he was safe; for only within the matrixes themselves could their minds range beyond the Veil that protected them from outsiders. Moving resolutely, holding his weariness at bay, he went through the cluster of buildings at the foot of the Tower, past the air field, and toward the streets of Arilinn.

His plans were inchoate, indefinite. Where could he go? The Terrans had not wanted him; now, there was no place for him on Darkover, either. Yet perhaps after all that was best—back to the Terrans; let them deport him. He could stop fighting his fate. . . .

Yet if the Terrans had planted him on the Com'yn, a giant booby-trap . . . What when he came back to them, resolved to sabotage their long-laid plans . . . What then?

Did it matter?

Did anything matter now?

He raised his eyes and looked straight into the great red eye of the sun. It was sinking slowly, almost behind the great and looming mass of the Arilinn Tower; and behind it came the swift and scooping darkness, the rapidly lowering chill and silence. The last gleam of the Bloody Sun went out. The Tower lingered a moment, an after-image in pale ultraviolet on the inside of Kerwin's eyelids, then dissolved in the fine rain. A single light lingered, battling valiantly to pierce the mist, then was wiped out and vanished. Kerwin wiped the rain from his eyes and turned his back resolutely on the Tower of the Com'yn, and walked down into the City.

He found a place where he would be recognized neither as Terran nor Com'yn—where they looked only at the color of his money and gave him privacy, a bed, and enough to drink to blot out memory, to blur the vain, unavoidable re-living of those weeks in Arilinn. Plans and futures could wait. For the moment he only wanted to be freed of thought. He slept at last, but the darkness was blurred with voices and faces, cloudy half-memories, nightmarish and painful. Then he came dimly up to consciousness out of a long forgetfulness that was more stupor than sleep, struggled up to awareness of who and where he was, and saw them all standing at the foot of his bed.

For a moment he thought it was the aftermath of the bad whisky, or that his overloaded mind had cracked. Then Taniquel made an uncontrollable sound of dismay and pity and flung herself down at his side, and he knew that they were really there. He rubbed a hand across dulled eyes, wet cracked lips with his tongue, and shook his head.

Rannirl said compassionately, "Did you really think we would let you go like this, Jeff?"

He said thickly, "Auster—"

"—doesn't know everything, even about us," Kennard said. "Jeff, can you listen to us sensibly now?"

He sat up. The squalor of the hideout room, the empty bottle lying at the foot of his tangled blankets, the ache in his knifed arm, all seemed part and parcel of the same thing, and the presence of the Com'yn in this room, newly incredible. Taniquel, holding his hand; Corus, looking troubled; Rannirl, friendly but reserving judgment; Auster, bitterly aloof.

Elorie, her face a white mask, the eyes red and swollen; Elorie, in tears!

He sat up, gently disengaging Taniquel's hand. He said, "Oh, God, why must we go through all this? Didn't Auster tell you?"

"He told us a lot of things," Kennard said. "All rooted in his own fears and prejudices."

"I don't even deny that," Auster said. "I ask if the fears and prejudices weren't justified."

Taniquel said, "We can't let you go, Jeff. You're a part of ourselves, and where will you go? What will you do?"

Kennard motioned the girl to silence. He said, "Kerwin, bringing you to Arilinn was a calculated risk. It was a stroke against dark magic and taboo, a first step toward making matrix mechanics a science, not a—a priesthood."

"Speak for yourself there," Rannirl said. "I don't agree with Kennard on that, Kerwin, but he's right about one thing. We knew it was a risk, and we were willing to take the risk."

"But can't you understand—I'm *not* willing to risk it?" Kerwin's voice cracked suddenly. "When I don't know myself what they might make me do—how I might destroy you."

"Maybe *this* was how you were meant to destroy us," Corus said bitterly. "To get us to trust you, put all our faith in you, and when we depended on you, walk out on us!"

"That's a damnably unfair way of putting it," Jeff said hoarsely. "Can't you understand, I'm trying to *save* you? I can't risk being the one who destroys you."

Taniquel bent her head and put her cheek against his hand. She was crying, without a sound. Auster's face was hard. "He's right, Kennard, and you know it. You're only hurting us all, by prolonging this."

Kennard got painfully to his feet, looking on them all with contempt and repressed anger. "Cowards, all of you! Now that we have a chance to *fight* this damned nonsense—"

Auster said, "You're defending him because of your own half-Terran sons, Kennard. You're too transparent."

Kerwin put his hands over his eyes. How could he say—*I love you all, don't torture me this way?* He said, thickly, "Now you know it can be done, you'll find someone to take my place."

"No!" Elorie flung herself forward; automatically, fearing the girl would fall, Kerwin caught her, and she clung to him, her face dead white, her hands gripping his shoulders. "No!" she whispered, again. "No, I can't let you go. Stay with us, Jeff, stay with us, whatever happens—" her voice trailed off; Kerwin held her, agonized, whispering, "Oh, God, Elorie, Elorie!"

Then, steeling himself, he put her gently away. He said, almost whispering, "Now don't you see why I *must* go, Elorie? Don't make it harder for me."

He saw shock, comprehension, anger, compassion dawning in the faces around him. Taniquel came to take Elorie in her arms, murmuring, but Elorie flung off the touch, and her voice was high and shrill. "No," she said, clearly. "If this is what Jeff has decided, then I have decided too, and it's over. I—I can't give my life for it any more."

She whirled to face the Com'yn, pale and shaken, her eyes looking bruised in her white face.

"Elorie," Taniquel pleaded, "you don't know—"

"You—you dare to say that to me, you who have known his love?" Elorie sounded frantic, beside herself.

"Elorie, you're—you don't know what you are saying," Kennard said gently. "You know what you are."

"I know what I am supposed to be," she flung at them. "A Keeper, a *leronis*, a puppet, a sacred virgin without a soul or a heart or a life of my own."

Kennard's lined face was white with shock. He turned, outraged, on Kerwin. "We brought you here, and you have done *this* to us, this to *her!*" He was shaking with rage. "This is worse treachery than the Terrans could compass!"

Rannirl's voice was hoarse. "And I defended him! So history repeats itself. Cleindori again, with this filth of a Terran!"

"Yes," Elorie cried, almost hysterical, "because now I know what Cleindori knew."

"Bitch! Whore!" Rannirl struck Elorie, hard, across the mouth. Kerwin leaped and grabbed his raised arm, but Rannirl shook himself free, with loathing.

"In days past," he said grimly, "it would be death for you, Elorie, and death by torture for *him!*"

In shock and dismay, Kerwin realized the mistake they were making. He stepped quickly forward to defend Elorie. *I've never touched her, I swear she has been sacred to me.*

Elorie flung back her head, white and defiant. "It's no use, Kennard," she said. "I'm—I'm no more use to you as a Keeper." She turned and flung her arms around Jeff, holding herself to him with desperate force, clinging helplessly. He saw the shock on their faces deepen to revulsion and disgust. Elorie was trembling violently in shame and terror. In

153

consternation, Kerwin realized that if he spoke a word in Elorie's defense, it would be a repudiation of the girl.

Deliberately, accepting, he bowed his head and put his arms protectingly around her.

"They should die for this!"

Rannirl spat. "What's the use? They've sabotaged everything we've done. Nothing we can do now will make any difference. Wish them joy of it!" He turned his back on them and walked out.

Auster and Corus followed; Kennard lingered a moment, his wrinkled face miserable; at last, shaking his head, he followed the others. Stunned, still shaken by the force of her lie, Kerwin heard the door close behind them. It sounded like a closing tomb.

Elorie began to sob. She cried brokenly, like a child, clinging to him; Kerwin held her, numb, still not understanding.

"Elorie, Elorie," he entreated, "why did you do it? Why? Why? Why did you lie to them?"

Sobbing and laughing at once, almost hysterical, Elorie leaned back to look up at him. "But it wasn't a lie," she wept. "I couldn't have lied. Oh, yes, I know you'd never have touched me, because of what I was, because of the law and the taboo, and yet when I spoke to them they knew the truth! It's because I cared so much—" her sobbing almost drowned the words. "I'd come to love you so—to want you so—so much that I knew I couldn't bear to go on—being a Keeper."

"Oh, Elorie!"

"So now—now you've lost everything and you're not even free," she said wildly. "But I—I have nothing and no one else, if you don't want me."

Kerwin picked the girl up in his arms, like a child, cradling her close, awed at the immensity of her trust, with what she had given for him. He laid her down on the tumbled bed, knelt by her side.

"Elorie," he said, and the words were a prayer and a pledge, "I don't care if I've lost everything else, now that

I have you. My only regret in leaving Arilinn was in leaving you."

The words were not true, and he knew as he spoke them that they were not true, but for the moment nothing else mattered. He leaned forward, kissing Elorie on the lips and gathering her childish body into his arms.

CHAPTER THIRTEEN

THENDARA, in the dying light, was a mass of black towers and shapes; the Terran HQ was a single brightly lighted spike against the sky, and Jeff, seeing it through the window of the plane, pointed it out to Elorie.

"It may not be very beautiful to you now, my darling. But I'll find a world somewhere to give you."

She leaned against his shoulder. "I have all the world I want."

The pilot of the plane—mountain Darkovan he was but wore the uniform of Terra—circled for landing, and Elorie put her hands over her ears; she was not used to the roar of the spaceport below them. He put his arm around her, holding her tight.

The last three days had been days of discovery and joy for both of them, even through their shared sense of being outcast, driven from their only home. Neither spoke of this; they had too much else to share with each other.

He had never known a woman quite like Elorie. Once he had thought her aloof, passionless; then he had come to see that calm as control, not as absence of passion.

She had come to him frightened, desolate, innocent almost to ignorance; she had given him her fear with the rest of herself, without pretense and without shame. That utter trust almost terrified him—how could he possibly be worthy of it? But it was part of Elorie that she could do nothing by halves or meanly; as Keeper she had kept herself wholly free even from the fringes of emotion, and having discarded that place, she gave herself as wholeheartedly to Jeff as, before, to her traditional office.

155

As they landed, she drew her cloak over her bright-sunset hair; he held her arm against the hard and unfamiliar steps. He must seem resolute, even if he was not. "It won't seem strange for long, darling."

"No place will be strange where you are. But will they let you stay on Darkover? They—won't separate us?"

On that he could reassure her. "I may be Darkovan by your laws, but by Terra's, I have Empire citizenship from my father. And any woman who marries an empire citizen is automatically a citizen as well; all that's necessary is for me to acknowledge you on any public document as my wife." He added, gently, "It's true that we may have to leave Darkover, though."

She nodded, biting her lip. The Com'yn might be as anxious to drive them out as, before, they had been to save Jeff from being driven.

Kerwin secretly felt it might be best that way. Darkover could never be, for either of them, more than a reminder of what they had lost. And there were worlds enough, out there. The compulsion that had driven him back to the Bloody Sun had nearly destroyed him, but it had given him Elorie.

He approached the barrier, rather nervously. He might, just possibly, be taken into custody as a deportee. There were legal formalities and rights he could invoke. It hadn't been worth it, for himself, but for Elorie's sake he would do all he could to delay the summary judgment; turn it in his favor.

"The Com'yn played hell with both our lives, darling. Try to forget," he said, knowing the words were empty, as they approached the gate. The Spaceforce guard there stared at Kerwin's Terran clothes, the shrinking veiled girl on his arm. Jeff gave him his spaceport identifications.

"And the girl?"

"My wife."

"I see," the guard said slowly. "In that case there are certain formalities."

"Just as you like."

"If you'll come into the station, please." He led them into

the terminal. Jeff followed, squeezing Elorie's arm reassuringly. He felt apprehensive, and he knew she sensed that apprehension; the records would immediately go through the main HQ and immediately identify him. He had half considered returning to the Terran Zone anonymously, at least for a day or two. But the peculiarity of Terran laws concerning native women made that unthinkable where Elorie was concerned. She had insisted, when he explained, that she did not care. But he had asserted himself, for the first time, "*I* care." He had left no room for argument.

The Empire civil service consisted largely of single men; few Terran women cared to accompany their men halfway across the galaxy; which meant that on every planet, liaisons with native women, both regular and informal, were taken for granted. This was unavoidable. But in order to avoid endless legal complications with planetary law, the Terran Empire made a very clear distinction between the two sorts. A Terran could marry a woman of any planet, by her own customs, provided the laws of the planet permitted it, which was a matter between that Terran, the woman, her family, and her laws. The Empire had no part in it. Whether the marriage was formal or informal, temporary or permanent, or no marriage at all, was a matter for the private morals of the people concerned, but that man was still considered single on the Empire laws, provided the woman concerned was never legally registered as his wife.

But it went both ways. Once he signed any formal Terran document speaking of a native woman as his wife, she was so in fact; he was obligated to her by all the laws of the Terran Empire, and she and her children were citizens. Hence, Terran Empire men thought twice before practicing the social hypocrisy common on Terra itself, of casually referring to a mistress or a pick-up as a wife. The wife brought into the Terran Zone, was so for all time.

The spaceforce guard turned them over to a registry official. Kerwin gave up his identity card, his thumbprint, and signed forms; the official turned to Elorie.

"Name?"

"Elorie Ardais," she whispered.

He wrote down the name, blinking slightly at the double name, which meant Darkovan aristocracy, and adding *Kerwin*. He took her thumbprint. A capsule whisked away through a pneumatic tube and after a delay, came back. The official spoke to Elorie, before they left the place, as "Mrs. Kerwin." Kerwin, knowing he had probably set trouble in motion for them both, still did not regret what he had done. Now there was no way for the long arm of the Com'yn to reach out and seize Elorie from him.

He hoped.

He wasn't happy about going into the Terran Zone; but just at the moment, he sensed, it might be safest for them, even though he was sure that within a few hours they would have questions to answer, and might be facing deportation. He'd have to arrange to regularize his status, possibly face inquiry and, in general, make arrangements about a living. There were a hundred things to decide—whether to go to Terra or take a chance on a new world, for one—but they could wait.

Most of his knowledge of the spaceport zone was a knowledge of bars and similar places, where it would be unthinkable to take Elorie; he could have claimed quarters in the HQ, but he wouldn't do that until it was necessary. Equally unwise would be to find a place in the Darkovan Zone, risking recognition of the girl—he had had a taste, in Arilinn, of how the Com'yn were treated when recognized. A hotel in the Terran Zone was the obvious temporary solution.

He pointed out to her, as the surface-car took them there, the white walls of the spaceman's orphanage. "There's where I lived until I was twelve years old," he said, and let the silent puzzlement strike him again. *Or did I?* If it was true that the Terrans had arranged the peculiar train of circumstances which put the Com'yn on his trail—

"Elorie," he asked her, when they were alone again, "did the Com'yn have anything to do with destroying my records at the Spaceman's Orphanage?" A matrix, he supposed, could wipe out data on a computer. And if anyone concentrated on that—

158

"I don't know," she said. "If so, it was before I was Keeper. I know Auster was taken from the orphanage when he was five years old."

Kennard had referred to that as a "curious story." But Kerwin had never heard it.

And this wasn't the time to ask.

But long after Elorie slept, he lay awake thinking about it. He had followed a trail of his own background, through a diminishing number of false leads and blind alleys. When the Com'yn found him, he had abandoned the search—after all, he had found out the main thing, the secret of his parentage. But there were still mysteries to be solved, and before he left Darkover forever, he was going to have a last try at solving them.

He told Elorie a little, the next day. "There was no record of me there," he said. "I saw what the machine gave out. But if I could get into the place and check—"

"Would it be dangerous to try and get in?"

"Not dangerous to life and limb. But I'd probably be thrown in jail for breaking and entering."

"You were not trained in so many things," she said. "If I were still—" She bit her lip, saying, "I could barricade you—throw what we call a *glamour* over you—so that you could pass unseen."

She looked pale and wretched, and Kerwin felt his heart turn over at the thought of what she had given up for him. But why? Why should it make so much difference? He said, "Is that true? Have you lost all your powers as a Keeper, Elorie?"

She said, not too steadily, "I have always been told, since I was a child—the Keeper must be a virgin."

Her acceptance surprised and startled him. He thought of her defiance of so many of the Com'yn superstitions, of her refusal to accept her ritual authority, but this one she had never questioned.

Kennard had called it *superstitious drivel*. And yet, he knew, himself, the terrible exhaustion and nervous draining of matrix work; it made sense, that the Keepers must be protected, isolated from the danger of such contacts, when

159

they had to be at their peak of strength for the difficult and dangerous Keeper's work. He leaned over and took Elorie in his arms, holding her tight, thinking, *At least that danger isn't with her any more. . . .* He was thinking of the day she had collapsed while building the matrix, and how he had lent her strength.

Had that destroyed her as a Keeper?

"No," she said quietly, sensing his thoughts as she so often did. "I knew from the beginning that I cared for you. But I was sure I could keep my self-control. And there was Taniquel, so that you were not lonely." Her eyes suddenly brimmed. "I shall miss Tani," she said softly. "I wish it could have been different."

"You're not jealous of her? Because she and I—"

Elorie laughed softly, "Oh, you Terrans, you Terrans! No, if—" she swallowed, her gray eyes wet, "if things were different, if we could have been together among our own people, why, it would be Tani that I would send to your bed, if I was ill, or bearing your child with all my love for both of you. Does that seem so shocking to you?"

He kissed her, without speaking. Darkovan customs might be idealistic, but they took some getting used to, and he was just as glad to have Elorie to himself. But he returned to the subject.

"But Taniquel was part of the rapport circle, and no virgin—"

"Nor was she a Keeper," Elorie said soberly, "and she did only minor, simple things. She had never been trained, or intended, to do more. So for her there was no danger."

Seeing Elorie's troubled face, Jeff did not press the point. He said, taking the matrix from his pocket, "I may be able to do some things still."

"I can," she said. "I'm sure there are still some things I can do. It's only that I feel so strange. Not like myself. I don't seem to belong to myself any more."

"You belong to me," Kerwin said firmly, and she smiled. "I'll try."

Kerwin wanted to tell her he didn't give a damn, he wouldn't risk letting her touch the thing, she was too precious to him—and then he saw her eyes. Elorie loved him, she had given up her whole world for him, all she had been and would be. If she needed this to give her confidence even if it killed her, he had to let her try.

"But promise me, Elorie," he said, taking her shoulders between his own, and tipping her head back to look into the gray eyes, "no risks."

He felt that she hardly heard him. Her slight fingers were holding the matrix. She said, not to him, "The shape of the air here is different. We are in the mountains. I must take care not to interfere with his breathing." Then she looked up, moving her head with an imperious small signal, and he felt her drop into rapport; intangibly, like a caress.

She said, not aloud.

I don't know how long I can do this when there are Terrans around, but I will try. Look in the mirror.

Rising from her side, Jeff glanced at the mirror on the door. He blinked and looked again. "Where am I?" he demanded. He could see himself perfectly well—but not in the mirror!

"Oh yes, and if anyone bumps into you, they will know you are there," she said with a sting of a smile. "So don't think you've become a ghost, my love of a barbarian. I've only changed the look of the air around you—that's as close as I can come to saying it in words. But I think, if you want to get into the orphanage unseen, it will stay with you for a little while."

He left her there, in that room of a Terran hotel, passing silently and unseen down the corridors. There was a strange feeling to it, an almost dreamish feeling when in the lobby people passed him without seeing. No wonder the Com'yn were almost invincible—

But at what cost? Girls like Elorie, giving up their lives . . .

The spaceman's orphanage looked just as it had looked—was it barely two months ago? Two or three of the boys were doing something in the grounds, kneeling around a patch of flowers, supervised by an older boy with a badge on his arm. Silent as a ghost, feeling like one, Jeff hesitated before walking up the white stone steps. What should he do first? Go unseen into the office, investigate the records himself? Quickly, he dismissed that notion. He might be unseen, but he could certainly not rummage through files, punch buttons for printed information; all that would happen would be that he'd scare the people in the office to death, seeing drawers and papers moving of their own accord, and sooner or later they'd start investigating.

Then he remembered. On the third floor, in the dormitory where he had slept with six other boys, he had carved his initials into a window frame. The frame might have been repaired or replaced. If it wasn't there, it would prove nothing. But if it was . . .

And it might be. The dormitory was an old one, and many of the boys had done the same thing. The Darkovan nurses and the children's counselors had left them a good deal of freedom in some areas. In his day the dormitory had been battered, the old walls clean, but bearing the imprint of many childish experiments with tools.

He almost ran up the last flight of stairs; he paused at the top, out of breath, trying to get his bearings. Finally he turned toward what he thought was the right room.

It was quiet and sunlit, eight small neatly-made cots in little cubicles around the room, and in the open space between, a group of toy figures, men and spaceships, arranged on a small rug. Carefully stepping around the set-up toys, Kerwin saw that a small white skyscraper had been built at the center, and sighed; the children had built the Terran spaceport which loomed so large in all their thoughts.

He was wasting time. He moved to the windows, ran his fingers along the molding. Yes, there were some rough spots—in the soft wood, rough crosses, hearts and tick-tack-toe shapes, and he felt along them with his hands. They had been about eye-level—

Suddenly he realized he was looking in the wrong place. When last he saw this dormitory he had been a child of twelve, and eye level would not be six feet above the floor.

He bent down, looking first to one side and then to the other, searching through the tangle of blurs and scratches and rough-carved emblems. And then, at the edge of the frame, roughly approximating the squarish letters of the Universal Alphabet taught to the orphanage children, he saw the childish work of his first pocketknife: JAK JR.

Not until he saw the initials did he realize that he was shaking. His fists were clenched so hard that his nails hurt his palm; he let them go. Then it had been a lie. He did not realize until now that he had ever doubted; but as he stood there touching the deep gouges in the windowframe, he knew that he had doubted and that the doubt had gone shakingly deep in him. Now it was sure; they had lied.

"They lied, they lied," he said aloud, and turned toward the door.

"Who lied," asked a quiet voice, "and why?" And Kerwin saw, standing in the door, the slender, gray-haired form of a man, and realized that Elorie's illusion had worn off. He had been seen, and heard—and found.

Now what?

CHAPTER FOURTEEN

THE MAN'S eyes, intelligent and kindly, rested on Jeff Kerwin without anger.

"We never allow visitors in the dormitories," he said. "If you wanted to see a particular child, you could have had permission to see him in the playrooms!" His eyes narrowed suddenly. "I know your face," he said. "It's been a long time, but—your name is Jeff, isn't it? Kerradine? Kermit?"

"Kerwin."

The man nodded. "The one we called *Tallo,*" he confirmed. "What are you doing here?"

Abruptly, Jeff decided to tell the truth. "Two months ago I came here," he said, "and they told me, in the office, that there were no records of my parentage—that they had no records of my living here—that I was lying. The computer had no record of my fingerprint. I started to wonder if I was crazy." He pointed to the carved initials. "I'm not. I cut those there when I was a kid."

"But why should they do that?" the man demanded. He

held out his hand, suddenly flushing. "I'm called Barron. I used to teach mathematics to the younger boys. I still do, as far as that goes."

Jeff clasped his hand. "I remember you, sir. You stopped a fight I got into once."

Barron chuckled. "You were a young rowdy, all right," he said. "Yes, I remember you, well enough. I remember when your father brought you to us. You were about four, I think."

Had his father lived so long? *I ought to remember him,* Jeff thought; it was like the elusive perfume of Cleindori's rooms in the Arilinn Tower. . . .

"Did you know my father?" he asked, almost holding his breath.

The man said, regretfully, "I saw him only that once. But for goodness sake, come downstairs, young Kerwin, come and have a drink or something. I suppose computers do get out of order sometimes, but it seems impossible."

But if there were people who would *remember* him here, why had the front office been unable to tell him more? He should have waited and demanded.

"Is there anyone else who would remember me?"

Barron thought that over. "A couple of the maids, perhaps. But most of the nurses and teachers are young. We try to keep them young. I go on and on, old fellow that I am, because it's hard to get good teachers to come out from Terra and the Empire wants someone who speaks the language without accent," he gave a deprecating shrug. "Come on down to my office. Tell me what you've been doing, young Jeff. You went to Terra. How did you happen to come back to Darkover?"

In the old man's austere little office, filled with the open-window noises of children on a playground, Jeff accepted a drink he didn't want, fighting with unspoken questions to which, he supposed, old Barron wouldn't have the answer.

"You say you remember my father bringing me here. My mother?"

Barron shook his head. "He said nothing about her, or about having a wife," he said, almost prissily.

But he acknowledged his child, Kerwin thought. "What was my father like?"

The old man frowned. "It was a long time ago. But I remember because he seemed so—well, so shaken up. He'd been in a fight of some sort. His nose had been broken, and he was wearing Darkovan clothes, but he had his spaceport identifications. We asked you questions about your mother, but you couldn't talk."

"At four?" Kerwin demanded in amazement.

"You didn't talk for six months; for a long time we thought you were mentally deficient," the old man said frankly. "That's why I remember you so well. You couldn't speak either Terran *or* Darkovan, at least no language any of the nurses knew, and you never said a word in any other."

Kerwin let the old man talk on. "Kerwin finished up all the formalities for having you taken in here," he said. "Then he went away, and we never saw him again. We asked a few questions. You didn't look much like your father, I remember. You looked like a Darkovan child, except that you had red hair, and they don't. I remembered that especially because that same week we'd taken in another little red-headed boy."

Kerwin said, grasping at a quick straw "Was his name Auster?"

Barron frowned. "I can't remember; he was only here for a couple of years. That was very odd. He was kidnapped. . . . I'm an old man, and I talk too much. It's nothing to do with you, that story, unless—why did you ask his name?"

Kerwin said slowly, "Because I think I know him."

Barron said, "His record would be downstairs. Let me look."

"Don't bother," Jeff said. That made no difference now. How had Auster come to the Spaceman's Orphanage? *A curious story*—one they might never know. It was unlikely that he would be listed as Auster Ridenow. And somehow the Com'yn had recovered this child of theirs, born of two of the Com'yn, traitors, who had fled with the renegade

Cleindori and her Terran lover. . . . Did it matter how?
Auster had been brought up with the Com'yn and he had
inherited all of their powers. And Kerwin, brought up on
Terra, had come among them and he had betrayed them. . . .

But he wouldn't think of that. He thanked Barron, sub-
mitted to being shown around the new buildings and speaking to some of the teachers, approving the work of the
orphanage, and finally took his leave, filled with disquiet and
new questions to replace the old ones.

Cleindori died. And how and why had Jeff Kerwin, Sr.
battered and bruised from a terrible fight, his nose broken,
brought his son to the Spaceman's Orphanage, and where
had he gone after that?

Why had Jeff Kerwin, Jr., at four years old been unable
to speak a word for six months?

Why had he no memory . . .

Except the curious half-memories of walls, arches, doors,
a man who strode proudly, cloaked, through a long castle
corridor . . . a woman . . . a child's scream. . . .

Shuddering, he cut the memory off. He had found out at
least part of what he wanted to know.

Now Elorie was waiting for him.

When he got back to the hotel, she was asleep, flung
across the bed in exhaustion, gray smudges under her long-
lashed eyes, but she woke as he came in. She said quickly,
"Jeff, I held it as long as I could."

"It's all right," he quickly reassured her.

"What did you find out?"

He hesitated. Should he tell her? Would the questions
that surged in him, only stir up unhappy memories? What
did she know of Cleindori, save that she had been taught to
despise the memory of the "renegade?"

Her hand closed over his. "What would really hurt me,"
she said, "is if you refused to share . . ."

He sat down close at her side, then, and told her everything. Everything that had happened since his first moment
on Darkover, when he had encountered Ragan and learned
what his matrix was, his experience at the orphanage, the

matrix mechanics who had refused to help him—and then all the rest, including what Barron had told him.

He concluded, setting his teeth, "I suppose I've got to face it—I'll never know. It's a matter of hours, now, until that report they made on us at the spaceport gate goes through, and they'll pick me up as a deportee. For all I know, they may already—"

As if in answer to his words, the buzzer sounded, and when he picked up the communicator, the metallic voice at the other end said, "Jefferson Andrew Kerwin, Jr.?" It was the voice of a recorded communication.

"Speaking."

"This is Co-ordination and Personnel," said the taped voice. "We are informed that you are within the Terran Zone and that a civil charge has been placed against you of unlawful flight to avoid deportation. Your whereabouts are known. You are hereby notified that the Council of the City of Thendara, Darkover, has placed you on record as *persona non grata* and you are officially forbidden to leave the Terran Zone. This prohibition applies also to your wife, since legal proceedings have been initiated to give her Empire citizenship and status. This is an official order. You will not leave your present accommodations for more than one hour or go more than one mile from their location, and within forty-eight hours you will surrender yourself to the appropriate authorities, on penalty of the issuance of a warrant for your arrest. Please acknowledge and comply or file a legal reason for refusal, or a legal request for an appeal."

Jeff muttered, "Damn!"

The recorder repeated patiently, "Please acknowledge and reply, or file a legal request for an appeal."

Jeff said "Acknowledged," and put down the receiver. That ended it, then. He wouldn't stand a chance on an appeal; now that the Com'yn had turned against him, not a soul on Darkover would stand in the way of having him deported.

Now I'll never know the truth. . . .

Elorie rose and came to him. She had put the matrix

crystal, on its fine chain, about her neck. Now she said, "I could, perhaps, get past that block in your memory, with this. Only, if the block is very strong, Jeff, why do you want to know? Why not let it pass? We're done with the Com'yn, probably leaving Darkover—"

"Elorie, all my life I've had this—this compulsion, this hunger, to get back to Darkover, like an obsession. I could have made a life on other worlds, but Darkover was always there at the back of my mind, calling me. Now I begin to wonder if it was really me, or if the pushing-around really started way back during the time I can't remember anything."

Because, if his hunger for Darkover was not real, what was he? A hollow man, a pawn, a passive tool driven by the Terrans. Take away that and what did he have left, of the thing that had shaped and molded him?

"I'll try, then," she said, gravely. "Not now, I'm still tired from the illusion."

They went out of the hotel, walking about the Terran Zone for a little, stopping at one of the Terran-type cafés near the spaceport, where Elorie ate one of her enormous meals (reminding Jeff of the tremendous physical drain of telepathic work). He made a gesture at showing her a few of the sights of the Terran Zone, but neither of them really cared.

Jeff found that his thoughts returned, obsessively, to Arilinn. What would this failure mean to Darkover, to the Com'yn? They had located, clarified the various mineral deposits in their bargain, but the major operation, the tremendous task of lifting them to the surface of the planet, remained to be done.

He knew Elorie was thinking of it, too; he heard her murmur, once, "There are a few matrix mechanics who might—" And once she said, irrelevantly, almost at random, "After all, they have the matrix patterns and the molecular models all built and established. They might be able to handle them." She added, "Yet, without a Keeper—"

Jeff pulled her to him. He whispered, "Regretting?"

"Never." Her eyes met his clearly. "Only—oh, wishing it might have happened another way."

He had destroyed them. He had come to the world he loved and he destroyed its last chance to remain as it was.

Later, when she took his matrix between her hands, he felt sudden misgiving. He was remembering the woman who had tried to read his memory; she had died. "Elorie, if this harms you—I'd rather never know."

"It won't hurt me." She cupped the matrix between her hands, brightening the moving points of light. Her fair hair fell like a soft curtain along either cheek as she gazed into the matrix; then she raised her eyes to Jeff.

He was feeling uneasy. The breaking of a telepathic block, or barrier—as he remembered from his first days with the Com'yn—was not an easy process.

The light in the crystal thickened and seemed to pour thickly over Elorie's lowered face; Kerwin shaded his eyes from the brilliance, but he was caught in the tension of the pattern. And suddenly, as if printed plain before his eyes, the light thickened and darkened here and there, and he was seeing the inside of a room. . . .

Two men and two women, all of them in Darkovan clothing, seated around a table; one of the women, very frail, very fair, bending over a matrix crystal. . . . *He had seen this before!*

He froze, a curious sense of apprehension clawing coldly at his heart. Something . . . something . . . the door was opening. . . .

He heard his own cry, hoarse, shrill and terrible, the shriek of a terrified child from the full throat of a man, a moment before the world dissolved in spinning darkness.

He was standing, swaying, both hands gripping his temples; Elorie, very white, was staring up at him, the crystal dropped heedless in her lap.

"Zandru!" she whispered. "What did you see, Jeff? Gods, I never dreamed of such a—such a shock," she breathed deeply. "I know now why the woman died . . ." she swayed, fell back against the wall. Jeff moved to steady her, but she went on, not noticing. "I'm not even an empath, but whatever you saw—whatever struck you dumb as a child—whatever it was, that poor woman evidently caught the full backlash of it. If she had a weak heart, it probably stopped. She was, literally, frightened to death by something you saw more than twenty years ago!"

Jeff took her hands. He said, "It's too dangerous, Elorie."

"No. I'm trained, there was no danger for me," she said, and he realized that she was just as eager to know as he was.

"Let me try something else," she said. "You told me, once, that you had a few memories before the orphanage. Let me go back to those . . ."

The lights brightened. There were colors, swirls like mist; there was a blue beacon shining somewhere, a low building gleaming white on the shore of a strange lake that was not water, a ghost of perfume, a low and musical voice. . . .

Wrapped in a cloak of fur, he was carried through gleaming corridors in the arms of a man with blazing red hair—a man clad in green and gold, tall, commanding. *My father*—

Elorie's voice, from very far away, murmured, "And wearing Ridenow colors . . ."

Jeff's consciousness drifted, changed. He saw himself playing childish games with two smaller children, like as twins except that one had blazing red hair and the other was dark-haired and dark-eyed. And there was a big burly black-haired man in strange dark clothing, who spoke to them in a strangely accented tongue, treating them with kind roughness. More hazy were the glimpses of the fair-haired woman with the musical voice, drifting dreamlike in these vague memories. . . .

Jeff knew, unsurprised, that he was approaching the point of peril. His breath choked in his throat, he felt his own blood pounding in his ears, and suddenly he *was* his childish self, he was . . .

The tall man in Terran clothing stood up, letting the toy ship fall from his hands to the rug where the three children were playing. The smaller boys grabbed for it; but the child who now called himself Jeff Kerwin watched the man's drawn face as he pulled the door closed. The room was a big one, high-ceilinged, vaulted, with large windows.

"You know best, Cleindori," said the man with the Terran accent, "but still I think this is not wise."

The tall, fair-haired woman, standing behind the long table, said firmly, "I have done nothing my conscience forbids. They are fools and fanatics—no more. Am I to run and hide because madmen yell in the streets?"

A smaller, darker woman, red-haired, like Cleindori, only less beautiful, said, "That is true. But fools and madmen—and fanatics—can be more dangerous than wise men."

Cleindori leaned on the table, her fair face defiant.

"Are you so much afraid, then, that you want to run and hide—beg for protection from the Hasturs who have called me abominable things? Arnad? Jeff? Cassilde?"

The Darkovan in the green-and-golden cloak came up behind Cleindori and laughing, put his arms about her. He said, "If any of us had any such thought, we would be ashamed to show it before you, Golden Bell! But I think we must be realistic, and you know it as well as I do—or why have you and Cassilde brought the children here, at an hour when they should be long asleep?"

"Arnad is right," said the man in Terran clothing. "Believe me, Cleindori, I know how you feel. It's like a confession of defeat, to you. But it's only a little while—a year or two on another world. And that's our only choice—unless, as you say, we want to ask the Hasturs for protection. Or, worse, the Terrans!"

Cleindori shrugged. "As you wish, then."

"I can make the arrangements most safely," the Terran said. "I'll go now but—" he hesitated. "Are you safe here?"

The Darkovan, Arnad, with an arrogant gesture, dropped his hand to knife-hilt. "I have this, if anyone dares!"

Time seemed to spin out and drag after he had gone. The smaller children dozed on the rug; Cleindori and Cassilde talked in low tones; Arnad paced the floor restlessly, hand on sword-hilt. At last Cleindori said, uneasily, "He should be back by now."

"Hush," Cassilde said. "Did you hear—"

"I heard nothing." With an impatient gesture, Cleindori drew the matrix from her breast and laid it on the table. The others gathered close; the child who now knew himself as Jeff Kerwin tiptoed closer, unobserved, closer to the center of the glowing light. The three of them bent over the glowing matrix. . . .

The child whirled at some slight sound; he raised his head in terror, staring at the turning handle of the door. He shrieked—

Arnad turned, a second too late; the door had burst open and the deadly thrown knife struck him in the back. He fell, with a gurgling cry, sprawled across the table and lay still. The room was suddenly filled with dark forms, hooded and masked. He heard Cassilde shriek aloud, and saw her fall. Cleindori, snatching the knife from Arnad's dead body, was fighting like a cat, struggling with one of the masked men.

The child ran, shrieking, pounding at the dark forms with small fists, biting, kicking, clawing like a small wild thing. Scratching, kicking, he actually ran up the back of one of the men, shouting and sobbing wild threats. Cleindori screamed, bursting away from the men who held her and snatching the child to her breast. She held him tight, and he felt her terror like a physical agony, her eyes met his. . . .

There was one instant of burning, blinding, blazing rapport, in which the child knew exactly what they had done, and why; knew all of Cleindori's story, knew the full truth. . . .

Then rough hands seized him; he was flung through the air, landing hard on stone flooring. A heavy foot struck him in the ribs; pain exploded in him and he lay still, hearing a voice crying out:

"Tell the barbarian that he will come no more to the plains of Arilinn . . . and so we deal with all renegades, Golden Bell!"

Unbelievable, unbearable agony thrust a knife into his heart; then mercifully the rapport burned out and the room went dark and blind and the world vanished around him, into silence and darkness. . . .

There was a heavy pounding at the door. The child who lay unconscious on the floor stirred and moaned, seeing only darkness before his eyes. Painfully he moved, trying to speak, to call out . . . then memory flooded over him, in horror. With eyes like a trapped rabbit, he clutched his small fingers over his mouth, squirming painfully under the table, cowering there. The pounding increased; something thudded against the door. It broke open and the cowering child heard voices.

"Zandru's hells," someone muttered, with a long whistle of consternation. "Someone got here before us. Those murdering fanatics . . ."

"I told you we should have tried to approach them before this, Ragan," one voice said.

"Damn it, I tried, but Kerwin wouldn't listen to me! As for those——" he swore, shockingly, "well, *you* know what the sons of the Seven Domains think of us. I knew it would come to this, although I never guessed it would be murder." A fist struck the table, in impotent wrath, and the child in hiding quivered and clasped his fingers more firmly over his mouth to smother back his sobs. "And when I think we could have protected them—"

Another man was walking around the room. They spoke Darkovan with the mountain accent from beyond the Kara-din; this voice was rough and hard. "Lord Arnad," he said, "and Cassilde Aillard, and Cleindori. Where's Kerwin? Dragged away alive for torture, most likely—Zandru's hells!" He broke off with a cry. "What's this—*children!*"

"At least those fanatic devils had decency enough not to harm the brats."

"Maybe they didn't see them," retorted the first man.

The child in hiding crept to the edge of the table and peered out beneath the hangings. The twins had wakened and the newcomers were bending over them. They were tall men, Darkovans, dressed in the mountain fashion. "Neither of these is Cleindori's child," said the first man. "I wonder what they did—"

"Murdered the poor brat, most likely," said the other. He whistled suddenly. "But these two have Com'yn blood! Listen, do you know what the Terrans—" he lowered his voice suddenly and whispered.

He broke off, listening closely. "Someone's coming," he said, quick and low. "Bring the kids, and keep them quiet!"

The child in hiding watched, paralyzed, as the men caught up his two playmates, wrapped them quickly in their cloaks, and a door opened, closed. The room went dark.

Then there was an opening door, a terrible cry, and the tall dark man in Terran clothes burst into the room. He was swaying on his feet, his clothes torn, his face bloody; the child hiding under the table felt something break apart in him, some terrible pain. He tried to scream, but he could only gasp. He thrust the folds of the tablecloth aside, staggering out toward the man; he heard the man cry out, and then his legs gave way and he fell into darkness again. . . .

He was wrapped warmly in a blanket; thin fine snow was drifting across his face; he was wet through, and in pain, and he was being carried in someone's arms and it hurt; he tried to speak but his throat would not form words. After a long time he was in a warm room, and gentle hands were spooning warm milk into his mouth. He opened his eyes and whimpered. He was lying in a woman's lap, and the bleak-faced man in Terran clothing sat bent over in a chair, his face bloody and his eyes terrible.

"Murdered them, all three," he was saying, in a thread of voice. "And my own boys—God knows what those murdering devils did with them."

The child Jeff opened his mouth, trying to say, *They didn't, the other men took them away,* but he could only make a little whimpering sound. The man looked at him, his face working, and said in a low voice, "Poor little tyke, he was hiding under the table—he must have seen them all die. They took—they took my boys, but they left this little fellow for dead, he'd been kicked around as you can see."

"Poor little thing." The woman shook her head. "What will you do, Jeff?"

The man reached out and lifted the child into his lap. He said, grimly, "Cleindori died for what we've worked for these six years. They murdered Arnad and Cassilde, just for following her, and did their damndest to kill me, and they even murdered a pair of innocent children. This is all that's left—" he dangled the matrix crystal in his hands. "This, and this poor kiddie here." He slipped the chain over the child's head and rose to his feet.

"I wanted to keep away from the Terran authorities until I could make my own terms. That's why I never—" his voice strangled in his throat, "never did anything about Cassilde and the twins. It's too late for them, but I can protect this one. For Cleindori's sake, I owe her that. I'll take him to the Terran orphanage. They'll never look there for him."

"Will they take him in?"

The man said, grimly, "They will if I say he's *my* son. Time later to clear it all up, if I live that long. For the time being, I'll leave him there as Jeff Kerwin, Jr."

He looked down, kindly, at the child in his arms and said, "If the poor tyke could only tell us, but he hasn't said a word. I hope the shock hasn't turned his brain! God, what a thing for a kid to see!" He beat, impotently, on the door-frame.

"Devils! Filthy, murdering devils!"

Then it was cold, again, and he was being carried in the big man's arms, each step jolting his broken ribs, through heavy rain and sleet that felt icy on his face. . . . And then he was gone. . . .

He was standing, shaking and white, in his room at the Terran Hotel, still trembling with a child's terror; Elorie, her eyes filled with tears, was staring up at him. Jeff put a hand to his face and discovered it was wet with tears. He struggled to speak, for a moment the old paralyzed terror striking at him and was unable to force a word through his tight throat. . . .

175

Elorie said quickly, "You're here. Jeff—Jeff, it was twenty-five years ago! *Come up to present time!*"

"So that was it," he whispered. "I saw them killed—my mother, my father."

Jeff couldn't get a word out. It was too overwhelming. The story was clear to him, now. . . .

Cleindori, beautiful and rebellious, had tried to alter her world, and had found a Terran ally in Jeff Kerwin—but not a lover. When she fled from Arilinn, two of her kinsmen had gone with her; Cassilde Aillard, Arnad Ridenow. For a long time they had worked together, the four of them, discovering matrix mechanics as science, not superstition, slowly stripping it of the old trappings of magic and taboo.

They had worked in hiding; the Com'yn had sworn vengeance—and both the Terrans and the anti-Com'yn faction of mountain Darkovans were trying to get wind of what they were doing. They had been hounded from place to place, too proud to ask protection from Terra or from the Hasturs.

They had been more than co-workers. Cleindori had found support, and trust, and later love, in her fellow-exile, Arnad Ridenow. While Jeff Kerwin had learned to love the merry, gentle Cassilde, Cleindori had borne a son to Arnad. And twins had been born to Jeff Kerwin and his wife—

Elorie said, almost inaudibly, "Cleindori did *not* run away with Jeff Kerwin! You're not the son of Jeff Kerwin at all—you're not a Terran at all!"

And then the murder . . .

The child of Cleindori had seen it, and had been shocked voiceless by the terrifying moment of rapport—his inborn empathic gift torn prematurely open by Cleindori's dying terror—and by the rough handling. He had managed to hide.

"And then the final complication," Jeff said. "The anti-Com'yn faction found them, just too late. They knew the Terrans would be glad to have children from the Com'yn—hostages. They thought what everyone else thought—that the Earthman was Cleindori's lover, that the other children were Cassilde's children by Arnad Ridenow. They took them to the orphanage for safe-keeping."

Elorie said, her voice shaking, "Twins. Later, we got one of them back; we thought he was Arnad Ridenow's child, and gave him the name of Auster Ridenow—" she gasped suddenly. "You're not Jeff Kerwin, Jr. at all! We've had the real Jeff Kerwin, Jr. in the Com'yn all along! And the spy, Ragan, is Auster's twin brother—and Auster doesn't even know it!"

For a moment the room reeled around Kerwin. Kerwin? He had no right to that name. Son of Arnad Ridenow?

"And full Com'yn," Elorie whispered. "It's true the Terrans thought you were Kerwin's son, and sent you to Terra to be out of harm's way after Kerwin was murdered. They thought they had the child of an Earthman by a Com'yn Keeper, and they hoped you might, some day, be useful to them. They'd already arranged things so we had Auster back—after they had established a psychic bond, a hypnotic command between the twins! Auster doesn't even know it—but you weren't the spy, Jeff! *He was!* You were just—the catalyst!"

"Strange," Elorie said, "and sad, that when children were in danger here, two different people had the same idea—they knew that only with the Terrans would the children be safe. It makes our world look rather strange by comparison."

"I lived on Terra," Jeff said slowly, "the Terrans aren't monsters. And it's true that they're less likely to drag children into adult affairs. There's no feud tradition there." He fell silent. Strange, now that he knew he was Darkovan, he almost regretted the Terra which had become part of his existence.

Yet legally he was Terran. Under the law, when Jeff Kerwin took this child to the Spaceman's Orphanage and entered him there as Jeff Kerwin, Jr. the child had become a citizen of the far-flung Terran Empire. And the Empire had the legal right to send him where they would. . . .

"Jeff," said Elorie slowly, "your father was Arnad Ridenow. It explains why you have the empath Gift, and we didn't expect it. Jeff!" she turned to him. "You still don't see what it means! It means we've got to warn them at Arilinn—somehow! They may try the Lifting operation, and Auster's still in contact with the spy Ragan, and doesn't even know it!"

Cold struck at Kerwin's heart. "Elorie, how can we? That's *there,* and we're here. Even if we could get out of the Terran Zone, which I don't think we can, Arilinn is almost a thousand miles away. Unless—do you mean telepathically?"

"No. I couldn't do it without the special communication relays—not now," she said. "But have you forgotten? Just outside the Terran Zone lies Thendara, and in Thendara is the Castle of the Com'yn. There is always a Keeper there. There is always someone there who can handle the relays. And Old Hastur."

Hastur! Kerwin remembered, almost with longing, that stern and sensible old man. If he could have told *him* . . . maybe none of this would have happened. But he said, painfully, "Have you forgotten, Elorie? The Com'yn—all of them, not only Arilinn—have turned against us; surely Arilinn will have told the others."

She nodded. "I hadn't forgotten. But we've got to try, or it means certain failure. Oh, I know failure is almost certain, if they should be mad enough to try the Lifting operation without a Keeper, or with a half-trained one. But at least there would be a chance! And you—now that we know you're *not* a pawn for Terra, *you* could go back into the matrix ring!" Her face was pale and eager. "Oh, Jeff, it means so much for our world."

"Darling, I'd try anything," he said, wrung, "but do you understand, we're prisoners! That notice I got, forbade us to leave the Terran Zone or to be absent from this hotel for more than an hour! Just because we're not behind bars doesn't mean we're not under arrest!"

"What right have they—" The arrogance of the princess, the favored, half-worshiped Keeper, was in her voice now. She caught up a hooded gray cloak—Jeff had bought it for her in Arilinn, to conceal her golden-red Com'yn hair—and said, "If you will not come, I will go alone!"

He seized her arm as she turned toward the door.

"Elorie, you're serious about this?" Her eyes answered him, and he made up his mind. "Then I'll take the chance, too."

When they were out in the streets of the town, she moved so swiftly that he could hardly keep up with her light steps. It was late afternoon; the light lay, blood-red, along the streets, and shadows crept, long and purple, from the feet of the tall houses. As they neared the edge of the Terran Zone, Kerwin began to wonder if this was insanity. They'd certainly be stopped at the gates, if his description had been put on the list. He wanted to warn Elorie, to know what she meant to do, but she moved quickly and so decisively that he felt all he could do was to follow at her heels.

The great square that separated Terran Zone from the old Town was half-empty. Across the square, on the Darkovan side, he could see the little cluster of shops and markets, bars and stalls; the gate was perfunctorily guarded by a man in black, lounging half-asleep beside it, but as Elorie and Kerwin approached the gate, he sat up, looked at them briefly and said, "Sorry. I'll have to see identifications."

Now what? Kerwin started to speak, but Elorie prevented him. Swiftly, she straightened up, flinging back the gray hood that covered her hair, and the light of the Bloody Sun lay red and dazzling around it, as she sent a clear cry ringing across the square. Kerwin had never heard the words before.

But across the square, Darkovans looked round, startled at that ancient rallying-cry. Someone cried out:

"Ai! A Com'yn *vai leronis*—"

"Com'yn!"

Elorie turned and with a quick gesture she threw back Jeff's hood. She seized his arm. The guard got slowly to his feet, bewildered, protesting . . . but the crowd, assembling as if by magic, was already streaming out into the square, crying out. The sheer weight and number of them rolled over the Terran guard; Elorie and Jeff were borne along on the surface of the riot, a way opening for them through the crowd as if by magic, deferential murmurs and cries following them. Breathless, startled, Kerwin found himself standing at the far end of the square, the whole brawling mob between themselves and the Terran guard at the gate. Elorie, laughing shakily, her eyes alight, seized his hand and pulled him into one of the side streets.

"Quick, Jeff! This way, or they'll be all round us again wanting to know what it's all about!"

He blinked, following the girl, admiration mingling with astonishment. Clever of Elorie—to use the prestige of the Com'yn to create a riot—yet it could have repercussions. The Terrans had ways of retaliating for riots held too close to their doorstep.

Elorie turned, facing him. "I had to," she said in an undertone. "Jeff, don't you understand, even now, how important this is?"

He didn't, quite. But for the moment it was a question of trusting Elorie, trusting her as much as she had trusted him.

"Where are we going?"

She pointed. Poised high above the plain, white and iridescent against the dark mountains, the rainbowed towers looked down aloofly at the town lying below.

"The Com'yn castle," she said quietly.

Kerwin whistled. Except for a few of the highest dignitaries, no Terran had ever set foot there, and then only by invitation.

But I've got to get used to the idea—I'm not a Terran!

A week ago, knowing that would have made me very happy. Now I'm not so sure. . . .

Neither of them spoke on the long climb upwards, through the darkening streets, toward the Com'yn Castle. Kerwin was holding thought at bay. He was still numbed by the import of the new discoveries.

He wondered if Elorie had a specific plan for when they got there. The Castle looked both big and well-guarded, and he didn't imagine they could walk in at leisure on one of the highest dignitaries of the planet.

He had reckoned again, however, without the enormous

personal prestige of the Com'yn themselves. There were guards, in the green cross-belted uniform of the City Guard, but at the sight of Elorie—afoot, humbly clad, but her copper hair blazing in the last sunlight—they fell back, murmuring "Com'ynara, you lend us grace."

"Say to the Lord Hastur that Elorie of Arilinn would speak with him."

"At once, *vai leronis*." The guard looked askance at Kerwin's Terran clothes, but even so he did not question. He went. Less than a minute later, one of the soft-footed furry nonhumans padded through the doorway and beckoned to them. He led them through broad corridors and into a long pillared passageway. . . .

Jeff stiffened, shaking. Again he saw himself, a child, carried through a long pillared corridor. . . .

Elorie looked around and held out her hand. He took it, gratefully. He felt as if he were moving into a dream.

The nonhuman ushered them into a room walled with translucent swirls of curtain and then stole softly away. Almost at once, the curtains at the far end parted, and Dantan of Hastur strode into the room.

He saw Elorie, and bowed, then stopped, his brow ridging briefly in displeasure as he saw Kerwin, but almost at once the displeasure was gone. He was reserving judgment. He came and took Elorie's hand.

"Well, child?"

She said, "It is good of you to see us." She hesitated and said, "Or—don't you know?"

Hastur looked dispassionately at Kerwin, but his voice was courteous and grave.

"Twenty years ago," he said, "I refused to listen when one of my kindred begged me to understand. I was a fool, and blind with prejudice—and at the back of my mind, Elorie, I have never felt quite guiltless of Cleindori's death. Oh, I had nothing to do with the evil fanatics who killed her, but I did not stretch out my hand to guard her, either. I told myself she had forfeited all right to our protection. I don't intend to make the same mistake twice. Why have you come here, Elorie?"

"Now just a minute here," Kerwin interrupted, before Elorie could answer. "Let's get one thing straight." His jaw had a belligerent twist as he said, "We didn't come here to ask for anybody's protection, or for any favors. The Com'yn threw me out, and when they threw me out Elorie stuck with me, so they turned on her, too. Coming here isn't my idea, and we're not asking for anything!"

Hastur blinked rapidly, and then, over the calm and austere face, an unmistakable smile spread. He said, "I stand reproved, then. I'll let you tell it your own way."

Elorie looked at him in appeal. She said, "The important thing is this—he's not Kerwin's son. He is Cleindori's child, yes. But his father was Arnad Ridenow."

Hastur looked startled. He looked sharply into Kerwin's eyes, then said, half aloud, "Yes. Yes, I should have known." Then, gravely, he bowed to Elorie and said, "Arilinn has done you a wrong, Elorie. Any Keeper may give up her high office at her own will, if she wishes to take a lover or a husband from among the Com'yn. May all your children be gifted with *laran*—"

"The hell with that," Kerwin said, in a sudden rage. "I haven't changed one damn bit from four days ago, when they thought I wasn't good enough for Elorie to spit on! So if she marries a Terran she's a bitch, and if she marries one of your high-and-mighty Com'yn, all of a sudden she's—"

"Jeff! Jeff, *please*," Elorie entreated, seizing his hand, and he caught her frightened thoughts, *no one dares speak like this to Hastur . . .*

"I dare," he said, shortly. "Tell him what you came to tell him, and then let's get out of this, Elorie! You chose me thinking I was a Terran—remember that. I'm not ashamed of the name I wear, or the man who gave it to me!"

He broke off, suddenly abashed before Hastur's steady blue gaze. The old man laughed, a gentle, merry laugh.

"There speaks the pride of the Ridenow," he said laughing. "Yes, and the pride of the Terrans too, Jeff Kerwin. Take pride in your double heritage, my son. My words were to ease Elorie's heart, no more. And now tell me, tell me in your own way, why you came here."

182

His face grew graver as he listened, and at last he frowned, looking troubled.

"I knew Auster had been in the hands of the Terrans," he said, "but he was so very young when he was taken back. It never occurred to me that they would—or could—use so young a child in any way."

Kerwin said, "I thought I'd been used for the—the time bomb, Hastur. I thought it was *my* brain Ragan was picking. And all the time it was Auster."

"Auster, who grew up among us. Auster, who—" Hastur shook his head, in bewilderment. "But he has *laran!* He is full Com'yn!"

"He thought he was," Kerwin corrected, and suddenly a curious excitement began to boil in him, and he began to see something else, something exciting and new, beneath the surface of this—new implications to the whole thing. "Hastur, that's the answer, don't you see? He had *laran* because he was told he had it, because he expected to have it, because he never developed any mental block against thinking he had psi powers."

A vague glimmer of understanding began to dawn in the old man's eyes, but Elorie interrupted, "Hastur, can't you see now why we—why we have to warn them at Arilinn? They'll try the Lifting operation—and Auster's still linked with Ragan—and they'll fail."

Hastur's face turned white. "Yes," he said, low. "They were going to try it without you. We had one of the younger Keepers here, not much more than a child, but we sent her to Arilinn. It was a risk, but we thought it was worth risking. And we heard by the relay, a few hours ago, that they meant to start tonight."

"Tonight!" Elorie gasped. "We've got to get to Arilinn! We've got to warn them! It's their only chance!"

Kerwin's thoughts were bitter as they flew through the swiftly darkening night, rain beating against the little ship. Elorie sat at his side, wrapped in her gray cloak, silent, even her thoughts withdrawn from him; in the control cabin, a slender, strange young Com'yn knelt, controlling the ship against the beating elements, but Kerwin no longer had any curiosity about it.

He was going back to Arilinn, after all. Going, to warn them, perhaps to save them—for there was no question that this, the greatest of the Com'yn experiments, was the primary target of the Terran spies.

Elorie's hand felt cold as ice in his. Without asking, Kerwin wrapped his own fur-lined cloak round her. He could shelter Elorie in a Darkovan cloak, but now that he knew he had no more right to his Terran name than to the Com'yn, where could he take her? What would come after this?

She pointed through the window of the plane to lights below. "Arilinn," she said softly, then drew a sharp breath, clutching at his fist with icy fingers. "Look, the Tower!"

As Kerwin's eyes followed the direction of her gaze, he made out the dark squat upthrust of the Tower toward the sky, and faintly, around it, a pale bluish iridescence that shimmered and wavered and burned. . . .

"We're too late," Elorie whispered, "they've already begun!"

CHAPTER FIFTEEN

KERWIN FELT as if he were sleepwalking as they crossed the airfield; Elorie moved dreamlike at his side, and he felt her trembling. *They had failed, then?* Behind them the little airship was surrounded by the red-and-yellow-clad guards of Arilinn, others walked around them, but neither Jeff nor Elorie paid the least attention to them. They passed through the cluster of low buildings; Elorie caught his arm, saying, "It's no use, Jeff," but Kerwin moved steadily on. He didn't quite know why; there was no need to face rebuff and humiliation here, now that it was too late to warn them. But some half-guessed intuition kept him moving toward the Tower, led him through the many-colored sparkling Veil.

When he had passed it, he sensed the tremendous charged

force in the Tower tonight; it emanated, tingled, radiated from that high and hidden room where the energon ring had formed. Incomplete, yes, but still holding unguessed, unguessable power. It beat like a pulse in Kerwin; Elorie trembled, and the man saw her face working convulsively, like a small child's about to cry.

Was this dangerous for Elorie—now?

Swept on, dominated, by that mysterious center of force, Kerwin slowly climbed the Tower. He stood outside the matrix laboratory, reaching out, sensing what lay within. . . .

He sensed Auster's barrier like a wall of mist; passed it. With senses beyond his physical eyes he was within the room, seeing them there: Taniquel, her touch light and secure on each member, guarding them; Auster; Corus and Rannirl, intent, visualizing in the great crystal screens, while Kennard at their center stood before the screen itself, and holding them together, frail and tense as spiderweb silk strands, an unfamiliar touch, almost like pain. . . .

The girl was slight and frail, barely out of childhood, dark-red hair braided on her shoulders, a little triangular face smoothed to so great an intentness that it was wholly passive, inhumanly calm, yet trembling with effort. She sensed his touch and the rapport wavered, like a web shaken by a harsh wind. . . .

Rapidly, with swift, sure telepathic touch, Kerwin made the rounds of the circle again. Corus. Rannirl. Kennard. Taniquel. Auster.

Auster . . .

He sensed, like a sticky and palpable black cord, a *something* that beat out from Auster, through the barrier, a line that chained them down, kept the matrix circle from closing their ring of power. *The bond . . . the psychic bond between twin brothers . . . and Auster's Terran twin clung to the fringes of the matrix ring, spying. . . .*

Like water beaten into waves by a harsh wind, the rapport trembled and turned on the intruder. Auster sent a harsh thrust in his direction; almost idly, Kerwin parried it.

Terran, spy—

No!

Beneath the surface of the rapport, Kerwin reached out for contact with Auster and deliberately, steeling himself, threw the memory open:

The room where Cleindori, Arnad, Cassilde, had been murdered . . .

Auster screamed noiselessly, twisting in anguish. With sudden, intuitive knowledge, as Auster's barrier dropped, Kerwin caught it up and erected the guarding circle around the energon ring, and with one swift, deliberate psychic thrust (a black cord slashed through, sizzling, scorching) cut the intruder away. . . .

(Miles away, a swart little man who called himself Ragan cried out in agony and collapsed, to lie senseless for hours.)

Auster's mind was reeling under the shock of that impact; Kerwin steadied him, dropping into deep rapport. . . .

Bring me into the circle!

Like a clasped hand, he fell into the closed ring. There was a brief moment of dizzy timelessness, where he was no more than a bodiless speck floating in an atomic ring somewhere, a speck of light in a crystal, and then . . .

Far down below the surface of the world, lie those strange substances, those atoms, molecules, ions known as minerals. His touch had searched them out, through their crystal structure in the matrix screen; atom by atom and molecule by molecule, he had sifted them apart from impurities, from alien substances, so that they lay pure and molten in their rocky beds. Now the welded touch of power was to be stretched forth, the vast Hand that would bring them, in streams, to the surface, to the place prepared for them. . . .

The formed circle welded together, poised, concentrated on the gigantic matrix that would give them power. The fragile spiderweb strand that held them together, the trembling touch (*such a frail hand to wield so great a weapon!*) poised and hesitated . . .

Kerwin, deeply now in rapport with Taniquel at the margin of the circle, felt the child-Keeper's weakening touch, her gradual slipping from consciousness. He was one with Taniquel's despair—

No! It will kill her!

And then, at the moment when the welded ring shimmered like a breaking rainbow, ready to crystallize from a single unit into seven severed separate minds again, Kerwin felt a firm, sure, familiar, beloved touch—

Elorie, no! You cannot!

Cleindori did! That was the secret she discovered! Cleindori was no virgin—she had even had a child, yet she lost none of her powers!

Then, with infinite gentleness—a steadying arm slipped around childish, frail shoulders, a falling and spilling cup steadied and held in place—Elorie slipped into the rapport, gently displacing the spiderweb-touch of the little Keeper— so gently that there was neither shock nor hurt . . .

Little sister, this is my place. . . .

And the sevenfold, complete circuit suddenly flamed like a bright star in the depths of the screen; the sense of tremendous, waiting power seemed to glow, fuse, burn and brighten.

Kerwin was no longer a single person; he was not human at all. He was part of a tremendous glowing, burning, flowing river of molten metal, surging upward, impelled by great throbbing power. It burst, spilled, flamed and gleamed and then . . .

Slowly, slowly, it cooled and hardened and turned solid and lay, inert again, dead and non-sentient again, awaiting the tools and hands that should shape it into the life of the planet.

Slowly, slowly, gently, one by one, the forged rings of awareness unlinked magically and were separated again. Kerwin rubbed his eyes, stretched cramped, painful muscles. Taniquel's eyes, blazing with triumph, met his: Kennard, Rannirl, Corus, they were all around him, Auster dazed, his face swollen, deep shock centered in the cats' eyes, but burnt clean of hatred. . . .

The young girl with braided hair, the Keeper who had failed, lay dazed in a chair at the center of the ring. She was blinking, her eyes filled with tears, her face white.

Elorie—

Kerwin's heart sucked and turned over. He flung the door open into the hall.

Elorie lay there, sprawled white and lifeless at his feet. Kerwin dropped to his knees at her side. And all his triumph, all his exaltation, melted into nothing, into hatred and curses, as he laid his hand to her motionless breast.

Elorie, Elorie! She had won for the Com'yn, and for Arilinn . . . but had she paid with her life?

And if it is, I killed her.

He had brought her back here, knowing how Elorie felt about it; knowing she would never be content to let them fail.

He had known how this work drained vitality, how it had sapped Elorie's strength and exhausted her nearly to the point of death, even when she was guarded and isolated, her vitality and nervous force carefully guarded in sacrosanct purity. No, she had not lost her powers—and knowing that, she had dared to use them.

And this was the result!

Barely conscious, he knelt by Elorie, racked with despair and anguish. He could not even protest when Taniquel gently moved him aside, and at first he did not hear her speak.

Kennard lifted him, roughly, saying in urgent tones, "Damn it, listen, Jeff! She's not dead, not yet! There's a chance! But you've got to let us get to her. Let us see how bad it is!"

"Haven't you done enough!"

"He's hysterical," Kennard said dryly. "Hang on to him." Dazed, Kerwin felt strong hands restraining him and realized that he was being held by Rannirl and Auster. Elorie was taken by force from his arms.

Then, through some unspoken, sensed, direct contact, through their very touch on him, it penetrated. Elorie wasn't dead. They were only trying to help. Gradually, he grew calmer, standing at last between Rannirl and Auster, quiet, only his shaken breathing betraying his fear.

"I know," Auster said, in a low voice, "but easy, Jeff. They'll do everything that can be done." He raised his dark eyes, and suddenly Kerwin saw that Auster was trembling from head to foot.

"You—I failed, Jeff. I would have broken, if it wasn't for you. I never had any right to be here at all," he said, shaking his head as if dazed. "I'm not Com'yn at all. I'm a Terran, a Terran. You have more right here than I have."

Unexpectedly, to Kerwin's shock and horror, Auster dropped to his knees. His voice was just audible.

"Everything I said of you was true of myself, *vai dom*. All I deserve at the hands of the Com'yn is death." He bowed his head and waited there, broken, silent, resigned to doom. Kerwin stared at him, in appalled disbelief.

Suddenly, his overflow of emotion broke loose. He jerked Auster roughly upright by the shoulder.

"Listen, you damned fool," he said angrily, "don't you realize, even yet, what this means? All it means is that you've got to change a few of your ideas about the Com'yn. So Auster was born of a Terran father—so what? He has the Ridenow gift—*because he was brought up believing he had it!* He could pass the Veil—*because he believed he could!* I went through hell in my training—*because you all believed that my Terran blood would keep me from developing the gifts easily and quickly!* Yes, the power is inherited, to some small degree, but not nearly to the extent you have always believed. It means that Cleindori was right, even though they killed her for it—that matrix mechanics is not a secret for a given caste, but a science—Darkover's own science, to be used in the right way!"

"You're right," said Hastur, quietly, coming up the long stairs to where they stood. "You've won for us, Jeff Kerwin, or whatever you want to call yourself. Darkover has its own way—"

"A period of grace," Kerwin interrupted, "not a final solution." And Hastur nodded.

"You're right. This experiment may have succeeded, and the Darkovan Syndicate has pledged to be guided by the council. But there was a failure, too. We know, now, that the Tower circles can never be brought back as they were in the old days. Life can only go forward, not back. The cost is too great, in human terms. It's better to ask help from the Terrans, even, than to let all such work rest on the shoulders of a few gifted men and women. Better that the people of Darkover should learn to share the effort with one another—"

"—and even with Terra," Kennard said gravely. "But then—"

Kerwin said, "Cleindori and Jeff Kerwin, and my father, were working for that. They intended to make an even exchange with Terra: Darkover's matrix powers for those things where they could be safely used, even for the Terrans, and in exchange, Terra would give such things as she could give. But they would be equals. Not the Terran masters and the Darkovan suppliants. A fair exchange between equal worlds, and each world to keep its own pride and its own power."

"They died thinking they had failed," Hastur said. "It took their sons to complete the work they had begun."

Kerwin turned to Auster. Auster stood up, and stretched out his hand. He said, "Then the compulsion that brought you back to Darkover—"

"Was for the best," Kerwin said, "for *our* world."

There was a feather-light touch on Kerwin's arm. He looked down to see the pale childish face of the little-girl Keeper; she murmured, "Will you come? Elorie—"

Kerwin thrust his way past them and into the room where Elorie was lying. White, pale and strengthless, she opened her eyes and stretched her hands to him, and Kerwin reached for her, not caring that behind him the rest of the Com'yn had crowded into the room, frightened, anxious. He knew, when he touched her, how deep the shock had been, how much it had cost her. Elorie had indeed come very near to death, and many suns would rise and set over Darkover before her old merry laughter would be heard in the tower of Arilinn, but her glowing eyes blazed out, in triumph, from her white face.

"We've won," she whispered, "and we're here."

And Kerwin, holding Elorie in the curve of his arm, knew that they had indeed won, for Darkover and for the

Com'yn. The days that were coming would bring change for them all; Terran and Darkovan would struggle with the inevitable changes that time would bring. But a world that remains the same, can only die. They had fought to keep Darkover as it was, and had, instead, fought through to awareness that their victory was only the victory of determining what changes should be made so that it should live.

He had found what he loved, and he had destroyed it, because Darkover, and the Com'yn, would never again be the same. The mold had been broken.

And yet, destroying it, he had saved it from complete and final destruction.

The Com'yn were all around him, his brothers and sisters in Arilinn. Taniquel, so white and worn that he knew how recklessly she had spent her strength to bring Elorie back to herself. Auster, like Jeff himself, the mold of his life broken, but it could be forged again. Kennard, Corus, Rannirl . . .

"Now, now," said the sensible voice of Mesyr, calm and level, "what's the sense of standing here like this, when your night's work is done and well done? Downstairs, all of you, for some breakfast. Yes, you too, Lord Hastur, and let Elorie get some rest." With brisk hands she drew up the covers beneath Elorie's chin and made shooing gestures at them all. Kerwin met Elorie's eyes again, and suddenly burst into laughter. Weak and shaky as she was, Elorie began to laugh, too, and the great vaulted spaces of the Arilinn Tower rang and echoed with shared mirth.

Life in Arilinn was back to normal.

They were home.

PHILIP K.DICK

The Crack in Space	95c
Eye in the Sky	$1.25
The Man Who Japed	95c
Solar Lottery	$1.25

Other Recent
Science Fiction Releases!

$1.50 each

Noah II Dixon

Science Fiction: What's It All About
Lundwall

Time and Again Simak